RAVEN

A NOVEL

ROBERT T. KELLEY

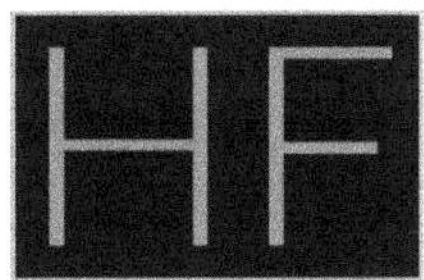

HIGH FREQUENCY PRESS

For Margot, the better maker

WEDNESDAY, DECEMBER 27, 1989

STEPPING OFF THE NUMBER 66 BUS IN THE ALLSTON neighborhood of Boston, Kenneth felt a prickling on the back of his neck, a feeling of being watched. It wasn't, like, threatening, though, more like, *interesting,* he thought as his grin spread into the wide, cheek-burning smile that first hit of cocaine always delivered.

The spitting rain started to turn to sleet, and Kenneth broke into the loping jog he'd learned in his time in the Army Signal Corps. Only now, years later, he was woefully out of shape, knees twinging and breath short, the result of piles of coke, countless joints, and a lot of shitty luck.

He opened his apartment door, wheezing and buzzing, still smiling, thinking about a cigarette. Then he felt a strong hand on his back, pushing him inside.

He wheeled to face a hulking man who filled out a Bruins jersey without hockey pads.

"Hey man, be cool," Kenneth said, slightly disoriented but working to settle into his professional pose.

He fished a creased packet of Newports from the pocket of his damp field jacket and shook one out, his long fingers straightening the slight kink in the cigarette, stroking it until it was just right. He lit it and drew in the smoke, the nicotine and menthol on top of the coke brightening the room and focusing his attention back to the guy standing in front of him, arms crossed.

Kenneth exhaled the smoke. "You looking to score, man? I mean, it's cool if you are. Like, that's my thing. I've got some good stuff on me, and I can say with tremendous certainty . . ." He really liked the word "tremendous." "*Tremendous* certainty that it will wind you up tight!" he said, punctuating his words with his arm raised, the cigarette pointed at the ceiling.

Clients adored Kenneth. Thought he was fun, often sharing coke they'd just bought from him while they got high together. That wasn't this guy's vibe, but it was all good. Kenneth always delivered outstanding customer service.

"You into something else? I can get other stuff. A few calls, that's all. I am connected as hell. What you need?"

"For you to do the job you're gettin' paid for," the man said.

Kenneth's wide smile dimmed. Was the dude about to jack him? The uncertain feeling he had as he got off the bus might have been right after all. This wasn't a customer. This was something else.

Actually, *fuck,* this was that other thing.

He lit another cigarette from the first one. The room brightened again, though not quite as much as before. Still, the action of lighting and inhaling gave him a moment to try to focus.

The man was pacing the apartment in silence, picking up the rotary desk phone on the milk crate next to Kenneth's futon, hefting it, evaluating it, before putting it down. Stopping in front of Kenneth's computer, the man stabbed two blunt fingers down on random keys, the loud keyclicks the only sound other than Kenneth's blood rushing in his ears.

He'd run into tricky situations before, and he'd always come to an understanding, everybody cool. Sometimes you just had to smooth the waters, that was all.

"Look man, like I told the professor dude, I'm a pro here. This is serious business. And the money he's paying ain't cutting it. Cops are going after people for this stuff now. Feds too. It's, like, all over the news. Plus," Kenneth leaned back against the kitchen counter, took another long drag on his cigarette, spread his hands, and summoned his most winning smile. "I've got a lifestyle to maintain here."

Kenneth paused, preparing to tell it like it was. The truth of the matter was that the professor was too anxious, too needy, which told Kenneth that he wasn't charging enough. After all, he was a business-man, right?

"It's the principle of the thing, you know?" Kenneth said. "You want people to respect your work. You understand respect, am I right? Yeah, of course you do. People look at you and see you're a serious dude. Same here. I mean I'm really good at what I do. I just need a little more respect, a little more cash, and it will all be cool."

The guy stood still, as if waiting for something, while Kenneth was thinking of another cigarette, and another bump once he got this guy out of here. He'd burned too much of his high already on adrenaline. This dude was cramping his style and his space.

"So, we're good right?" Kenneth said as he put his hand on the man's upper arm to gently nudge him toward the door.

Instead, the man grabbed Kenneth by his shirt, lifted him completely off the floor and hurled him backward. Taken off guard, Kenneth flew into the cheap kitchen cabinets, then dropped, cracking his head on the sharp corner of the Formica counter, breaking his fall and apparently his skull as he slid down the cabinet wall, eyes glazed, unmoving.

The other man checked Kenneth's pulse. Nothing. He riffled through Kenneth's pockets and found the large bag of cocaine. He scanned the apartment, identifying the only other thing of obvious value: the Compaq computer tower. He unhooked the cables and phone line from the back and hefted it under his arm. He closed the apartment door behind him, then planted a booted kick next to the lockset. The door splintered and swung open, making it look like a break-in.

That would have to do.

MONDAY, JANUARY 29, 1990

MEV HAYES HADN'T PICTURED THE PROMISED LAND AS A sallow brick office building surrounded by sooty January snow piles, yet here it was in Cambridge, Massachusetts. MIT Building 38. The Fairchild Building. Home of the Advanced Concepts Lab. And her salvation.

She'd driven two days to get here, her first time outside Maryville, Missouri. Born there, thrived there, shamed there, stuck there.

Then she got the call.

And got the hell out.

Despite that urgency, she was later than she'd expected, and the afternoon light was already coming down under a low sky. Snow, traffic, and her desire to avoid any encounters with police all conspired to slow her down. She was supposed to meet with her new boss at noon today, a few days before the start of the semester. Now, it was almost 3:30.

Shitty first impression, Mev.

Her anxiety increased as she searched in vain for a parking spot, finally finding a tiny metered one on the left-hand side of the street that she fit into after several attempts. She ended up parking too close to the filthy snowbank and had to shimmy out. Sorting through the change at the bottom of her bag, she found enough for two hours, the maximum the meter allowed. She'd have to remember to come back and refill it. One more thing to worry about.

She was uncertain of her exact destination, and anxiously searched for building numbers on Vassar Street. She felt like an idiot, gawking at the buildings to determine her destination. But between looking foolish and being even more late, it seemed like a good trade-off.

Inside, she stomped the snow off her boots onto an already soaked mat and searched the directory for her destination. She took advantage of the long walk to the lab on the other side of the building to extract herself from her winter coat and smooth her hair and blouse. With a deep breath, she opened the door.

And walked into Oz.

Spread about the lab was the most diverse collection of computers she'd ever seen anyplace except *Byte* magazine. An array of desktop and minicomputers filled the room, some she didn't even recognize, many she did: the sleek new Sun Microsystems workstations, Digital Equipment MicroVAX systems, putty-colored IBM AT PCs, a few newer IBM PS/2 PCs, Compaq PC clones, Commodore Amigas, even three cute Apple Macintosh IIs on a table in the corner. The drone of all the cooling fans was a constant low level hum, vibrating through the room. And anything that could be networked together was, with a web of Ethernet and Token Ring network cables covering the floor. She shook her head, amazed.

Not that she hadn't benefited from a wired-up campus before. Northwest Missouri State University was an early "electronic campus," with many classrooms connected and VAX terminals in every dorm room. Not that she'd been able to enjoy that. She'd lived at home.

At the far end of the room, a knot of people huddled in front of the largest computer monitor she'd ever seen. It had to be almost forty inches diagonal, and probably weighed a couple hundred pounds. When a few of the folks noticed her, a man in a midnight blue three-piece suit rose and walked toward her, discreetly checking his watch, then extending his tanned hand in greeting. She tried not to let it rattle her.

"You must be Mev. Randy FitzRoy. I can't wait for you to get started with us."

"Thank you so, so much, Dr. FitzRoy," Mev replied, her voice meeker than she'd intended.

"Oh, please, Mev, call me Fitz. All my friends do," he said with an inviting smile.

He was tall and fit, with a ruddy complexion as if he'd just been skiing, and floppy blond curls framing his face. "Fitz" was an absolute celebrity within the computer science community for the work coming out of his Advanced Concepts Lab at MIT. *This lab.*

The Institute of Electrical and Electronics Engineers, IEEE, had called him "a guiding light in computing innovation, leading us into the twenty-first century."

And she was about to join his lab.

"Everyone, this is Mev."

The crowd around the monitor watched her quietly.

"Mev came to my attention recently as someone who could both benefit our team and benefit from it. I've convinced her to transfer from Northwest Missouri State to MIT to finish the few hours left on her undergraduate degree, then she can enter the graduate program with all of you while she continues to refine her research."

That version of the story sounded far, far better than the actual one. A week earlier she had been taking extra shifts at the Maryville Kmart, still in shock after being expelled from Northwest Missouri State. She'd left under a cloud, without a degree, figuring she was done with college, or at least it was done with her. Late one evening, after a double shift, she'd come home to find a note from her mom on the kitchen table, the only way she was communicating with Mev since she had "brought even more shame to the family."

All it said was to call a guy about school. The number was for the Department of Electrical Engineering and Computer Science at MIT. The caller? A Dr. Randall FitzRoy, III, Director of the Advanced Concepts Lab.

"I heard about your dismissal from Missouri State," he'd said on the phone that evening. "A travesty that they would let such talent go. Come to MIT. In my lab we cherish unorthodox thinkers."

Her very next call was to Kmart to quit. She packed her car that night, left a goodbye note for her mom the next morning, and hit the road.

Fitz pulled out a chair for Mev and, once she was seated, retook his own. He turned to a Latino guy in a preppy pink polo shirt and khakis sitting at a keyboard in front of the enormous monitor.

"Hector, please proceed."

Hector started a code walk-through, outlining what his program did and how it worked. He'd gotten only a few sentences in before Fitz interrupted him.

"Good God, Hector! After the whole Morris Worm debacle, you can't possibly expect me to approve research on computer viruses."

Mev knew well the furor Fitz was talking about. A little more than a year earlier, in November 1988, a Cornell student named Robert Tappan Morris released a computer worm, accidentally taking down 10% of the machines connected to the internet. Morris said it was just a test to prove he could make a self-replicating program, but it multiplied unexpectedly, bringing servers all over the world to their knees. And now he was back in the news as the first person indicted under the Computer Fraud and Abuse Act of 1986.

"It's not a virus, it's a self-replicating . . ." Hector tried to object.

Fitz talked over him. "It's ignorant and irresponsible, that's what it is. Your final proposal for your dissertation research was due back in the fall. I give you extra time, and this is what you come up with?"

Hector paled. He looked as if he wanted to retort, to defend his choice. Instead, his shoulders slumped. "What now?" he asked, not to anyone in particular.

"See me tomorrow during office hours. We're done here."

Another awkward silence fell as everyone watched Hector pack and leave the office, dismissed in shame. Mev's own face flushed in sympathy. She knew precisely how he was feeling.

The team broke up and Dr. FitzRoy turned to her; his anger with Hector evaporated as if he'd flipped a switch.

"Did you drive in today? You must be exhausted. Do you have a place yet?"

The answer to that was a definite no. She'd tried to arrange something over the phone, but Campus Housing said they couldn't help her on such short notice. She figured she'd grab a cheap hotel room and find a place over the next few days.

"Not yet," she said.

"Check *The Phoenix*," one of the other students shouted from behind a cubicle wall. "Free newspaper. Stacks everywhere. People advertise for room shares."

Mev cringed at the intrusion into her personal affairs, then took a deep breath and tried to let it go. That was a remnant of her old life, of her old fears. This was a completely new start.

"Take the rest of the day to get yourself settled," Fitz said. "I have great plans for us."

MONDAY, JANUARY 29, 1990

MEV RETURNED TO THE LOBBY OF BUILDING 38 AND found a messy stack of newspapers: *The Boston Phoenix.* Flipping past news, advertisements for concerts, bands, record stores, ski resorts, escort services, and explicit personal ads, she found the real estate classifieds: Rooms to Rent.

She scanned the ads, working to interpret the expense-saving abbreviations and realizing most were outside of her price range. Fitz was going to be paying her in the lab, but she'd still need to eat, buy books. Live. She had no idea how much money she'd need, only that it would be a lot more expensive than home. Though, she supposed, Cambridge was now home.

One caught her eye: CAMBRIDGE/PORTER. 1M/F to shr with MIT/Hrvrd grad students. Inc. ht/hw, Shrd meals. $299. 499-2038.

She consulted the Cambridge/Boston map she'd bought at a rest stop on the Massachusetts Turnpike and oriented to Porter Square. It was only a few MBTA stops from MIT and, even better, it was cheap.

Mev went through three pay phones before she found one that worked, checking each coin return for change, like her dad had always done despite their wealth. Their *apparent* wealth. Only now did she realize it had been a clue, among so many others no one had seen.

The phone rang several times and an answering machine said, "It's the '90s. You know what to do." Before the beep someone picked up the phone, panting, out of breath.

"I'm calling about the room," Mev said, unsure about the protocols for looking at a rental. This, too, was new for her.

"Oh, cool! Sure, absolutely. Nobody's claimed it yet. I'm here now if you want to come by."

He gave her directions from Building 38 and she followed them, down Massachusetts Avenue through Central Square, getting turned around in Harvard Square, circling it twice, then continuing west toward Porter Square. A final turn brought her to a turreted, painted cedar shingle house: 39-1/2 Linnaean Street. It was big, a little shabby. And much nicer than anywhere Mev and her mom had lived since everything went sideways.

Mev's knock was answered by a guy in cutoff camouflage shorts, Doc Martens, and a black Warren Zevon concert T-shirt. Inside, the vestibule mirrored the house's exterior. Once grand, now it looked a little tired, with scratched baseboards and worn hardwood floors. The light, though, was amazing.

Her host extended a hand.

"I'm Jack. Jack Kane."

With a sharp, gnomon-like nose, medium brown wavy hair, and round tortoise shell glasses, he looked like someone who could blend into a crowd here in Cambridge, a thing Mev, just shy of six feet with long red hair, had often dreamed of doing.

"Mev Hayes."

"Mev?" he asked as he took her coat and expertly tossed it onto an overloaded coat tree.

"Margaret Evangeline. Family name. My mom shortened it when I was little." *That* was as much personal history as she intended to share.

He walked her through the first floor, giving running commentary as he went, talking over some kind of punk music on the stereo.

"It's a little banged up, sure, and it's a bitch to heat, but there's lots of space. So, I embrace it." He continued the tour to the rear of the house.

"Kitchen," he waved his hand grandly, as if presenting a masterpiece. "Note the resplendent harvest gold."

The kitchen décor and appliances clearly dated from the '70s, when harvest gold and avocado green had managed to rule the design world. They'd had similar appliances in one of the nicer double-wides her mom had rented outside Maryville after dad went to prison. While still ugly, this was much nicer. And cleaner.

Jack opened a door and pointed down a narrow staircase. "Basement. Mostly dry. Plenty of room for your stuff."

Not an issue. Mev's worldly possessions fit in her Ford Pinto.

"How many people live here?" she asked, following him up the stairs.

"Three. No—two, now. Our former roommate lost her Harvard fellowship and had to leave school."

Mev could relate.

"Bathroom," he gestured to a narrow open door.

A beautiful claw-foot tub sat in the center of a spotless black and white hexagonal-tiled room. She could imagine soaking in that.

"This is yours."

He pointed into a bedroom that was the second floor of the turret. Round, spacious, well-lit, if a little chilly. The room had a simple twin bed, a desk, a low bookcase, and a dresser, leaving plenty of open floorspace. It was the largest room she could call her own in years.

"You're MIT?" he asked.

She knew she didn't quite fit the advertisement, so she might have to fudge a little. "Yeah, I'm not in grad school quite yet. I got placement for my last semester of undergrad and a lab job. I'm working on my application to grad school right now." It sounded better than the reality, much like Fitz's characterization. And seemed to satisfy Jack.

He continued the tour, leading her to another bedroom. "This one's mine." Equally large, and dark, the only window covered with ugly damask curtains. The room was spotless, with books piled neatly to the side of the crisply made bed. The sole decoration was a Boston Red Sox pennant over the bed.

"Yeah, that was from my brief baseball phase. My dad got it for me for memorizing Ted Williams' career hitting stats. Didn't like the actual baseball part that much though, much to my dad's dismay."

At the back of the house was another door.

He knocked. "Hector, put on pants, OK?"

Hector?

Sure enough, when Jack opened the door, there was the student Fitz had humiliated, Hector, his face lit only by the glowing green phosphors of a workstation screen. He looked up, more composed than he'd been in the lab after Fitz's withering comments.

"Mev, right?"

"You two know each other?"

"We met all of an hour ago. Mev's working for Fitz now."

"What are the odds?" Jack said.

"Pretty good when you beg me to put your stupid flyers all over MIT," Hector said.

"Bulletin boards at Building 38 or the Coop?" Hector asked, pronouncing what Mev had thought was the "co-op" as if it were a chicken coop.

"I didn't see the flyer. I got it from *The Phoenix*."

"Gotta hit all the channels," Jack said. "Killer marketing."

"Let me finish what I was working on, and I'll join you guys downstairs," Hector said, returning to his keyboard.

In the living room Jack plopped into an overstuffed chair covered with a flowered bedspread.

"$299 a month. Utilities included," he said.

Mev sank into an aqua faux leather chair. It was as garish as the rest of the furniture in the house, yet also surprisingly comfortable. And she felt surprisingly comfortable here.

"I'll take it."

"I can help you move in whenever you want."

"I don't have much."

"Then we'll have it done before Hector finishes his code!" Jack trumpeted, striding onto the porch. In T-shirt and shorts, fists on hips, he surveyed the neighborhood, not looking cold at all.

Her meager possessions organized and put away, Mev joined Jack and Hector in the harvest gold kitchen, where they were drinking wine and talking. The stereo in the living room was playing more music she didn't recognize. "What is this?" she asked.

"The Pixies. *Doolittle*. Great album."

She admired the CD case featuring a monkey with a halo inside a geometric figure of some kind. More punk than Mev was used to.

Not horrible.

"They're a Boston band," he added.

Jack was wearing an apron and stirring a tomato sauce.

"That smells amazing," she said.

"If Jack didn't cook every day, I think I'd starve," Hector said.

"Wine time for you too!" Jack declared and began to pour a glass of red for Mev.

She hesitated to take it, and he tilted his head.

"How old are you?" Jack asked.

"Old enough," she said. "Twenty."

"Wait, you're a twenty-year-old undergrad, and you got a research position with Fitz?" Hector asked. "I had a 4.0 at Stanford, got an award for my thesis, and I still had to beg Fitz to agree to be my advisor."

Without comment, Jack put the wine in front of her.

"I have work tomorrow," Mev said.

"Me too," Jack said. "But there's wine time every night. Life needs rituals, and this is one of mine."

"One of his many rituals," Hector added, laughing.

"What can I say? I bring order to a chaotic world."

Jack returned to the counter, pulled a ball of dough from a covered bowl, and fed it into a hand-cranked device that flattened it.

Mev's idea of pasta with red sauce was that it came from a jar and a box. Her mom had stopped cooking after the court made them forfeit everything. Mev figured it was some kind of passive aggressive reaction to losing their chef, who her mom thought of as a friend and confidante. Another person who'd disappeared from their lives. Just like everyone else after the arrest.

Mev stood behind Jack, wine glass in hand, as he fed the thin cream-colored sheets back into the cutter cylinders on the device, resulting in a pile of square cross-section spaghetti. He tossed them in flour then dropped the pile into a pot of boiling water. He pushed tiny buttons on his Casio digital watch, gave the red sauce a stir, then sat at the scarred kitchen table, his chin in his hands.

"OK, Mev, tell us everything."

She sat down slowly, taking a moment to consider what to share. She explained about Fitz's call, though omitted her earlier, troubled history. Each time she paused, however, Jack asked more questions. She needed to turn the focus away from her.

"What about you?" Mev asked.

Jack's watch beeped and he held up a silent finger. He rose, tested the pasta and, satisfied with its doneness, drained it, tossed in sauce, then served all three of them.

Mev took a bite of the pasta, the sauce rich with complex meaty flavors that Mev had to guess weren't the fatty hamburger she might have put in it.

"This is really good," she said.

"I know," Jack said, clearly pleased. "So, I'm in the English PhD program at Harvard, working on my dissertation on the potential for storytelling in computer games. It's called *A Maze of Twisty Little Passages All Alike.*"

"I don't get it," Mev said.

"You know, like from *Zork.*"

Mev shook her head.

"*Adventure? Colossal Cave?*"

She shook her head again.

"Seriously? *Colossal Cave* was one of the first computer games ever. It was designed right here in Cambridge at Bolt Beranek & Newman. I can't believe you haven't heard of it."

Mev had heard of Bolt Beranek & Newman, of course. BBN was one of the founding firms of what had become the internet. But the game? Not at all. She hadn't had much time for anything beyond work and school since her dad's conviction. Fun and games had been in short supply the last few years, a fact she didn't intend to share.

"That's a valid dissertation topic?" Mev asked instead.

"It is at Harvard," Hector snorted, and Jack laughed along.

"Even C-squared thinks it's nonsense," Hector said.

"C-squared?"

"A friend." Jack waved his fork in the air. "In any case, it's as good as anything my esteemed colleagues are doing."

Jack continued pointing with his fork. "It's ridiculous to think that stories only exist on paper. We have movies, television, why wouldn't we add computers to the mix? They have their own tropes, devices, motifs, just like any other medium."

Jack turned to Hector. "Your turn."

"Well, Fitz killed my project today. He just won't give me a break." He looked pointedly at Mev.

It was true: Fitz had given her a huge break. But she wasn't going to feel bad about that. Her luck was finally starting to turn, and she was going to take complete advantage of it.

Jack tried to ease the tension. "What will you be working on in the lab?"

Mev hesitated, again unsure how much to say. They might think her college thesis project was cool, worth pursuing, but it had cost her an expulsion after all. Her mom always said it was better to keep their business private, and Mev had generally followed that advice.

"Not sure yet," she said.

"Hey Hector, remember telling me about the artificial intelligence program you were playing with?" Jack said. "You could expand that ELIZA thing for your dissertation."

Hector glowered at him.

Jack laughed. "He wrote a version of that psychologist program ELIZA. Except it talks dirty to you. You know, like those 1-900 phone sex lines."

"Jesus, Jack!" Hector said and got up to start the dishes.

After Jack wandered into the living room, Mev grabbed a flowered towel and joined Hector to dry. He glanced at her, then handed her the pasta pot. His hands were soft. Programmer's hands.

"So, what are you going to do?" Mev asked.

He shrugged. "I'll figure something out on my own. Fitz sure as hell isn't going to help me."

They finished the dishes in silence. Hector went upstairs, and Mev sat with Jack, who was, unsurprisingly, playing a computer game. A long cord extended from the keyboard on his lap to a tidy pile of game consoles and a PC computer tower, all tied into the TV.

"What are you playing?" Mev asked.

"SimCity. Just got it. Basically, you're an urban planner. You take tax revenue from the citizens, set zoning, and build services like police and fire. The citizens, 'Sims,' decide what to build, and where. They do it on their own. It's so cool."

"How do you win?"

"You don't really win. You can create a nice orderly city the citizens approve of. Bad stuff still happens though: fires, floods, tornadoes. Or you can go bankrupt. It's like real life."

He didn't have to tell her about that.

Mev watched as Jack tried to extinguish fires after a nuclear meltdown in Boston in 2010. They got away from him after a while, and he did indeed go bankrupt as the city burned. He handed the keyboard to Mev, and she played Rio de Janeiro in 2047 with global warming causing the city to flood. Jack watched, drinking wine, and occasionally making suggestions on where to put roads or how to zone a city block.

When she finally looked up from the game it was late.

"I've got to get to bed; I'm with Fitz first thing. Hey, don't I need to sign a lease with the landlord?"

"I sort of am the landlord," Jack replied. "I own the house with my parents. I didn't want to live in the dorms or share a house with ten random strangers," he added, "so my parents and I figured if I was going to stay in Cambridge it made more sense to buy."

That kind of money was a distant memory for Mev. At one time her father had made—well, stolen—millions.

"Thanks, I guess, for letting me stay here."

"No problem. It's way more fun to have smart people hanging around in the house." He turned back to the game.

"I think I can save Boston this time."

MONDAY, JANUARY 29, 1990

A FEW MINUTES BEFORE 9:00 A.M., SPECIAL AGENT PAUL Ostrowski stood before his new boss's closed door in the Boston FBI Field Office in the John F. Kennedy federal office building. Assistant Special Agent in Charge Mitchell Weaver's secretary wasn't in yet and Paul didn't think he should be sitting when Weaver arrived. The rest of the office was silent except for the rumble of the heating ducts.

At 9:00 sharp, Weaver's door opened, startling Paul. He'd been in there the whole time.

"Ostrowski?"

"Yes sir," Paul answered, reflexively straightening his tie.

Weaver didn't offer him a seat.

The office was spare, and the desk, a large expanse of mahogany, was completely devoid of items, save several file folders squared to the far-right corner. Weaver looked like the prototypical drill sergeant: graying hair in a flat-top buzz cut framed a square face, permanently tanned.

"Ostrowski, let's start with how I run my operation. Agents do what they are told, they keep their noses clean, they look and act like real FBI. This is a by-the-book office."

He opened the top file folder but didn't look at it. He clearly already knew the salient details.

"D.C. contacted me and asked if I could partner one of my new agents with one they were transferring here. That agent was you. Make no mistake, you would not have been my first, second, or second-to-last choice."

He paused, his gaze sharpening from a grunt-intimidating glare to a soul-piercing stare aimed right at Ostrowski.

"Son, I don't get it. Your work record was excellent. Your supervisors gave you high marks. You were on a path for leadership. That incident with Agent Knightly stands out like a clown in church. If I'm going to have you on my team, I need to know what the hell that was about."

It was all in the file. In detail. Ah well. Paul told the story enough times it almost didn't make him angry anymore. Almost.

"Yes, sir. Knightly was harassing a member of my team, Sara Abramson. Last August, he confined her in his office and attempted to assault her. I stopped him. He wrote me up. When the Office of Professional Responsibility investigated, I was suspended. I did the mandatory counseling. That's it."

"That's not quite it," Weaver said. "You struck him."

"I decked him, sir. He had it coming, and I delivered."

Was Weaver old-school FBI, the kind of guy who thought women agents were an abomination and yearned for the black and white—mostly white—days of J. Edgar Hoover? Or was he part of the new FBI who led by example?

He sure played the part of the old-style G-Man.

"OPR cleared you after counseling. Headquarters sent you here. Your file says you are fit for duty, so we'll go with that for now. You feel the need to punch anyone in the face, you lock that crap down. Got it?"

"Got it."

"You screw up, son, and you'll be chasing seal thieves in Anchorage."

"Absolutely, sir."

"Sit," Weaver said, the interrogation phase apparently over. He opened another of the neatly stacked folders. "How are you on Counterintelligence work?"

Paul was too seasoned to sigh, at least on the outside. He'd completed a refresher on CI at the Federal Law Enforcement Training Center in Georgia which had only reminded him how much he didn't know. He'd been in the Criminal Investigation Division his whole FBI career until now, and had absolutely no interest in Counterintelligence. Or in leaving Washington D.C. The whole thing felt like an affront, a pile-on. First the investigation and reprimand in his file, then required counseling, then the transfer, his already-troubled marriage stumbling under the strain.

"No field experience sir. Though, I did take a refresher course down at FLETC last month. I'm good to go." He didn't need to give more reasons for his new boss to doubt him.

Weaver grunted and handed Paul a thin case folder.

"There are a series of events we are working to either connect or dismiss. We think they're all related to computer crime. 'Hacking', it's called."

That subject was not covered in any of his refresher classes.

"You may be aware of the problems with the AT&T long distance network on Martin Luther King Day."

He'd seen a story about it in *The Washington Post*: "AT&T Long Distance Lines Fail." Except for the fact that it happened, Paul hadn't attributed any importance to it.

"The outage was the result of malicious activities by so-called 'hackers' who intentionally brought down the system. A form of technology terrorism the White House will not tolerate. There is an ongoing investigation to address this kind of crime, the Chicago Fraud and Abuse Task Force. It's being led by Secret Service and supported by the U.S. Attorney's office, the FBI and other DOJ personnel."

"Sorry, sir. The Secret Service? How are they involved?"

"Has to do with how the Computer Fraud and Abuse statute was written. They wanted the spotlight. What's important is they've indicted several known hackers over the last few months. They believe these hackers are responsible for that phone outage as well as numerous other crimes including interfering with the 911 system."

Paul nodded, but he wasn't following. He knew little to nothing about computers. This kind of technology stuff just wasn't interesting to him. Not that anyone was asking his opinion.

"Over the last year, a hacker who goes by the alias 'Raven' has cropped up in several incidents here in Boston. CIA has evidence of technology stolen from local companies and universities ending up in Soviet hands. Secret Service doesn't cover cases involving espionage or foreign counterintelligence. Since it's domestic, CIA handed it to us. And with the phone system break-in and the rising perception of threat from these hackers, this case has been assigned a higher priority by the Director, so I have to take this seriously. Which means you'll be taking this seriously. You'll be partnered with another agent transferred from D.C. for this assignment. Carl Philips."

"Sir, I really don't know anything about computers. I'm not sure this is a good case for me."

"I'll decide what's good for you while you are here. You'll do what you're told. Clear cases and we'll see if you deserve more leash. Philips will be giving a briefing for agents later today that will bring the team up to speed on computer crime. That's all. Dismissed."

Paul left with the thin folder and a great weight. He knew he was going to be under scrutiny. He'd assumed he could be a solid agent, close a few cases, and the dark clouds would clear, sending him back to D.C.

This case though? He didn't know crap about computers. Computers plus Counterintelligence. Was this a setup to make him fail? To quit?

Weaver's secretary was outside the office now, typing briskly on an IBM Selectric. Paul asked where Philips sat, and followed her directions through the sea of metal desks. He found Philips heads down reading a report, oblivious to his presence. Paul knocked on the desk corner.

"Paul Ostrowski. Weaver sent me over."

"Cool," Philips popped up from his chair and extended his hand. "I'm Carl."

Philips was a tall skinny Black man. Kid, really. This had to be one of his first postings.

"I was sent to Boston specifically for this case, and there's a ton of work to do. I was super excited when the ASAC told me I'd be getting a partner." Philips said, talking quickly.

Paul rolled over a desk chair. Philips pointed to the codename on the file Paul was holding: "Longbow."

"What exactly is the work?" Paul asked, hoping he'd understand it better than when Weaver told him.

"It's really cool. Stealing computer technology and selling it to the Russians. It's different from other espionage cases, though. This isn't like John Anthony Walker and his family, walking military technology secrets off a Navy base, stealing anything they can get their hands on. No radar plans, no fighter jets in this instance. This Raven dude only steals commercial computer technology."

Paul was almost afraid to ask, knowing he'd likely not understand the answer. "What kind of computer technology?"

"See, that's the interesting thing, it's all kinds, some of it stuff the Russians can't even use. One was an advanced microchip design."

"Why couldn't they use that?"

"The design alone isn't enough, you need the FAB plans, and you need to be able to build it."

"FAB?"

"Fabrication plant, where you turn silicon into integrated circuits. The CIA report said this stood out because there's no intelligence saying the Russians could even use the chip design."

"They'd still want it, right?"

"Sure, I guess. It's export-restricted tech, so why not? Maybe if we uncover more intelligence, we can answer that. The interesting thing though is the hacking. It's not some random disgruntled guy grabbing stuff from work and hoping Moscow's into paying for it. This is targeted. Purposeful. At least that's what the CIA is telling us from their sources."

"Which are?" Paul paged through the thin file.

Carl shrugged. "Classified. They say they've given us everything they know about the US side of this operation, which isn't much. A reference to the hacker's handle—Raven—and the fact that most of the research they are stealing seems to originate around Boston."

"That's not much at all."

"We don't need much. That hacker who broke into Lawrence Berkeley Labs, Markus Hess?"

Paul shook his head.

"He was looking for military secrets to sell to the KGB and was discovered because of a seventy-five cent discrepancy in the computer accounting log."

This assignment was sounding less attractive by the minute.

"Think about it. Hess did the hack from Germany. Now you can steal global military and industrial secrets from thousands of miles away. No fingerprints, no trace. No record anything was taken. At least if you're good."

"So—this may not even have anything to do with Boston?" Paul asked.

"Who knows? That's what's so cool." Carl said.

Paul considered his next statement. He needed this job to work, but he didn't want to screw his new partner. "Look, Philips."

"Carl."

"Look, Carl. So, we're clear, I don't know anything about computers. I mean, nothing, nada. I type with two fingers," he said holding up his thick index fingers.

"I'm pretty good with computers. We'll be just fine."

Paul was crushingly bored and completely lost. Well, that wasn't entirely true. About once every thirty minutes something came out of Carl's mouth that Paul thought he might understand. He tried—and failed—not to look at the clock.

"If you don't understand the mind of the hacker, his motivation, you can't *grok* his actions," Carl said.

Paul glanced around the agent-filled room to see if someone could translate *grok*. Everyone looked as confused as Paul. Carl continued talking.

He began by saying how woefully behind the FBI was in dealing with computer crime. Paul didn't dispute that; new ideas, new technology, new policing procedures needed to be part of the FBI toolkit. Paul knew there was a team in D.C. that did computer forensics: the Magnetic Media Program. He'd met one of them at FLETC, though to be honest, he didn't understand exactly what they did either. Nor, he suspected, did anyone else in the room except for Carl. Change at the FBI did happen, just at a glacial pace.

"How many of you have read William Gibson's *Neuromancer*?" Carl asked.

No one replied.

Incredulous, Carl shook his head then trudged on, describing the novel and how it captured the "essence of living in computers."

The seminar finally broke at 5:30, and Paul rolled down his sleeves and put his suit coat back on. He wanted to look like he was taking his new position seriously: Special Agent, Counterintelligence. Might as well be the "rubber gun squad." Instead of pursuing, catching, and arresting criminals, now he'd just watch suspected spies and write reports.

Paul took a long breath, held it, then slowly exhaled. Anger management had at least been good for something. And it had been mandatory.

Paul congratulated Carl on the seminar and asked if he wanted to grab a drink. "I need to cool off these brain cells," Paul said.

Carl chuckled. "Sure, I think one or two of the other guys are going out; I can introduce you around."

In the lobby of the JFK Building, two more agents joined them.

"Guys, this is Paul Ostrowski, posted here from D.C. Paul, this is Allen Connor and Kevin Morrison."

"Everyone calls me Morrie," Morrison said as he shook his hand.

"Connor," the other agent said, nodding, not offering his hand, and ignoring Carl completely.

Old school bigot. Still rampant in law enforcement. Paul had learned how to deal with them. It angered him that Carl had to.

"I know just the place to take the edge off," Connor said. Carl navigated for Paul as he drove ten blocks or so, twisting through the maze of downtown Boston streets, then parking in a pretty seedy part of town. He looked at Carl as they trudged down LaGrange Street.

"They call this the 'Combat Zone,'" Carl said.

Paul could see why. Strip bars, street walkers, cops, dope dealers, everything from sleazy clubs to adult bookstores. The nattily dressed Connor led them into the less-than-classy "Glass Slipper," where the bouncer knew Connor by name and whisked them to a front-row table. The air in the club was stale, with a pall of cigarette smoke hugging the ceiling. A plump, bored-looking blonde was on stage, giving a half-hearted striptease a few feet from them.

Paul thought the choice of location said a lot about Connor.

"Just up from headquarters?" Connor asked.

"Yep. They moved me into CI."

"Morrie here is in CI, chasing spooks like you."

Carl didn't raise an eyebrow at the intentional slur. Connor was equally straight-faced, as if he hadn't intended the double entendre. Paul was getting an exceptionally clear picture of the man.

"What were you doing in D.C.?"

"Criminal Investigation Division."

"That's my beat. Organized Crime," Connor said. "Any cases I would know?"

"Nothing earth-shattering, mostly smuggling, drugs."

"I thought they were transferring people out of CI into CID? 'End of the Cold War' and all that crap?"

"Just lucky, I guess."

"Family come with you?" Morrie asked.

"Not yet. Wife and kid back in D.C."

"Ah, cat's away, eh? You want a little distraction?" Connor said waving a hand at the stage, and the girls working the room, "I can hook you up."

No doubt.

"That was a heck of a lot of computer talk for one day," Morrie said, trying to be friendly and engage Carl, trying to offset Connor.

"Good luck with that computer stuff," Connor said. "I have no idea why Weaver made us sit through that. The FBI is going to hell, man. I mean most of the kids going into Quantico now never held a gun before, don't know shit about policing. You know shit about *law enforcement*, Ostrowski?" he said, drawing out the words and jabbing the lit end of his cigarette at Paul.

This guy needed that anger management seminar so much more than Paul had.

"Four years with Chicago P.D., then Quantico."

"See, that's what I'm talking about. You're on the streets, you know what goes down."

"I wasn't a cop first," Carl said.

Paul wasn't sure it was a good idea to bait this guy, but Carl was a Special Agent like the rest of them. And he deserved respect like the rest of them. You didn't make it through the FBI Academy if you didn't have some iron in your spine.

To Carl's credit, his comment took Connor off balance. "True," he said, "you're a smart little fucker though. Brass seems to think we need your kind, too."

They fell silent, and for lack of anything else to talk about, watched the tired performer as she finished her act, and another listless girl took the stage. After her performance ended Connor checked his watch, drained his beer, and threw a fistful of ones onto the stage.

"Can you believe they want to tear all this down? Build some new 'Midtown Cultural District?' I mean, we already got all the culture we need right here," he said opening his arms expansively. "Gotta get going. Wife number three and I are supposed to go to dinner."

Connor shook his head. "That had to be the most boring shit I've ever had to sit through. No offense." The thing every asshole said when they meant every offense. "Naw, I take it back. It wasn't as bad as that stupid sexual harassment session last year," Connor laughed.

"Asshole," Carl said, barely loud enough for Paul to hear.

TUESDAY, JANUARY 30, 1990

MEV FOUND HER WAY TO THE MBTA STATION IN PORTER Square, fortunately only a few blocks away from Jack's house on Linnaean. Her brief time driving in Boston had convinced her that she'd rather leave her car parked.

Passing by a huge metal sculpture of red balloons, she followed fellow passengers down the long escalator to a ticket booth, bought a few dollars' worth of brass tokens and dropped one in the turnstile slot to access the platform. She boarded a Red Line Braintree-bound train and was soon at her stop, scrambling to her feet when the crackly speaker called Kendall/MIT.

Her umbrella did little to stop the needles of sleet blowing sideways on her walk to Building 38. She could hear activity in the building, but at 8:30 a.m. the door to the Advanced Concepts Lab was locked. She waited on the cold hall floor for half an hour before one of the grad students showed up and opened it.

"No one's here this early," he said.

Mev was trying to remember his name. Roger? Rick? There were so many new faces, and most were always turned toward a monitor.

"Fitz usually gets in around ten," he said. "You might wanna ask him for a key." He turned and proceeded to a terminal in the far end of the lab, ignoring her and leaving her in silence. Mev shrugged off her parka and fidgeted outside Fitz's office.

Hector came in not long after and nodded to her. He sure as heck could have given her a heads up on the lab start time.

When Fitz finally arrived, he steered straight toward Mev. "Good morning! I'm going to want to work closely with you during your first few months, so let's get right into things." He gestured toward a desk in his office and handed her a folder. "Here's the graduate program application. It's due soon, so make that your first priority, then we can grab lunch and chat."

It felt only like minutes had passed when she sensed Fitz standing behind her. It had been two hours.

"Lunch?" he asked.

The damp, gray morning had given way to a dazzlingly sunny winter day. Mev followed Fitz to a dark blue BMW. Academic work appeared to pay better than she'd thought. On the drive, the MIT campus gave way to central Cambridge, filled with double and triple decker row homes and single-story brick commercial buildings. In Inman Square, Fitz turned into the cramped parking lot for the S&S Deli. The line moved quickly despite the crowd, and they were soon seated.

Before he looked at the menu, Fitz ordered a glass of white wine for himself and one for her. "Working lunch," he said by way of explanation.

Mev hoped they didn't card her. That would be a humiliating start to their relationship.

"I knew when I first talked to your advisor that you were meant for MIT. I read about the Ada Promise Prize winners in *IEEE Spectrum* and had to discover who this young woman from Northwest Missouri State was. Dave Franklin couldn't say enough about you."

Dave Franklin, her advisor at NW Missouri. Mentor and friend. He pushed her harder than anyone had before. As generous a teacher as she'd ever worked with. Even kind of a father figure.

He'd nominated her for the Ada Promise Prize for Rising Women in Computing based on her academic achievement and had been thrilled when she'd won one of the coveted awards.

"So, what do you want to focus on once you're in the graduate program?" Fitz asked. "Expand your thesis? Work on network administration and security, maybe multi-factor authentication? I might be able to land you outside research support from RSA. I know the guys over there and they're about to get significant government funding."

She knew the names—Rivest, Shamir, Adleman—RSA. The deans of computer security. Fitz knew them *personally*.

Dave Franklin had continued pushing her even after the award, making her do a thesis, rejecting her first few half-assed proposals as "simple-minded," only accepting the one he thought was going to change the face of network security.

"And what about after your PhD?" he asked. "With a doctorate from MIT and my recommendation, you'll be able to write your own ticket."

Maybe she'd be able to afford her own BMW.

"I haven't even applied yet."

"Trust me, you'll get in," he said and finished his wine in one big gulp.

He ordered another wine. Mev declined. Waiting for the drink, he was quiet, less exuberant, perking up only when a female undergrad waved to him.

His second glass of wine came with their food, a corned beef Reuben for Fitz, a chef salad for Mev.

"Of course, you'll be busy working on your classes," he said between bites. "And we can review your schedule later today. First let me talk to you about what I want you working on in the lab."

He wiped the grease from his fingers onto his napkin and leaned toward her, his voice low. "The work you were doing at Northwest Missouri was quite innovative, and I want to see you to continue it with the support you deserve."

Her thesis. She had called it DEMON: Distributed Exploit Monitoring Over Networks. A play on the Unix operating system term "daemon," describing any program that ran in the background.

Her DEMON would catalog all the known vulnerabilities—"exploits" in hacker terms—in the operating systems running on the target network. Systems administrators were notorious for failing to apply patches and system upgrades in a timely fashion. To help with that, DEMON would traverse a target network, probe each computer, and identify if it had any known vulnerabilities or outdated software that could be exploited.

Basically, DEMON could help make computers safer by breaking into them. The widely unpatched Sendmail exploit, one of the vulnerabilities the Morris Worm used to spread itself through—and cripple—the internet, was what inspired her.

"I would love that," she said. She'd been proud of the work, as had Dave Franklin. Too proud maybe.

In her early testing, she'd gone to the Northwest Missouri network administrator with it. Unlike Dave, he was unimpressed, saying it was a gimmick, useless to professionals like him who kept their networks patched and current. But with Dave's support, she was feeling sure of herself and bet the admin she could find a vulnerability. She did. And to prove it, she broke into the admin's email, sending him back evidence in the form of a set of steamy love notes between him and a student twenty years his junior.

He was not amused. Nor was the Dean.

The Dean was as outraged by her "theft" of school property as by the name DEMON itself, more of the "satanic panic" B.S. causing parents all over America to hyperventilate. He raged on about the school's reputation, saying he had no choice: he would be forced to expel her, given her violation of the honor code—and that she should count herself lucky that they hadn't involved the FBI.

In that moment, Mev hadn't felt lucky.

Then Fitz called Dave Franklin to find the girl who won the Ada Prize. And Dave, being who he was, pitched Mev hard to Fitz. She couldn't help wondering if he'd actually reached out to Fitz first to find her a safe haven.

Mev owed Dave for this opportunity. Even so, no matter what Hector might think, she deserved to be here.

"You know better than most that what you are investigating could be seen in a bad light," Fitz said. "I want every advantage for you, so let's keep the work between us for now."

She saw the wisdom in that. Keep her head down. Do the work. Embrace this opportunity.

Fitz finished his sandwich and his second glass of wine. "Between classes and your research, you've got a lot on your plate. Let's meet on Fridays to check in and make sure you're getting what you need."

What she needed was to shine.

FRIDAY, FEBRUARY 2, 1990

WITH HELP AND ENCOURAGEMENT FROM FITZ, MEV plowed through her grad school application, submitting it just before the deadline. Classes were starting the next Tuesday, so she was using this tiny respite to clean up her work on DEMON, which she hadn't touched in months. The list of exploits powering it would be out of date. And it still wasn't fully automated.

Her first Friday meeting with Fitz had come much too soon. He'd be expecting an update on her progress, and she didn't have much. Considering what she'd say as she stared at the unfinished code, she felt a presence behind her. Expecting Fitz, she was surprised to see Jack.

"What are you doing here?" she asked.

"I was going to have lunch with Hector, only he's too busy stressing about a new dissertation topic. When's the last time you ate anything?"

Despite living in the same house, she'd barely seen Jack or Hector all week. Her meals had been sandwiches from one of the cafés on campus or snacks from the vending machines. She looked at her watch: 1:15 already.

"Um, maybe last night?" she said.

"That won't do. Come have lunch with me."

They bundled up before venturing into the cold. "What the heck are you working on anyway?"

"Just some research Fitz has me doing." It felt strange keeping it secret, but she trusted Fitz's judgment.

"You know all work and no play makes Jack a dull boy."

She laughed. "I'm trying to make a good impression."

"On Fitz? He recruited you. I think you're all set there."

Mev tried to read Jack's tone. Was he siding with Hector on Fitz's generosity toward her? Maybe it wasn't fair, the break she'd been given. Despite that, she believed she deserved to be at MIT.

After a frigid walk to Central Square they arrived at Harvest, a small natural foods co-op with a café. It smelled of a combination of spices that suggested the Middle East, though truthfully, Mev had no idea what that would actually smell like. The only international cuisine she knew of in Maryville were a Taco Bell and the storefront Chinese Panda buffet. Not that she and her mom ate out very often.

Mev picked a sandwich with cream cheese, cucumbers, and bean sprouts on a bagel, not certain she'd ever had bean sprouts. Jack got some kind of bulgur wheat bowl and led the way to a wobbly table next to the steamy front window. The sun had come from behind the clouds, and Mev felt warm enough to take off her coat.

"You know, you'll burn yourself out if you don't take some breaks, have a little fun. I've seen it happen."

Mev considered Hector, who was working his ass off, without the extra help from Fitz. While he might enjoy eating dinner with Jack, otherwise he was on his computer, working, clearly struggling. Jack, on the other hand, certainly took his own advice, listening to music, playing computer games, cooking. Maybe MIT was just harder than Harvard. Or maybe Jack was smarter than she gave him credit for.

Mev nodded occasionally as Jack prattled on, talking about live shows he'd seen in Boston, ranging from Timothy Leary doing comedy at Catch A Rising Star to an upcoming Laurie Anderson concert.

She had an event of her own on the calendar that very night: the monthly meeting of 2600, named after the magazine *2600: The Hacker Quarterly*. From its founding a few years before, it had featured articles on hacking computers, phone systems, switches, routers, and anything else that digital explorers might be curious about. Boston had one of the only chapters in the United States, and she was thrilled at the chance to meet other hackers.

It was part of the appeal of MIT, of Boston. Along with Silicon Valley, this was one of the hubs of technology development in the United States. Some of the brightest, most talented innovators worked at and around MIT. And where technology flourished, so did those who liked to test its limits.

In college Mev had discovered Usenet newsgroups, the message boards created by the early architects and users of the burgeoning internet. It was where they debated Requests for Comment, RFCs, the documents that became the rules of the growing network. Newsgroups were synchronized across servers worldwide, including discussions of science like *sci.research* and computing in forums like *comp.programming*. Users also shared other, less professional interests in the *alt.* domain, where Mev found *alt.2600*, a hotbed of hacker culture, and discovered that these were her people. People for whom the world of computers had no boundaries.

The afternoon went quickly, with Mev reacquainting herself with DEMON and researching new exploits identified since the last time she'd touched her application. The list was extensive and she began the detailed work of adding them to the code.

"It's been a long week," Fitz said when he entered the lab at the end of the day. "I've noticed how diligently you're working on your research, and I'm looking forward to an update. For now, however, it's time to unwind. Let me buy you a drink."

Mev was grateful he was cutting her slack. Watching Hector's experience, she knew this was a rare opportunity, and she was determined to make the most of it.

"That'd be great."

Back in Fitz's BMW, they drove into Harvard Square. Despite the cold, it was busy with students, buskers, and onlookers. Mev marveled at the diversity and energy with street musicians, punks smoking and talking, and tweedy academics rushing to their next appointment. What a contrast to the Midwest, where "different" was a not-so-subtle insult.

At the Charles Hotel, a valet took Fitz's car, and they walked up to the Regattabar.

"Happy Friday, Dr. Fitz," the bartender called as they entered.

"Pedro, my man!" Fitz replied. When they were seated, Fitz waved over an attractive, older waitress, who also clearly knew him. "Connie, my usual, and one for my colleague here."

How cool was it to grab a drink with a work colleague? To be in a place where being smart wasn't weird, but respected, even revered. This was Fitz's element, and now hers as well.

"Tell me about your week," Fitz said. "Sorry I haven't seen as much of you as I'd like. Hector tells me you've been putting in long hours."

Hector was certainly paying close attention.

Connie delivered two gin martinis with extra olives. Fitz took a generous sip. Mev took a more tentative one and tried not to grimace. It tasted like lighter fluid.

She'd deliberated all afternoon what update to give Fitz, eventually deciding being straight with him was the best way to earn his trust. He'd made a big deal of the research when he'd invited her to MIT, and she felt vulnerable having to admit that she wasn't as far along on it as he might believe.

"I hadn't fully finished the automation on my thesis project before everything, you know, unraveled. I'm working on that now and catching up on new developments," she said, taking another trial sip of the martini. Still terrible.

"I'm impressed with your focus," he said, taking another long slow sip from his own glass, then eating an olive, surveying the room before turning his attention back to her.

"You're not like other students, Mev. Half of them don't even know why they're at MIT. Only a few stand out: the ones with talent and the drive to make use of it. To do what it takes to be successful. You know, I don't invite just anyone into the program. And not everyone I bring in earns the right to stay. You've got that kind of drive. I can see that. You belong here."

He raised a glass, and she clinked it, trying not to spill the still-full martini.

"Your research shows amazing promise, and we'll likely be working together on it for several years."

The silence lengthened and Mev grew uncomfortable as he waited for her to speak. He didn't sound disappointed in her progress, so what was it? Then it hit her. "They haven't released admissions already, have they?"

"No, not yet. I've already had a few conversations behind the scenes, of course. I've made sure you'll be accepted into the graduate program."

She began tearing up, shocked by the news, then embarrassed. She mopped at her eyes. "Sorry."

"It's fine. And congratulations. Well-deserved. Don't tell anyone I told you," he said, giving her an exaggerated wink. "I'd get in big trouble."

He drained his glass. Connie had two more on the table in a minute.

"Drink up," Fitz said, raising his glass. "To a wonderful partnership."

Mev went to take a tiny sip of her martini and yawned. Then yawned again.

"Oh my God, I'm so sorry," she said again.

Fitz paused, a look of disappointment crossing his face. "No problem. You've had quite a week."

He put money down on the table and grabbed their coats, waving to Pedro and giving Connie a peck on the cheek before taking Mev's arm.

"Let me drop you. Where did you find a place?"

"Linnaean Street."

Mev was quiet on the drive back, the BMW's efficient heater making her even sleepier. As Fitz arrived at 39-1/2 Linnaean, Mev opened the car door, the cold air shocking her back to wakefulness.

"We've got great work ahead of us, Mev. I can't wait to get back to it. Meet me in the lab Monday at 10:00."

Hector was on the porch steps smoking a cigarette, watching her as Fitz drove away. He said nothing as he stubbed it out in Jack's empty planter on the porch and brought the butt inside, letting the door close behind him.

Mev followed, determined not to let his snub kill her mood. She might be tired, but she had places to be.

She ran up to her room, dropped her backpack on her bed, then came back down to the living room, where Jack was reading while, somehow, also watching MTV playing Sinéad O'Connor's "Nothing Compares 2 U."

"How do I get to the Prudential Center?" Mev asked.

"Doing a little shopping?"

"No, I have a meeting at the food court there."

"In a food court?"

"2600. It's a kind of computer programmer collective."

"Cool. Can I come?" Jack asked. "I can show you the way. Plus, I think I know one of the guys who kind of runs it. We play D&D together sometimes."

It occurred to her that Jack might have more geek credentials than Mev herself did, despite her chosen profession.

On the T, Jack asked to look through the Autumn 1989 edition of the *2600: The Hacker Quarterly* she was holding in her lap. He pointed to pictures of telephones from behind the Iron Curtain.

"They sure like their phones."

"Phones are kind of the hacking origin story," she said. "Phone phreaking, hacking the telephone network, has been going on for years."

Jack kept reading. A long article on hacking academic computers, "Grade A Hacking," elicited a "that could be useful," from him. Flipping more pages, he found an article titled "Lair of the INTERNET Worm."

"Really?" he said, pointing at the bottom of the page where it read: "If you want a copy of the source code (with comnts), send $10 to 2600 Worm, PO Box 752, Middle Island, NY 11953."

"Even I know what that is and I'm an English major."

"Yeah, it got a lot of attention."

Mev didn't mention that she already had a copy of the code and had gone through it line by line. How could she not? If the dean at Northwest Missouri had known, no doubt there would have been yet another charge against her.

"Why 2600?" Jack asked.

"As you said, they like their phones. 2600 hertz is the frequency of the tone the long-distance network used for control commands. A hacker named Captain Crunch popularized it after he found that a toy whistle from the cereal hit that exact frequency."

They reached Park Street Station in downtown Boston and Jack led her through the maze of dank tunnels connecting the Red Line to the shabbier Green Line. She tried, and failed, to ignore the rats running along the tracks.

Exiting at Prudential station, they navigated to a large food court at the base of the skyscraper, hosting both a variety of food options and a diverse crowd. Clumped together at the edge of the court was a group that had to be 2600: angry-looking teenagers in surplus military coats with cigarettes dangling from their lips, cyberpunk aspirants with mirrored aviator sunglasses, gawky undergraduates who were badly dressed and badly in need of sleep. A few rangy guys who might be programmers or junkies or both.

What there was not was another woman.

A guy like a scarecrow, tall, thin, with lank blond hair and light chin fuzz was raging at the enthralled group. "This is an intellectual exercise, a battle of wits and mastery. They're acting like we're waging war. I mean, has anybody read *Cuckoo's Egg* yet?" Several voices grunted assent. "Makes out like he's a kind of war hero, catching the guy spying for the Russian military."

"KGB," someone corrected.

"Right. That's not us. I mean the cold war is over, right? Bush and Gorbachev said so. It's yet another excuse to whip the public into a frenzy about computers and demonize anyone who doesn't wear a suit and tie and sit at a desk at IBM."

"Fuckin' A!" erupted from the back of the group, and several parents with kids in the food court glared.

The tall blond speaker called to Jack. "Dude!"

He'd spoken to Jack, but the speaker's eyes—everyone's eyes—were on her.

"This is Mev," Jack said.

The speaker said "M.e.V.? As in Mega Electron Volts?"

"It's not a handle, it's my name."

"Too bad, that'd be a good one. I'm Tom." His offered hand was soft.

"No handle?" Mev asked.

"Tom B. 'Tomb.' Tom Bergstrom. I run a board called The Crypt. And help organize these degenerates," he said gesturing at the group.

An underfed undergraduate with thick glasses and a brown ponytail called the group to order, and got most of them to pay attention, though there was one cluster huddled by the payphones at the end of the food court, speaking in low tones and trading notebooks back and forth.

"I'm Party Phreak, for those who don't already know me," the wan undergraduate said. "I was supposed to talk about how to work a ROLM phone system this month, but given all the stuff that's been going down, I figured we could talk about it."

"Talk about what?" one kid asked.

"I'm sure you all heard about Robert Tappan Morris. RTM's facing five years on one felony count. And there are three bills in Congress right now making the construction of any virus, whatever that means, a felony. And now that Kevin Mitnick is out of jail, they have him in rehab like he's an addict. It's the 'War on Drugs' all over again. Next, they'll have a Hacking Czar in the White House."

That got a few wary laughs.

"The Cthulhu BBS said the Secret Service arrested a group of hackers in New York, blaming them for the AT&T crash this month even though AT&T now says they did it to themselves. Faulty software patch."

"It's a witch hunt," Mev said, and got universal, if surprised, assent.

"The stakes are getting higher," Party Phreak continued. "If you sneak into a government facility, they'll throw you out, maybe arrest you for trespassing, not put you in jail for five years."

"So don't get caught, dumbass," somebody scoffed.

Mev turned around to find the speaker, a serious young guy near the back of the group wearing mirrored aviator sunglasses and a long black trench coat. No, not a guy: a girl with short, cropped hair.

"They're not all stupid," Tom said quietly, aware that they were attracting attention. "The FBI, Secret Service, the NSA. They don't want anybody messing with the phone networks or any government or military systems. They'll bust anyone they can find to make an example of them."

As the meeting was breaking up, the girl in the mirror shades approached Mev and gave her a nod.

"I'm Hecate."

Her handle. Mev had experimented with a few aliases online, never really settled on one.

"I haven't seen you here before," Hecate said. "I'm usually the only one."

Mev knew what she meant: the only girl. The only girl in math class, the only girl in the computer lab, the only girl who wouldn't do what was expected of her.

Hecate's real name, it turns out, was Jamie, and they talked long after everyone, including Jack, was gone. As the food court closed, the staff encouraged them to leave. They'd barely scratched the surface.

As they walked down to the T, Jamie handed Mev a slip of paper with her pager number.

"We girls gotta stick together."

FRIDAY, FEBRUARY 2, 1990

CARL'S INITIAL BRIEFING HADN'T BEEN NEARLY ENOUGH. Paul had pages of notes from the session, most of it gibberish on re-reading. Since then, Carl had been putting him through twelve-hour days to bring him up to speed on "the basics." Honestly, Paul felt stupider than when he started. Carl had worked to explain the wild ecosystem of computing: networks connecting military and university computers, newsgroups anyone could participate in, FTP sites where you could upload and download files, dial-up bulletin board servers and commercial online services like AOL, CompuServe, and Prodigy. What a mess.

Carl answered every naive question Paul asked, never pointing out when he repeated, forgetting what he'd learned before. They'd worked straight through both lunch and dinner. The remains of food wrappers, coffee cups, and piles of files littered Carl's desk.

"Carl, it's Friday night. Don't you have anywhere to be? A wife? A girlfriend?"

"Nope. Just two bachelors here." Carl seemed untroubled about being alone. Paul missed having someone to go home to. He needed to fix things with Linda and get back to D.C. and his daughter Becky. First, he'd need to make serious traction on this case.

"Let's keep going. What's baud again?"

Weaver's assistant stood over them. She had her coat on, on her way home.

"ASAC Weaver would like you both in his office."

Paul and Carl both smoothed their ties on the way.

"Door," Weaver said as they entered, and Carl hurried to close it.

"Updates," Weaver said.

Paul was the senior agent, yet he wasn't sure he could string two coherent sentences together about what they had been doing the last few days. He waited a beat. Carl didn't jump in. Couldn't blame him.

"Agent Philips has been bringing me up to speed on the technical matters first, then we're going to dive deeper into the CIA's analysis. Their intelligence is awfully thin. The only domestic evidence we have so far is a lucky break with an individual who runs a bulletin board server and came forward claiming this Raven character broke into it."

At least Paul knew what a bulletin board server was now.

"You better get on the stick, Ostrowski. Secret Service has been making more raids the past few weeks. They're making us look like pikers. I want movement. Are we clear?"

He knew he should just say "yes sir!" and get the hell out of there, only he had no idea if he could promise anything so just said, "we're on it, sir."

It didn't seem like a good idea to go home quite yet given Weaver's dictate, so Paul let Carl familiarize him more with hacker bulletin boards. He had told Paul that if he was going to catch a hacker, he needed to understand how hackers talked, how they thought, and how they worked. Just like Carl, Paul figured.

Carl set up a putty-colored IBM personal computer on his desk. It took Paul several tries and help from Carl to start the program to make the modem box dial the 617-area code phone number Carl had given him. When it did, the box squealed and rang like an electric guitar being ripped apart. Only when the green screen read "connected," did it finally go silent.

Carl told him he needed to create a user on the board first.

"I need a username. Obviously not mine, and one that doesn't set off any bells with the other users. What do you use?"

"Master Blaster."

Paul laughed. "I certainly wouldn't picture you on the other side of that name. That's from a Mad Max movie, right?"

"See, you're not totally hopeless," Carl said.

"I saw that movie with my wife. She hated it." Paul remembered how Linda assumed that since Tina Turner was in it, the movie was going to be a musical. Things had still been good between them then.

"I know!" Carl said. "Agent Unknown."

"That makes it sound like I'm in the FBI," Paul said.

"I know. It's irony. Trust me, they like that kind of thing."

The bulletin board server was called Random Access. He could upload and download files, post messages, and peruse a list of other BBS phone numbers. Eight users were online.

Paul hit the "M" key and got a list of messages, many with large numbers of replies.

"Threads," Carl said, reading over his shoulder. "Messages and their replies are called 'message threads.' It's a kind of conversation. That's where most of the board activity is."

Paul read the message titles: Warez, Morris Worm, BBS numbers. Paul selected the Morris Worm message. At least he knew a little about that.

The message came from a user who went by the name "Doctor Death."

"I have the source code for RTM's worm. I've made modifications to make it stealthier and more stable. If you like it and make changes, share!"

Paul turned around in his chair. "Carl, is this for real? Are these guys spreading the worm that took down the internet? That got Morris indicted?"

"Technically, they are sharing the source code. Possession of the code itself isn't illegal, only using it to break the law is."

"Possessing this kind of, well, weapon—that isn't something we can prosecute?"

"If we could show it was military in nature, an illegal weapon of some kind, or a threat to national security, we'd have a leg to stand on. Just passing this kind of stuff around? Nope. We may face similar challenges when we chase down Raven. The law hasn't caught up with computers."

Nor have lawmen, Paul thought. He poked around in the bulletin board, finding requests for viruses, discussions of various hacks, a file on how to make your own lock-picks and explosives.

"Jesus," Paul sighed. "This is like handing a kid a loaded gun."

"Yep. And, unfortunately, there are a lot of kids on these boards. It's mostly harmless. You know—kids want to do stuff that's forbidden. Like showing your friends your dad's revolver."

"That gets a lot of kids shot."

"True. But it's not illegal."

"What about that movie, *War Games*? Could *you* do that?"

"Do I look like Matthew Broderick?" Carl asked, then turned more serious. "You know, they screened that in the White House, and it scared the bejesus out of President Reagan. He immediately demanded a new National Security Directive on computer security."

Paul wasn't sure if that should scare him more, or less. He returned to the BBS, reading one message ranting that Morris deserved to get caught because he was so sloppy. Paul picked that one to respond to. He figured he'd take a contrarian tone.

"Why should he be prosecuted at all? It was an experiment that got out of control."

Paul figured that would inspire good responses. He waited; impatient this conversation wasn't happening live. He was surprised nonetheless when replies came in from other users.

"Totally agree," one named Lord Lite wrote. "But he missed his chance. He should have taken more computers down. Too many back doors are closed now."

Another user asked, "I wonder what would happen if we all ran it at once?"

"How would I get started?" Paul replied. "I could use help."

Within minutes, Paul got several cranky messages directed at him, telling him to keep his newbie mouth shut until he knew what he was talking about.

Carl read over his shoulder and chuckled. "Lesson learned. This culture doesn't tolerate ignorance or inexperience. Do you want to move on to something else?"

"No. I got this."

Paul hated being a novice. He was the senior agent here, but could barely use the computer, much less understand what the hell people were saying on the boards.

He returned to the list of chat rooms, picked a new one, a "passwords" board.

"I'm looking for passwords for NASA." That felt like secrets a hacker would want. Everybody thought space was cool.

Immediately a reply came from "Admin."

"Are you a feeb? No direct asks for passwords. Board rules. Next time, you'll be permanently banned." Paul was abruptly logged off of the system.

Carl laughed again. "Feeb. Feeble. Or FBI. They made you either way, I guess."

Paul had to smile, despite the jab. This was going to take forever.

Later that night, sitting in his apartment, Paul found little hope in his future, his case, or his career. With the urgent move to Boston, he'd rented the crappy apartment sight unseen. Huge mistake. The realtor had crowed about the fact it was close to work and near the water. Yet the two mile drive to Government Center from his run-down triple decker in East Boston directly under the Logan Airport fly-over could take an hour on a busy day.

His destination was right there, but out of ready reach. His life in a nutshell.

Weaver had said it. Paul was a model agent, tackling every assignment with gusto, never complaining. His D.C. supervisor had told him his posting there was a sign that he was in favor and had great things ahead of him.

But Paul was a stickler for the rules. The real rules, the ones underneath the written ones. Right and wrong. He'd grown up Polish Catholic, and while he hadn't gone to church much since he was a kid, the moral compass he'd inherited from his parents still guided his life. He knew that was old fashioned. He didn't care.

Paul still believed in respecting people. And that's why he and his partner Sara Abramson had gotten along so well. Some FBI agents were certain a woman had no place in the Bureau. Paul, however, appreciated how hard she worked to be taken seriously.

When Rick Knightly had started hitting on her, making comments about her ass, Paul called him out. Paul encouraged Sara to report him. She said that would backfire, make her look too weak to make it in the FBI. Paul got it. Still, it burned. So, when he walked by Knightly's open office and saw him forcibly kissing Sara, he'd lost it. He barged in, and when she broke free, Paul stepped in and cold-cocked the bastard.

It had been so deeply satisfying in the moment. That feeling didn't last long. Paul believed in right and wrong, but the FBI operated on different principles: politics and perception. Knightly used his old boy connections and seniority to spin the story, implying there was something between Sara and Paul. In that context, the punch made Paul appear jealous, volatile, and that was the end of his upward career trajectory.

He opened a beer and sat in one of the chrome and cracked vinyl dining chairs that qualified his apartment as "furnished." Weaver might want instant results. Paul knew investigations had their own pace. Patience was required. You sit on suspects; you watch them.

They might have cut off his balls transferring him here. They didn't cut out his brain. *Cui bono.* Who benefits? Who is getting paid here? Raven? Who is Raven? No idea.

When you can't go around, go through. That's what he'd learned when he'd played football at Notre Dame. So, investigate, dammit. The motive had to be money, selling secrets for Russian cash. Next, means and opportunity. Who runs these bulletin boards? Who is letting Raven do his thing?

When you can't go around, go through. Time to put the hurt on these bulletin board admins, kick down doors, and brace these hacker punks.

SATURDAY, FEBRUARY 3, 1990

THE HOUSE WAS MORNING QUIET, AND MEV WAS THE first one up, pouring boiling water from the kettle over ground coffee in the French press pot when someone started banging on the front door and repeatedly ringing the bell.

Mev opened the door to find Tom Bergstrom, "Tomb," wild-eyed and out of breath.

"Where's Jack?" he asked, letting himself in. Mev looked down the street, wondering if Tom was being chased before closing the door behind him.

"He's sleeping. Though maybe not anymore."

"I need him. Can you wake him?"

She didn't need to. Jack was standing in on the stairs wrapped in a blanket. "What the hell, Tom? Couldn't you, I don't know, call first? And can you keep it down?"

"They raided me," Tom said, quieter now, his hands spread wide in surrender. "They took everything."

Jack looked at Mev, a questioning expression on his face, then finished walking down the stairs and sat on the aqua leather chair.

Tom was wearing a loose green sweatshirt and jeans over bright white tennis shoes. He was pacing.

"Chill out, man. You're making me nervous."

"Oh, well, yeah, sorry *man*, to make you nervous. Not like the FBI is at your door."

"The FBI? Tell me what happened. You want coffee or something?"

Tom sat on the matching aqua faux leather couch, his leg jiggling. "I got enough adrenaline for now, thanks," he said with a nervous laugh.

Mev went to finish making coffee and listened to Tom tell his story.

"A couple hours ago, the FBI pounded on my door with a warrant and took everything. All my computer equipment. They just left."

"That's insane," Jack said.

"I was asleep," Tom said. "I'd gone to bed like an hour before. Then at 5 a.m. there's this pounding. I figure it's the fraternity assholes next door cranking up their stereo. Then I realize it's the door. Two guys in suits and another couple of guys in those FBI windbreakers wave a warrant and carry in garbage bags and empty boxes. They took my computers, all my disks, anything that even smelled like computers to the idiots: binders, textbooks, all my electronic equipment. They even took my soldering iron for God's sake!"

"What did they say?" Jack asked.

"The Black agent said they were part of a national task force looking for hackers penetrating computer systems. They kept calling me 'Tomb' as if it was a secret identity they had uncovered. They asked me about The Crypt and wanted to know who had access to it."

Mev handed Jack a coffee, sat in the chair with the flowered bedspread and sipped her own.

"What did you tell them?" Jack asked.

"Nothing. I'm not a snot-nosed twelve-year-old stumbling around Ma Bell; I told them to take what they wanted and get the hell out. That seemed to confuse the young agent. He acted genuinely surprised I wouldn't cave just because they had badges."

Tom took a slow breath.

"I said I knew my rights, so they just ordered me to stay on the couch and forgot about me. They even dropped one of my servers, the gorillas. I'll sue them for damages!"

He'd been speaking faster and faster and took a moment to catch his breath. He pulled out a pack of cigarettes. Jack said, "not in the house," and Tom put it away.

"Once they had all the stuff, the two guys in suits came back in. New approach this time. The older white guy—Ostrowski—was less twitchy than the other suit. Now he did all the talking. He asked about all the folks who are regulars at 2600 and about a dude named Raven. He wanted to know what my relationship with him was, and why I was helping him break the law."

"Who's Raven?" Jack asked.

"No idea." Tom dropped his head into his hands and sighed. "I did this to myself. I was sure I had it under control."

"What are you talking about?"

"A while back I was doing admin on The Crypt and found a user account I didn't create. You know how I run it: access by invitation only. But there's this 'Raven' asshole who somehow made an account and was using UUCP mail to send email messages to other servers. I shut him down. Then he's back a few days later, new account, same username. I'm stumped; I keep that server locked down tight. Then I discover he's using an exploit in EMACS. Of course I missed it, only losers use EMACS."

Mev got it. She shared Tom's position in the "editor wars" that had been raging across Usenet the last few years. She, like him, was a fan of the text editor vi. Lean, mean, fast-loading, cross-platform compatible. The true programmer's editor. EMACS was a bloated Frankenstein's monster by comparison.

"I fixed it and that shut him out. The server is on the MIT campus, so I let the system admin know someone was breaking into servers in case it was happening elsewhere. The idiot called Campus Police, who freaked and called the FBI, giving them my home address."

"What was this Raven guy doing?" Mev asked, fully drawn in now. She couldn't help thinking about Morris, about her own DEMON program, about her near miss with the FBI after her hack.

"I'm not sure. He was connecting with other system admins, asking about getting access to public nodes, or guest accounts, mostly harmless stuff. Still, it felt like a hack. I think he was using it as a base for social engineering."

Social engineering, the human counterpart to the technical prowess of a hacker. Too hard to crack a password? Call a secretary at 5:00 on a Friday afternoon pleading to get the confidential modem phone number for the office network, saying you have to submit a report, or you'll get fired. Don't have access to a secure door? Tousle your hair, fill your arms with reports, and look so harried the employee with the key card holds the door for you.

In Tom's case, the hacker appeared to be doing the same thing, trying to look legitimate to fool more people into helping him. Mev knew the type: grifter, scammer, confidence man. In short, her father, Brian Hayes. Investment advisor, stockbroker, Rotary Club president, con artist. He could talk a great game, and his investment strategy—his Ponzi scheme—worked for years. Until it didn't. Until everything went to hell. Until he went to prison and they lost everything.

"So, he was using The Crypt to fool other admins into giving him access to their servers?" Jack asked.

"Maybe. I don't know. I was on top of it. Once I got the patches in place, I was able to keep him out, and, no surprise, detected multiple brute force password hack attempts against the server after that."

"Weird," Jack said.

"I know. Now the FBI is accusing me of conspiring with Raven, giving him refuge. They said Raven was a member of The Crypt and had used the bulletin board regularly. I told them that was crap. I was the one who'd reported him. Honestly, other than trying to intimidate me, and breaking my stuff, they were pretty random. They packed it all up, left, and said not to leave town."

"Now what?"

"They said they were reviewing whether to file charges against me in federal court. If no charges are filed, they'll return my stuff after the investigation. Whenever the hell that might be."

"You lost everything?" Jack asked.

"Seriously? No. I back The Crypt up onto another server on campus. I *am* pissed they took my first-generation Dungeons & Dragons books and Grateful Dead bootleg tapes."

"What if they find that server?" Mev asked.

"Good luck. Plus, even if they do, it's encrypted. Thing is, though, I keep notes on the 2600 meetings, usually with handles, with names if I forget. You're in the one from last night, Jack. You might be next."

"Was I on that list?" Mev asked.

Tom shrugged, embarrassed. "Sorry, no, I couldn't remember your name."

Mev was not sorry. She still felt anger at the FBI. At how they had paraded her father from their house in handcuffs, in front of the press, with Mev and her mom in the background of all the pictures. And the FBI's public statements, sneering at him, and the lifestyle they'd had, implying that she and her mom had been in on it

"Will your department do anything to you?" Jack asked.

Tom snorted. "Nah, I'm in Linguistics. I mean, Noam Chomsky's in our department, so I'm pretty safe. But I'd have expected MIT to have my back."

"You worried?" Jack asked.

"I'll be OK. I was pretty freaked out when it was happening. Now I'm mostly just pissed off. They'll probably come at me again. I'm not going to make it easy for them."

WEDNESDAY, FEBRUARY 7, 1990

CONFRONTED WITH THE SPRAWLING MIT CAMPUS, MEV barely made it to her first class on time. The seminar was in a small, stepped amphitheater fronted by a row of sliding chalkboards allowing the instructor to prepare the entirety of a complex theorem or demonstrate long solutions to difficult mathematical problems. Today the boards were perfectly clean, only the class name written in block letters: 6.045J Automata, Computability, and Complexity.

"Good morning, I'm Dr. Thomas Halloway. Let's begin with a question to get a sense of your mathematical maturity." He said the latter with his fingers hooked in air quotes.

"Who can tell us about Euclid's Algorithm?"

The class was silent. Everyone wondering if it was a trap or trick. It wasn't. The answer was simple.

"Greatest common divisor," she said.

Dr. Halloway looked to the back of the room, searching for who had spoken. "Again," he said.

"Greatest common divisor," Mev said, louder this time.

"Correct. Why do we care about that?"

"Factoring," she said.

"More."

"It has lots of uses. Search trees and encryption, for example."

He turned to the board and started writing pseudocode, a form of simplified programming language that demonstrates how an algorithm works. He outlined several versions of the algorithm, Euclid's original one based on subtraction, another one based on division, and one based on recursion, describing various refinements to the formula as he wrote.

"Efficiency of computation vs. complexity is what makes structures like encryption work. We will master these concepts in this class."

Encryption worked when information was easy to encrypt and really, really hard to brute force decrypt. Of course, you didn't need to break it if someone left the default system passwords unchanged, one of the exploits DEMON used with great effect.

The class seemed pretty straightforward, which was good because she really wanted to spend time getting DEMON up to snuff. Plus, she already knew the material. Dave Franklin, in another bid to keep her boredom at bay, had assigned lots of readings in math history, including the two-volume doorstop *Great Moments in Mathematics* by Howard Whitley Eves. She'd enjoyed the encyclopedic approach to math and Dave's unrelenting questions. He'd employed much the same approach Dr. Halloway took, emphasizing the practical uses of theories.

On her way out of class, Dr. Halloway signaled to her to come to the desk at the front.

"What's your name?" he asked.

"Mev Hayes."

"I look forward to your work in this class Miss Hayes," he said and turned to erase the board.

One of the great joys of being on campus was access to email. No searching for a payphone, no waiting for the postal service's "snail mail." Type an address at your university or bulletin board server and, with the right routing protocols, mail moved at the speed of light. Today when she checked it, she had one terse email from jbrennan@cfa.harvard.edu: "Coffee. Café Pamplona. Bow & Arrow. 3:00."

Mev's Cambridge map, already getting fuzzy at the folds, showed the curved Bow and straight Arrow Street that transected it near Harvard Square. Mev emailed Jamie in the affirmative and spent the intervening time researching new patches and exploits, hoping to show Fitz a complete catalog at the end of the week.

The café was a short walk from the Harvard Square T station, which was a relief, as the day had turned gray, and a stiff wind was blowing down the Cambridge streets. The café itself, however, was cozy with warm yellow walls, a black and white checked floor, small tables, and bent wood bistro chairs. It's what Mev imagined a European café should be like.

Jamie was already there, her hands wrapped around a cup for warmth. She smiled, a lovely transformation of her usual stern expression. Once again, she was dressed punk style, ripped T-shirt, a thin leather collar around her neck, and a black leather jacket on the back of her chair.

"This is cool," Mev said as she sat. The place was surprisingly crowded for the middle of the afternoon. A server pushed a cart through the tight tables with various unidentifiable foods in bamboo containers.

"I take my coffee seriously," she said.

Mev pointed at her cup, "what is that?"

"A *cortado*, half espresso, half steamed milk."

Mev asked a passing waiter for the same and perused the menu. She didn't want to ruin her appetite for whatever Jack was making tonight, but the menu was so tempting. When her coffee drink arrived, she ordered a fruit tart.

Mev told Jamie about her first class, then shared the events from the weekend with Tom Bergstrom and his encounter with the FBI.

"Who knows who they'll come after next?" Mev said.

"I'm sure we all have something we'd rather not have the FBI's grubby little fingers in. They dig around enough, and they'll find or invent something on anyone." Jamie said as she sipped on her drink.

True enough.

"I checked you out, by the way" Jamie said with a grin.

"Oh?"

"Yup. Wasn't hard. Northwest Missouri State's network security is shit. As, apparently, you well know."

Though miffed, Mev couldn't help admiring her style.

"I like to know who I'm dealing with," Jamie added.

"Me too."

"Hey, I'm an open book. And we have more in common than you might guess."

"How did you know my email address?" Mev asked. The question had struck her on the T ride from Kendall Square.

"There's no contact list or anything. I guessed. The format for email addresses is pretty standard at each institution, first initial, last name. Unless you're one of the original users like Marvin Minsky or somebody. He's minsky@media.mit.edu. Which made me wonder, how did this Fitz guy find you?"

Mev told her about the Ada Promise Prize she'd gotten in college. Sponsored by the Association for Computing Machinery, it was meant to promote women in computer science. Dave Franklin had nominated her, and it got attention, including coverage in the local newspaper. Fitz had seen the award and reached out to Dave, who had been so frustrated by her expulsion he'd probably pitched how she should be at MIT instead. It was just the kind of thing he would do.

"Fitz told me he finds promising students to bring into his program. I guess he stumbled on me."

Though they'd talked late into the evening after 2600, it had all been on the topic of hacking. If Jamie knew a lot about Mev, she knew little about Jamie.

"What about you?" she asked.

"I handle all the computers at the Harvard–Smithsonian Center for Astrophysics. The irony is, they'd never let me into Harvard, but man, they can't live without me at the center. I mean these guys are actual rocket scientists, but they can't remember their login IDs."

"That's awesome. Where did you go to school?"

"College? MIT. But I needed a job and answered a classified ad in *The Boston Globe*. And it was the kind of thing that would annoy my dad, so, added bonus." She didn't elaborate. "I don't need a degree to do what I do."

It was a thought Mev had never explored. Get the degree, get out of town, get her own life. That had been the formula, the obvious path to escaping her family's circumstances. Plus, she was so close to finishing her degree, and while she'd vaguely considered grad school before she'd been expelled, once Fitz put the idea firmly in her head, it felt like the right step forward.

"Well, I'm here. Only woman in my department and getting a lot of opportunity. Fitz is totally taking care of me, helping with grad school, giving me a job."

"Sounds like a dream," Jamie said in a tone Mev couldn't quite read.

Jamie waved to the waiter and asked for the bill. "I got this," she said.

She dropped bills and coins onto the table and rose, wrapping a long scarf around her neck.

"Thanks for coming," she said. "I needed a coffee to make it through the rest of the day. And in addition to being helpless when it comes to their computers, the rocket scientists can't make a decent cup of coffee to save their lives."

Jamie sounded a lot like Jack.

FRIDAY, FEBRUARY 9, 1990

DESPITE THE WHIRLWIND FIRST WEEK OF CLASSES, MEV finally had something to show Fitz: a simple command line interface and basic automation that would crawl a network, identify any connected machines, gather information on their operating system and installed software, and report any known exploits. Simple and effective, especially for larger networks with diverse computer hardware.

That diversity was exploding, and Mev wondered if it would be possible to keep up with new exploits in the future. Agencies like the newly formed Computer Emergency Response Team at Carnegie Mellon were tracking emerging vulnerabilities, but most of the time a computer was at risk because a patch or release to fix a known exploit simply wasn't installed, like at Northwest Missouri, or was thought unimportant, like Tom's EMACS oversight.

"Any breakthroughs?" was Fitz's greeting when he arrived later in the day.

"Actually, yes," she was pleased to say.

"Show me." He stood at her shoulder.

She attached to the Advanced Concepts Lab network and let DEMON run. It reported two Unix servers unpatched with the fix for the Sendmail bug that Morris had used in his internet worm, an IBM PC with no password protection whatsoever, and several other weaknesses.

"Impressive. And frankly embarrassing. We're going to have to fix those. You're keeping us all on our toes, Mev," he said, placing a hand on her shoulder.

"That's the whole point. It makes us more secure," she said.

"Here, demonstrate it on a network you are not familiar with. Show me on . . ."

He pulled a small bound notebook from his sport jacket pocket and gave her an IP address that was a gateway to a different network. DEMON found several computers, and one, a Digital Equipment Corporation VAX minicomputer, with a common, if careless, vulnerability. The program discovered that the machine still had the "SYSTEM" user that came by default when the computer was shipped from the factory. While the password wasn't the VAX default "MANAGER," it was the frequent lazy alternative, "OPERATOR."

"You're in?" Fitz asked.

"Yep."

He beamed as he wrote a few notes then put the notebook back in his jacket pocket. "Just amazing. I'm so pleased."

Mev's face burned with pride. She'd mastered everything she'd touched at Northwest Missouri, but this was MIT. And she was on top of it.

"You've been going full bore yet again this week, and you've made real progress. We need to celebrate your success, not to mention your impending admission to the grad program. Take the rest of the afternoon off. Recharge. And let me take you for a celebratory dinner. I'll pick you up at 7:30 at your place."

He went around to his desk, and turned on his monitor, which she hadn't seen him use much. Thrilled, and relieved, Mev got ready to leave.

As she did, Fitz looked her up and down.

"Oh, and Mev? Dress nice."

She put on the only dress she owned, a cocktail-length black dress she'd worn at her grandfather's funeral the year before. The dress was hard to zip and she couldn't quite manage it herself. Her mom had helped last time she'd worn it. She'd have to ask Jack or Hector.

Hector was laying on the hideous aqua couch, reading a book with a guy in a pink button-down shirt on the cover: *The New Peter Norton Programmer's Guide to the IBM PC & PS/2*. He was completely absorbed.

"Hector?"

He glanced up toward her. "Wow," he said.

"What?" she asked, guarded.

"I mean you look nice."

A compliment? She'd take it. "Thanks. Can you help me with the zipper?"

She turned away and held her hair away from her neck while Hector stood behind her and zipped her up, struggling with the hook-and-eye closure.

"That's harder than it looks," he said. He finally got it, sat back down, and looked her over again.

She'd undone her hair from her usual braid, letting it drape on her shoulders. She'd brushed it smooth, and in the bathroom mirror she'd been pleased with how her red hair shone against the black dress. She'd even put on a touch of her rarely used makeup and lipstick for the celebration.

"Where's Jack tonight?"

"He took C-squared for dinner. They went to the European."

"Where's that?" She wondered if she and Fitz would run into them. But that was ridiculous. This wasn't Maryville. There must be hundreds of restaurants in Boston.

"The North End. It's an amazing Italian restaurant. Jack says it's the best pizza in Boston, hands down. Plus, he usually gets lucky when he takes her there."

He cleared his throat. "What I mean is they go there on dates once in a while. Where are you off to tonight?"

"Fitz is taking me to dinner."

Hector's face hardened, any of his previous good will toward her draining away. "Seriously? I guess that explains it."

Mev was saved from having to respond when Hector slammed the book closed and marched upstairs just as someone knocked on the front door. Fitz.

"You look lovely tonight," he said.

It was a quick drive into Harvard Square. They parked and Fitz offered his arm, which Mev appreciated. She wore heels maybe once a year, and never felt comfortable in them, especially given the imperfectly cleared snowy sidewalk on Brattle Street. They turned into a short courtyard, arriving at a restaurant called Harvest.

"You'll enjoy this place," Fitz said.

The hostess asked to take her coat, which Mev was happy to relinquish. A parka was ridiculous over a dress. The maître d' gestured for her to follow and led them to a small table near the back. Mev admired another courtyard out the back glass doors, imagined it would be beautiful in summer. For now, she was happy to be inside.

A waiter approached, and Fitz immediately ordered two champagnes. When they arrived, he made a toast.

"To our great collaboration."

She clinked glasses with him and sipped, slowly.

"What do you think?" Fitz asked.

"It's amazing."

"It's Julia Child's favorite restaurant," he said quietly, as if sharing an insider secret.

The place was bustling, so much so that Mev was surprised Fitz was able to get a reservation on short notice. The people were elegant, including Fitz himself, wearing a well-tailored dark gray three-piece suit with a chartreuse silk tie and matching pocket square.

He, in turn, was openly admiring her. She was glad the dress still fit. If she kept eating Jack's cooking, it wouldn't for much longer. She smiled thinking of Jack, hoping he was having a good time.

"You have a lovely smile," Fitz said. "You know, you really are a beautiful woman. You shouldn't hide it."

Fitz drained his glass of champagne. "I can't tell you, Mev, how truly glad I am that you accepted my offer to come to MIT. You belong here."

"I'm grateful for the opportunity. I can hardly believe it."

Fitz flagged the waiter and ordered oysters.

She must have made a face. "Haven't had them before? They're from right here, down the Cape."

Any seafood that wasn't fish sticks was too many days out of the water by the time it got to Maryville. Mev had always found fish, and its accompanying acrid smell, disgusting.

"Trust me. You'll love them."

When they arrived, she watched Fitz use a dainty fork to loosen the flesh from the shell, then pour it and the liquid into his mouth. He gave it a quick chew and swallowed with obvious delight. He waited for her to do the same.

She tried to repeat his actions, spilling much of the liquid before freeing the oyster. Then she tipped the shell back and let the oyster slide into her mouth, giving it a chew before swallowing it. The texture was a little gross, but the flavor was what she imagined the ocean would taste like if it were slightly sweet.

Fitz watched her and when she nodded her approval, said "Trust me, I know what's best for you."

Mev took a sip of champagne, savoring the mixture of flavors in her mouth before reaching for another oyster.

"You know, despite having recruited you, I don't know that much about you," he said. "Of course, I read your transcripts. Early college admission and just short of finishing in under three years. Very impressive."

"I mostly studied and worked. It was just me and my mom." She wondered if he knew about her father. No doubt Jamie did.

"No time for a social life? I hope you can change that here. Trust me, Cambridge can be fun," he said, toasting with a refilled champagne glass.

The meal was delicious, and Fitz encouraged her to order a Courvoisier afterwards. Another new taste, cognac, one much more pleasant than the martinis he'd ordered at the Charles Hotel the week before.

After Fitz finished his own cognac, he said "I must tell you. I've rarely felt drawn to a woman so quickly." His smile was wide and warm. "I have a place here in Cambridge for nights I don't want to drive all the way back to Carlisle. A place I like to relax. Would you like to join me there for a private drink to properly celebrate your achievement?"

Mev sat in stunned silence. She wasn't sure what exactly she'd been expecting this evening. Drinks, good food. Not a proposition from someone like Fitz. He was unlike anyone she'd ever met: smart, wealthy, powerful, accomplished, sophisticated. He cared about her. He was taking care of her.

And while she wasn't the most sexually experienced woman, she knew where this was going. There would be consequences to accepting. She was on birth control. Her mother had insisted, preventing any further "shame to the family." That wasn't the real issue, though. The real concern was about screwing things up. Fitz was amazing. The opportunity even more so. This was her chance to break free and she needed it to work.

"I . . . I can't," she finally said.

"Of course," he replied, his hand covering hers on the table. "I don't want to pressure you, I just feel so strongly about you already. I knew you were special, then once I met you in person, well, that was that. We can take it slow. I just want to put you on notice that it doesn't change how I feel."

She could only nod, afraid to say anything more.

The ride home was quiet, the house on Linnaean dark.

SATURDAY, FEBRUARY 10, 1990

PAUL KNOCKED ON THE DOOR AT 39-1/2 LINNAEAN Street. He'd called several times during the week to make an appointment, getting the same annoying answering machine message each time: "It's the '90s. You know what to do." He'd left multiple messages, but never got a call back. Paul figured if he came early on a Saturday, he'd find Kane at home.

He knocked again and waited. No car in the driveway. He glanced into the picture window and listened at the door. Nothing. He was about to leave a card in the door jamb when a tall young woman answered. She was pretty, with long red hair in a braid, bare feet, and wearing U Missouri sweats.

Paul showed her his credentials. "I'm FBI Special Agent Paul Ostrowski. I'm looking for John Francis Kane."

The instant he'd showed her his credentials, she'd closed the door to a crack. "He's not here."

"Are you sure? Can you check?"

"Do you have a warrant?"

Paul was used to encountering distrust of law enforcement. In his experience, there were two types of people: those who had nothing to hide and were open to helping, and those who had something to hide and gave you crap.

"I need to speak with John Kane."

"He's not here," she said, and closed the door.

Again he went to put a card in the door jamb when a red pickup truck pulled up, double parking behind Paul. A twenty-something kid with round tortoise shell glasses got out and marched right to Paul.

"Is that your car?" he asked, pointing to Paul's FBI-issued Ford Taurus in the driveway.

"Yes," Paul said and showed his credentials again.

"Oh, you," the kid said. "I got your messages. Take the hint. And get your car out of my driveway. I'll get a ticket for parking like this."

"Are you John Kane?"

"Do you have a warrant?"

What was the deal with everyone this morning? "No, I don't. I'd like to ask a few questions."

"Huh," Kane responded, brushing by Paul, and entering the house. He left the door open, which Paul took as an invitation to enter.

"Are you John Francis Kane?" Paul asked again.

Walking away from him toward the kitchen, Paul saw the kid shrug.

"I'm following up on information we received relating to your involvement with a group called 'The Crypt.'"

"Hmm," he mumbled, while producing a bag of coffee beans from the freezer.

"What can you tell me about The Crypt?"

Kane responded by running an electric coffee grinder for a solid minute. The little shit.

"Look. I just want to ask questions, not haul you in."

Kane tilted his head—a cat spying a bird. Then he gestured for Paul to sit as he finished making coffee. The redhead hadn't moved, standing in the kitchen with Kane, her arms folded over her chest, glaring at him.

Paul sat in a chair covered with a particularly ugly fringed burgundy bedspread. The living room furnishings were a mishmash of 1970s kitsch and a tidy stack of computers, audio, and other electronics wired together. The furniture was more Paul's speed.

Kane served Paul a black coffee in a chipped Fiestaware mug. That *might* not be an insult, the mug as crappy as the furniture. Kane sat on an aqua leather couch, and the redhead sat beside him, rigid. She looked unhappy.

"Are you John Francis Kane?"

The kid nodded.

Paul pulled out his notebook. "Great. Can I ask you a few questions about The Crypt bulletin board system?"

"You say 'BBS,' or 'board,'" Kane said between sips.

"Right. A little background first." He turned to the redhead. "Miss? Your name?"

She remained silent.

"Miss? Can you tell me your name?"

Nothing.

"Miss, I'm only here to talk."

Her expression didn't change at all.

Paul turned back to Kane, "Does anyone else live here?"

"Why is that relevant?" Kane asked.

Time to take a different tack. "Now John . . ."

"Jack, for God's sake."

"Fine. *Jack.* Why don't you tell me about The Crypt BBS?" He spelled out the letters. What a stupid name.

Kane sat silently for a few moments, with a frown on his face.

"I don't think I'd like to do that," he replied.

"Mr. Kane, please. I'm following up on an investigation."

He shrugged again. Clearly his favorite response. Was the kid dumb, or just an asshole?

"You are not in any trouble here."

Kane still frowned.

"Do you know a Tom Bergstrom?"

The frown deepened.

"You may know him by his hacker handle, 'Tomb.'"

Kane rolled his eyes.

"I know The Crypt," Kane said, settling back into the couch, crossing his legs, and sipping his coffee. OK, this was progress.

Only then the woman's head snapped toward Kane. "Jack, you don't have to talk to him."

A moment passed and lengthened as they looked at each other. Paul waited. The key was to get a subject talking. Even deep cover spies, once they started talking, might spill long-held secrets.

Patience, his anger management coach had said, was about practice.

"I know Tom, 'Tomb,'" Kane said, using his fingers to make air quotes. The redhead turned away in disgust.

"What can you tell me?"

"I understand you rousted him last week."

Fine, let the kid vent. "So, you know him well enough for him to confide in you. What did he have to say about that?"

"Nothing good."

"Look, Mr. Kane, I'm sorry this subject seems uncomfortable for you. We are conducting a serious investigation."

"Witch-hunt."

Paul sighed and took another long slow breath.

"I would appreciate anything you can tell me."

"I'm sure."

"And are you a member of the hacker gang 2600?"

Kane chuckled. Paul was coming to despise this kid.

"That's wrong in so many ways. It's not a motorcycle club or drug gang. They sit around and talk about computers."

"About hacking computers. About committing crimes."

"Man, where are you from? What do they teach you people?"

Paul was weighing whether this kid was being cagey or a smart ass. And he was getting no help from the redhead, her face hard. He should have brought Carl.

But Paul waited, and true to his experience, Kane felt compelled to fill the silence. "Computer security experts share information there."

"And are you a hacker?"

"I'm an English major."

"But the rest of the attendees are?"

Kane rolled his eyes again. Paul sighed. This wasn't getting him anywhere.

"Do you know a Jamie Brennan?" The notes they'd pulled from Bergstrom's computer about the 2600 meeting had a list of attendees, most referred to only by handles. Only two actual names were used: Jack Kane and Jamie Brennan.

Both the woman and Kane reacted, albeit subtly. Paul wasn't sure what conclusion to draw.

"Do you know him?"

"I do not know him."

Maybe he was telling the truth. It wasn't as important as his next question. "And what about the hacker who goes by the alias 'Raven?' Do you know him?"

Both of their faces were noncommittal.

"I don't know everyone," Kane replied.

Had he seen another glimmer of recognition? This is why you had two agents in an interrogation: one to ask the questions, one to watch the suspect. He *definitely* should have brought Carl.

Paul kept at him for another ten minutes, then Kane must have hit a limit, repeating answers or shrugging, while the redhead remained stone silent. He was done here.

Paul had gotten almost nothing. He had a slightly better understanding of what The Crypt was. Carl likely knew more than that already. Leaving his business card on the scratched coffee table, he walked back out into the cold morning and saw a cop putting a ticket under the windshield wiper of the red truck.

Paul smiled all the way back to the office.

"WOW, I THOUGHT I WAS THE ANTI-AUTHORITY FIGURE in this house," Jack said as he came back inside after unsuccessfully arguing the ticket with Cambridge P.D.

"It's complicated." Mev said, her arms crossed over her chest, her shoulders so tight she feared she might rip her sweatshirt. She was back in Maryville, her father just arrested, the FBI questioning Mev and her mother, certain they were involved in his Ponzi scheme, threatening to keep investigating until they found something. She had a recurring dream about them showing up with fresh accusations. And now the FBI was back, in real life, sniffing around.

What had Jamie said? If they dig around enough, they'll find something. And now Jamie was on the FBI's radar as well.

"I'm not super happy about talking to the feds either," Jack said. "I don't want to do anything to hurt Tom. I also don't want them to believe I'm hiding stuff and come after me."

"It's not about that."

Jack waited. When Mev stayed silent he said, "I'll make more coffee."

It had started small, then accelerated. Rumors spread, a few of her father's clients wanted to check on their accounts, some wanted to cash out. Mev's dad demurred, tried to convince them "not to second guess the market."

Maryville was a small town, and the rumor caught fire in days. First Maryville P.D. showed, then the FBI, then the press: *The Maryville Daily Forum, The Kansas City Star, The St. Louis Post Dispatch,* even *The New York*

Times. It burned hot and fast, but eventually they all lost interest. The story and her father were forgotten.

Except in Maryville.

The town turned on them, and her mom grew bitter. Resentful at losing their wealth, their home, their reputation. Her dad faced his trial alone, her mom having expedited the divorce. The courts took everything; she and her mom were broke, bankrupt, and alone.

They worked multiple jobs and lived in a series of increasingly shabby locations, starting at the local Bearcat Inn, and ending in a double-wide near the Maryville Livestock Auction. Her mom worked for the first time in her adult life: a night shift janitor at the university, unseen, chewing on her anger in solitude and making sure Mev knew that she was only facing the indignity of cleaning toilets so Mev could get a tuition break when she went to college.

Now Mev had a new life, one she needed to protect. She didn't want complications. She didn't totally welcome Fitz's interest in more, and most definitely didn't welcome the FBI sniffing around because Jack tagged along to 2600.

She joined Jack in the kitchen.

"You don't have anything to worry about," he said. "Whatever that Raven dude did on Tom's server has nothing to do with us."

She had no idea how to explain her frustration and feelings of helplessness. And she still had to decide what to say to Fitz. He was amazing—smart, important, and generous. He took a chance on her, was mentoring her, helping her get into MIT. Should she have said yes? All she wanted to do was to keep the gains she'd made.

Exiting the Porter Square T station on her way back from the lab later that day, she was assaulted by the night wind, the cold biting her legs through her jeans. Home, desperate for warmth, she found Jack in the kitchen filling a Tupperware from a pot on the stove. Mev stood with her hands under her armpits next to it, trying to warm up.

"I made a beef stew," he said, "which Hector normally loves, only he didn't want to do dinner tonight. He's been cranky lately." He paused. "I was going to put it away and go out. Do you want to join me? We could go to the Wursthaus. Great beer selection."

"I'm not sure I want to go back into that wind."

"C'mon. I'll drive. And I'll even buy," Jack said.

Jack levered his truck on a snowbank covering a parking spot in Harvard Square in front of the Wursthaus. Inside, Mev took in the dark wood and barrel decor while Jack absorbed himself in the huge beer menu.

"I love this place," he said from behind the menu. "I'd come here every day. C-squared doesn't like German food, though, not to mention beer, so I find every excuse to drag other folks into coming."

The waitress arrived and waited while Jack considered the menu. "There're so many great beers. Has anyone tried them all?" he asked the waitress.

She shrugged. "Maybe the owner, Mr. Cardullo, has. I don't know."

"I'll have this Eisbock, and the bratwurst."

"Would I like that?" she asked Jack.

"It's kinda beefy. Get one of the Maibocks." He pointed on the menu.

"One of those and rouladen."

"Beef and pickles? My kind of girl!" Jack said.

They drank their beers in silence, the morning's events still hanging over them.

When the food arrived, Jack spoke. "You know, on the FBI business," he said between bites of his brat', "I just don't want to jam up Tom any more than he already is."

Mev wasn't angry at Jack, only frustrated that things were getting complicated. He was becoming a friend, and she didn't want to ruin that either. He'd trusted her. Maybe she needed to return the favor.

"I wasn't totally truthful when I told you how I got to MIT," she began.

She told him about private school, about being a rich, important family in a small town. About the arrest, the news articles, more cops, the FBI and their relentless campaign to drag Mev and her mom into the investigation. About losing their house and everything else. About the motels, then trailers, about trying to escape the furor of a community deceived and betrayed. While her mom could hide at the university, cleaning bathrooms, Mev had no such luxury, dodging bullies at high school, getting pushed into lockers and roughed up in the girl's bathroom.

That was until she found the one place her tormenters never looked: the computer lab. At least that's what Maryville High School called it. A tiny tutoring room with an HP 9800 series desktop computer using a cassette tape drive for storage. Mev taught herself the BASIC programming language in a matter of days, and what had begun as a desperate escape became a consuming passion.

"I was good at it, and for a little while, everything was OK."

She told him about acing math and science, then testing out of a whole grade and starting college classes. She harnessed her newfound power to kick ass and kept accelerating right into college, getting her high school diploma in the mail at some point along the way, and besting the other students with glee. It had led her to Dave Franklin, to DEMON, right before things fell apart: the bet, the expulsion, and her mother's unendurable and continuing humiliation.

Tears were welling in her eyes as she told it, reliving that shame.

Jack took a long sip of his beer and considered her. While she'd seen Jack be brash, quirky, and funny, this was new. He was grave. Concerned.

"I'm so sorry. That must have been hard. I'm glad you're here now." He reached for her hand, hesitated, then held it in earnest.

SUNDAY, FEBRUARY 11, 1990

AFTER HIS ABORTIVE ATTEMPT TO GET KANE TO COOP-erate, Paul figured he'd better bring Carl along to confront his only other lead, Jamie Brennan. As with Kane, his name had not come up elsewhere in the investigation. Given the paucity of other prospects, however, he hoped Brennan might add something to the few leads they had.

Parking was ridiculous in South Boston on a Sunday morning. He and Carl finally moved a lawn chair from a space not quite big enough for their car. The Ford jutted partway into traffic two blocks from the run-down row house where Jamie Brennan lived. Standing on a cement stoop, Paul took in the dingy gray plastic siding and the metal-bottomed screen door that hadn't been replaced with a proper winter storm door. He opened it to knock on the wooden door behind it. No answer. He knocked again.

"Maybe they're at church," Carl suggested.

"Maybe."

As they turned away, a young woman with short, spiky hair opened the front door and stared at them through the screen.

"Yeah?"

Paul showed his badge. "I'm FBI Special Agent Paul Ostrowski, and this is Special Agent Carl Philips. We are looking for Jamie Brennan."

The kid didn't even glance at the badge, and she didn't open the door. "Uh huh."

"Is Jamie Brennan your brother?"

The girl smirked. "No."

"Can I speak to Jamie Brennan."

"Yes."

Oh, right. "Are you Jamie Brennan?"

She shrugged.

"May we come in?"

"Not unless you have a warrant." She slammed the door.

"What the hell?" Paul said.

As they walked back to the car, and Carl said, "I'm guessing that was Jamie Brennan. Would've been nice if someone had told us she was a girl. Do we have a file on her?"

"Nope. And I'm not sure where the hell to go with this next."

The lawn chair was now on top of Paul's car, and someone had covered their windshield in road slush. Great.

When they got to the office there was a note on Paul's desk from Agent Connor to come see him. He hadn't seen Connor since that night out his first week. Today he was in his private office, nursing a coffee bright white with cream amid a haze of cigarette smoke.

"Ostrowski. Close the door."

Paul closed the door and turned to find Connor standing inches away, seething and reeking of sour cigarette smoke.

"What the fuck are you doing nosing around my informants? Keep away from Brennan. You've got no business there."

"Whoa, whoa, wait," Paul said, backing up until he bumped against the closed door, hands raised. "I was only following a lead in this hacking case. I got a tip to talk to Jamie Brennan."

"Jamie? You mean Jimmy."

"Jamie. Who the hell is Jimmy? And how should I know this was your case? There was no file on her."

"Above your pay grade."

"How about giving me the pay-grade version?"

Connor stepped back. "Yeah, I s'pose. Jimmy Brennan—'Jinx'—is a confidential informant. He's *my* CI. He's connected with Irish organized crime in South Boston and is helping us with a long-term investigation. I got a call from him this morning that somebody came looking for his kid."

"Jamie is the kid. That's who I was looking for."

"Well, stop. We gotta keep Jinx under wraps, so the Brennans—all the Brennans—are off limits. Clear?"

"She's one of the only leads I have."

"Well, then, now you've got one less. Screw that up and you'll regret it. I mean, computer hackers? Who the hell cares?"

"Washington cares. Weaver cares. I was sent here to pursue this case. I'm doing my job."

"No, you're fucking with mine, and that, my friend, is bad mojo. Look, you're new here, so you don't know how things work. Let me enlighten you. We're finally making progress against the Mafia here after years of trying. That's all me. Organized Crime is a priority for the Director, so it is for Weaver, me, and you. That's all you need to know."

Paul knew both the Italian Mafia and the Irish Winter Hill Gang were problems in Boston. Hell, they were trouble on the whole east coast. Drugs, gambling, loan sharking, the works. So, Connor wasn't *just* being an asshole.

"I've got Weaver watching me like a hawk," Paul said. "I need progress, too."

Connor sat back down. "Look, I get it. I didn't understand anything in that damn computer security seminar your guy gave, and I wouldn't want to be in your shoes. I'm sorry you're chasing your tails. But I can't have Jinx's cover blown. If you come up with independent evidence that Jamie is involved in what you are doing, then bring it back to me and we can talk. For now, back off."

He leaned back in his high-backed leather executive chair, the springs squeaking slightly. "No hard feelings, right? I can be a friend. You need tickets to a game, anything like that, you let me know. I've got connections. I can make stuff happen."

As if he'd ask Connor for a favor.

With no active leads, he'd have to go back to soliciting chat on the BBS's and getting tagged as a "feeb."

As he was leaving Connor said, "Oh, and Ostrowski? This is 'need-to-know.'"

This investigation was starting to suck.

MONDAY, FEBRUARY 12, 1990

MEV WAS NO STRANGER TO COMPLICATIONS, BUT THEY did seem to be stacking up. MIT, Boston, new friends. Awesome. The FBI's presence and Fitz's advances? Complications.

Still, way better than what she'd come from. Better than hiding in a high school closet with a glorified calculator, or in the stockroom at K-mart, or at home trying to stay out of the path of her mother's fury. It was complicated here, sure, but maybe that was adulthood. At least hers included new friends.

"Drink after work?" she emailed Jamie. Mev had looked up the Harvard Astrophysics Lab and Observatory, finding to her surprise that it was just down at the other end of Linnaean Street. Jamie would walk right by their place on her way to the T.

"Our place, 39-1/2 Linnaean, 5:00?"

Jamie's response was almost instant. "Done."

Mev arrived home from the lab to find Jack in the living room, facing a roaring fire. She hadn't realized the fireplaces in the old house worked.

"It's so cold today, all I could think about was a fire. Which is stupid because opening the fireplace flue lets all the heat in the house out. I just needed something to warm up after coming back from the library."

She had to agree; the walk from the Porter Square T station had been brutal. She'd left the MIT campus a little after 4:00, pleased to see Hector consumed with something in his cube. She didn't want his negativity filling the house, nor did she want him to hear what she needed to talk to Jamie about.

"I invited a friend over for a drink. Jamie, you know, from 2600." Invited to *her* place. It was nice to think of it as her place, as her and Jack's place. "She works just down the street at the Observatory. She's really interesting."

"I'm sure. You two were thick as thieves after the meeting."

"Just two girls planning the overthrow of the internet. No big deal."

He laughed. "Sounds like a plan," he said, closing his NEC Ultralight notebook-sized laptop. She coveted that computer, wanted one she could carry around. That little beauty, though, was a bit outside of her budget at five thousand bucks a pop.

Jamie knocked at exactly 5:00, and seeing the fire, immediately went to it, taking off her gloves and waving her hands in front of it.

"I should get the rocket scientists to fix something like this up. Maybe one of those spaceship nuclear generators that throw off waste heat or something."

In the kitchen, Jack had poured wine for himself and Mev.

"What's your poison," he asked Jamie.

"Beer."

"Sam Adams OK?"

Jamie's face lit up. "Kane, I'm impressed."

Mev looked at the bottle. She didn't know it. In Missouri, if a waitress told you they had *every* beer it meant Budweiser, Busch, *and* Michelob.

They settled in, Jamie hogging the chair Jack had previously occupied near the fire.

It was good Jack was part of this conversation, she thought.

Mev began. "I have to tell you, the FBI . . ."

" . . . is gonna pay me a visit?" Jamie said. "Yep, happened this weekend. They dropped by to see you too, I gather. That little chat with Tom Bergstrom seems to have woken the gremlins."

"Given my past, I wasn't too happy to see them," she said, and Jack nodded.

Jamie inexplicably smiled in response.

"What?" Mev asked.

"You see, I kinda was," Jamie replied.

"Happy to see them?" Mev asked.

"Yep. Turns out having that Ostrowski clown come to my house actually did me good." Jamie said.

"How's that?"

"You'll appreciate this. See, my dad, well, he's not the most sophisticated guy, but he does have connections. A made man, and proud of it."

"Made?" Mev asked.

"Connected," Jack said. "Irish Mob?"

"It's Boston," Jamie said with a shrug.

"OK," Mev said, the concept freaking her out a little, though Jack seemed to get it.

"So, they gave him a gas station to run. He's proud of it, 'cause it shows he's on the inside. I could care less about any of that. I'm nothing like my family or the other kids in my neighborhood. I like to read. I spend time on computers. He'd be happier if I was doing petty street crime. Still wouldn't fix the fact that I'm a girl, though. I was supposed to be Jimmy Jr. Sort of a disappointment, as you might imagine.

"Then the FBI comes to my house to ask me about computer hacking, and well, let's say I did the old man proud. It's messed up, but that's how these guys roll. Suddenly I have street cred because I've been questioned by the FBI. And about *computers,* which for all my dad knows are fancy toasters. My brother Mickey's only been hassled by the chumps at Boston P.D., so now I'm the golden child."

Mev appreciated the irony. Her own dad was in prison and her mom wasn't talking to her even though she'd been admitted to the most admired technical university in the world.

Jack laughed. "And I thought my parents had weird priorities about offspring achievement."

"He knows?" Jamie asked Mev. Knows about her past, she meant.

"He knows."

Jamie raised her glass. "In that case, to felonious parents."

Mev raised her wine glass in salute.

FRIDAY, FEBRUARY 16, 1990

MEV HAD FELT HER EQUILIBRIUM REBALANCED AFTER opening up to Jack then to Jamie. It didn't last long.

"Please read in private," was the title of the email from Fitz she'd gotten the next day.

"I meant what I said the other night and continue to think about it. Please, join me for dinner again Friday."

Mev knew exactly what he meant, and the implication remained a distraction from her programming, from her classes, all week. She knew that if anything happened, their professional relationship could be damaged. She didn't want to be known as the department slut. On the other hand, she wasn't chasing him; he was chasing her. He wanted *her*.

The week had been tense, with him being carefully polite, not pushing, not even asking, and her own thoughts on what she should do swinging wildly. She'd wanted to share her dilemma with Jack or Jamie, except when she imagined the conversation it sounded tawdry, desperate. And now it was Friday afternoon and she'd neither made progress on her research nor decided about dinner.

"How was your week?" Fitz asked when he breezed into the lab late in the day.

Mev took a deep breath. "Classes are heating up. I didn't get much time for research," she admitted.

"Both are important. In the meantime," he said, his eyes softening, "will you please join me for dinner tonight?"

She nodded and he clapped his hands together. "Excellent. I have the perfect place in mind. Pick you up at 7:30."

"That dress seems familiar," Fitz said as they pulled away from the house.

It didn't sound like a rebuke. Mev flushed anyway. "I know. I only have one. I never figured I'd go anywhere other than the lab and classes, honestly."

"Maybe we'll have to do something about that. What are you, a size six?"

Not even close. "A twelve."

"Hmm," he said.

Mev took in the city as Fitz drove through the dark Cambridge streets, steering his way past MIT then across the Longfellow Bridge toward Boston proper, a Red Line train passing them on the tracks in the center of the bridge.

In town, the Boston sidewalks were bustling with bundled winter shoppers and restaurant goers. And the Public Garden's trees twinkled with white holiday lights.

On Arlington Street, Fitz pulled to the curb, and Mev was surprised when her door was opened for her.

"Welcome to the Ritz Carlton, ma'am."

She carefully balanced on her heels and waited as Fitz came around the car. After relinquishing their coats, they were led to an intimate table.

Again, Fitz immediately ordered champagne, and as Mev sipped she registered the restaurant was even more elegant than Harvest. White tablecloths, upholstered chairs, photos of celebrities going back years. A jazz trio performing in the lounge. In the restaurant proper, a classical pianist. The patrons were equally elegant. Fitz fit right in with his dark blue double-breasted suit and paisley patterned red silk tie.

The waiter returned, and Mev realized that she'd barely looked at the menu she was holding, only now registering that it was in French with English translations. She was relieved that Fitz again ordered for them both.

"The Caesar salad and Chateaubriand for two, medium rare to rare. And a bottle of the 1982 Pomerol, *s'il vous plaît*," Fitz said. He tapped two fingers on his champagne glass, and the waiter gave a subtle nod in confirmation before gliding away.

The salad cart arrived, and Mev watched the waiter mix the dressing fresh, cracking an egg into it, whipping the ingredients, and tossing the salad before he served them.

The sommelier brought the wine, presented it to Fitz, then opened it, sniffed the cork, and placed it on the table with a flourish. He poured a bit into a shallow silver cup fastened to a chain around his neck. He sipped it, nodded, then poured a bit into Fitz's glass. Fitz swirled it around, breathing in then tasting the wine. He considered, then said, "Lovely." The sommelier poured for them both.

She reached for her wine, but Fitz spoke up. "Give it a moment to breathe. Enjoy your champagne."

The waiter cleared the salad and delivered their steaks. They were huge.

Fitz leaned back and considered his wineglass. "Mev, you're being so quiet. Is this all making you uncomfortable? It's important to celebrate our successes. As a team."

"I want that, too."

After they were finished, the waiter returned to ask about dessert. Mev refused, and Fitz passed as well. They finished their wine and Fitz handled the check. He pulled several hundred dollar bills from his wallet; she had no idea how much a dinner like this would cost.

Fitz got her chair and, rather than going for coats, led her into the lounge where the jazz trio was playing. Men smoked cigars, and the women with them sipped colored liqueurs and puffed at long, thin cigarettes.

"Do you mind?" Fitz asked, a cigar in hand. He'd pulled it from a leather case in his suit coat. He lit it with a small torch.

He ordered a Macallan 18 single malt scotch and a Courvoisier for her. It was warm in the lounge, and the woodsy smell of the cigar and the alcohol collaborated to make Mev's head swim. As she surveyed the room, she tried, and failed, to imagine the lives of the people who frequented this place, people for whom this was a typical Friday night. Certainly no one she knew, even when her family had been Maryville royalty.

She was brought back to the moment by Fitz's hand on her knee. "I reserved a room in the hotel. Would you like to retire there?"

She'd passed the evening not thinking of this moment, yet knowing it was coming. She didn't want to mess up, didn't want to say no, to reject him outright. After all, she was flattered. He wanted her. Why couldn't she enjoy good things coming her way for a change?

When the next step came, it felt natural. He put his hand around her waist in the elevator, and she put her head on his shoulder. When they got to the room, there was a fire going in the fireplace, two cognacs set out on a console.

He turned to her and kissed her, gently first, then more aggressively, pushing her back until she sat on the bed. Without a word, he unzipped his pants. Already erect, he pulled a condom packet from his pants pocket, put it on, then dropped his pants to the floor. When Mev didn't react, he pushed her onto her back, lifted her dress, pulled aside her panties, and penetrated her. He climaxed after a few thrusts, threw the used condom on the floor, then lay on the bed next to her and closed his eyes, falling asleep instantly.

After trying and failing to do the same, Mev wrapped herself in a blanket and watched the fire, sipping the cognac she hadn't touched until then.

Fitz woke after a bit and saw her sitting.

"Shall we get you home?"

"Yeah, I should get back."

She smoothed and adjusted the dress she'd never removed while Fitz pulled back on his suit pants.

They had to find a bellhop to open the coatroom, which had closed hours before.

And the valet kept them waiting.

SATURDAY, FEBRUARY 17, 1990

MEV HAD BEEN UP EARLY AND WAS ON HER THIRD CUP of coffee. Thinking. Brooding. Deciding. She'd been mulling over the events of the night before and her feelings about it all morning. It had been a mistake, sleeping with Fitz, but it wasn't too late to fix things. If she stopped now at least it wouldn't ruin her career.

Even though it felt cowardly, she plugged in a phone line from her desktop PC in her room and dialed into MIT's network to compose an email message. She knew she needed to get the words right and feared she wouldn't if she did it in person.

"Dearest Fitz." No. She backspaced.

"Dear Fitz, While I enjoyed our time together last night, I'm worried that it will become a problem for both of us. I find our work together challenging, and I look forward to continuing. I appreciate everything you have done for me and will be forever grateful." After a few tries with various warm and cold closings, she simply signed it "Mev." She read it again, then hit send, disconnected the modem, and got dressed.

She'd let the setting—his attention, the food, the wine—decide for her. Now she could see it was the wrong choice. A weak moment. His flattery and his attention were so warm and welcoming. She hadn't had anyone express that kind of care in how long? It felt good to be wanted. But it felt even better to be on a path toward something bigger. That's what she needed to protect.

Jack and Hector were still asleep, so Mev sat in the living room, staring out the first-floor turret window, sipping her coffee. She wasn't entirely surprised when Fitz's car pulled up an hour later and he marched onto the porch.

She didn't want this confrontation. She knew she had disappointed him, maybe angered him. Nobody liked a tease. She opened the door a crack.

"Get your God-damned coat," he said and turned away.

By the time she put on her coat he was already in the car. Once she got in, he revved the BMW's engine and took off, shifting through the gears so fast they were doing eighty by the time they got to the Harvard Observatory at the end of Linnaean Street. Gripping the armrest, she worried they'd slide off the slushy street as he turned, then turned again onto a side street and screeched to a stop. The engine was still running, the heat blasting, and he hadn't said another word. He didn't look at her, just stared through the windshield, his hands gripping the wheel so tightly she thought he might rip his leather driving gloves.

"Are you stupid?" he shouted at her. "'I will be forever grateful?' You're damned right you will be."

He sputtered into silence, choked by an anger she'd never seen in him. Mev wondered if she could exit the car fast enough if this escalated, fumbling at her seatbelt.

"Look," he said in a more suppressed tone, "I understand you are confused, but trust me, you want to be with me. I will take care of you, and I'll set you up for a great future. We'll forget this childishness and go back to the plan."

"It wasn't a plan for me, it just kind of happened," Mev said. "You are amazing, and I *am* grateful for everything you've done for me. I don't want this to ruin things."

"Don't you understand? I'm helping you."

"I know. I just don't think we should, you know, be together. I mean, aren't you married?"

His eyes narrowed. "You stupid girl. What do you know? I plucked you from that hick town, broken and forgotten. I made you; I can end you. If I throw you out of my lab, you're done at MIT. No one else will touch you. You'll be damaged goods."

Mev started to tear up, more ashamed than angry. She'd been so stupid.

"Fine. Do what you have to do," she said. "I'm an adult. Wouldn't be the first school I got booted from."

Fitz appeared truly surprised. He stared at her, mouth slightly open. The silence extended for minutes. Mev watched as his facial expressions evolved: surprise to confusion, confusion to anger, anger to something darker, something she couldn't place.

As she reached again to unbuckle her seat belt, he grabbed her wrist. Hard.

His voice a growl. "Not acceptable. There is a plan. I need you to do what you are told."

Now she was truly frightened. "Let go of me."

He let go. Bright red marks blossomed on her wrist where his fingers had been.

"You don't understand," he said.

"I do."

"You have to be with me, work with me."

"What, because you love me?" she said, more anger in her voice than she'd expected.

He laughed, though it was more like a bark. "No, because unfortunately I need you, and because you have no choice."

"I have a choice, and I choose to get out of the car. Let me go."

"Fine, go."

She unbuckled herself and opened the door.

"They'll be waiting for you, you know. I'll call the FBI as soon as you leave," he said as he pulled his car phone from the center console of the BMW.

"What?"

"The network you penetrated for me the other day? That wasn't a random MIT network. It was Thinking Machines, the supercomputer company. Hacking is a federal crime, you know." He put his hand to his mouth in mock surprise. "I'm horrified. You say she's a rogue hacker? That she did it before? I had no idea!"

Mev didn't know what to think, what to say. She sat back into her seat. "Why did you have me do that?"

"It's the new digital world, my dear. Anything not locked down is there for the taking by anyone with brains and balls."

"I won't do it again." She had to stop this now, had to walk away.

Mev gasped when Fitz dropped the phone and grabbed her again, this time by the forearm, shaking her once, hard, as if to wake her from a dream.

"You don't listen, do you? You're not done until I say you're done. You're implicated now. What do you suppose I'm doing with those servers?"

He waited, sneering at her. "I swear, you are dumb as a rock. I sell what I find. There are always buyers for high technology. Some pay better than others. The Russians, for example, pay very well." He released her arm forcefully enough that she fell back against the passenger door.

"You're a spy?"

He chuckled; his bantering persona restored. "No, Mev, sweetheart, *we* are."

"Why me?"

"Come now, Mev. Should the FBI come calling, who will they believe? The respected MIT professor or the reckless hacker dropout, who is also, wait for it, the daughter of a convicted con man?"

Mev felt the blood drain from her face; he had recruited her for this very purpose. He'd bought her, bought DEMON, bought the ability to hack computers. He'd bought all that plus deniability.

He watched her dawning realization with amusement.

"The dinners, the hotel, the email? That was all made up?" Mev felt ashamed that she even cared. The whole thing was horrifying.

"You're surprisingly bright. Just a little inexperienced. And not terrible looking." He appraised her body with a leer. "Don't get me wrong, I still expect to get together from time to time. As Bobby Knight said, you might as well 'relax and enjoy it.'"

Fitz turned away from her, looking straight ahead. "And Mev? Close the door behind you. It's getting cold in here."

MONDAY, FEBRUARY 19, 1990
PRESIDENT'S DAY HOLIDAY

FITZ NEEDED SOME AIR. IRONICALLY, THE HORSE STA-
bles, reeking of shit, was where he could get it. Alone, just him, a cigar,
and the fucking horses. Because after Donna took her early morning ride,
she was done with the stables, done with the other horses that kept her
"Lancelot" company, with the trainers, groomsmen, and stable hands.
Fitz had long ago lost track of how much money had gone into that
one ride each day. Still, he'd come to like the horses, despite the fact he
couldn't care less about riding. They ate, slept, ran, crapped. And never
talked back.

All part of what he'd promised when she'd forced him to choose
between her and his first wife. He got her, she got a horse farm in
Carlisle, private school for their twin daughters, custom jewelry, designer
clothing, and whatever else she demanded.

The deal had worked great until three years ago. Donna had money,
and he'd done fine. He'd been able to keep an apartment in Cambridge
for afternoon trysts with that year's hot student, buy the bespoke suits
he liked, acquire a new BMW every other year, and keep Donna quiet.

He'd had it all under control, right up until Black Monday in '87
when the market lost 22% in a single day. He'd been highly leveraged
with margin loans, and they were all called at once, forcing him to sell a
large portion of his portfolio just to cover them. It had been a slog to try
to recover his losses since. He still wasn't close to breaking even.

Walking back to the house, he could hear his daughter playing the
piano. Jessica or Amanda? He couldn't keep straight which one did what.

They were determined to be different from each other, and their hobbies changed so often he could never keep them straight.

"Where have you been?" Donna's voice grated. If he could get ahead of things, if he could put some money away, he could dump her. He wouldn't see Jessica or Amanda much. He could live with that.

He avoided her question. "I have to go out."

"Get some Stoli. We're running low," she said as she walked from the kitchen.

God forbid they run out of Russian vodka. It was the only thing keeping them from killing each other.

Fitz went into his office, closed and locked the door. He jiggled the molding at the base of his antique French desk and took from the cavity behind it an envelope containing a floppy disk. He put it in his jacket pocket and headed to the garage. He disliked having any evidence in his house or office.

His mind wandered as he drove toward town, thinking of Mev Hayes, of how naive she was. He'd given her a lesson in how the world worked, hadn't he? Power. You either had it or you didn't. Information gave you power, money gave you power. He had information and was turning it into money, the best kind of transaction.

He eased the BMW into one of the parking lots for the Greenough Land, a couple hundred acres with old farm buildings that the town of Carlisle had claimed for a park. Fitz chuckled as the mud slopped over the muck boots he used in the stables, imagining his effete Russian contact slogging through this thawing ooze in the fancy leather shoes that could only be bought in the West. A few hundred yards in, past the dam, he reached into a stump, removed a box and put in the plastic-wrapped diskette.

This was more spy craft than his Russian handlers had proposed, but he didn't want to take any unnecessary chances. He'd had to convince

Svitov—or whatever his real name was—that this was safer, higher tech. Much more in keeping with the way this kind of transaction should be handled, in Fitz's opinion.

Their relationship had been so promising at the start. He met Ekaterina, "Kate" Fedorova, a graduate student in Electrical Engineering, at a faculty-student mixer. Short red dress, blonde, legs to die for, she'd become his mistress that very evening. She was amazing in bed, giving him whatever he wanted. One night she'd told him about her uncle in the Soviet Ministry of Foreign Economic Relations, and how he was looking for smart connections in the US computer industry. That it could be very rewarding should he contact him. Fitz mailed a letter to Kate's uncle proposing they meet.

He'd traveled to New York and was connected with a man who never gave his name, telling Fitz only that he should call him Svitov. He'd shared the tradecraft they'd use: chalk on the back of a stop sign when he placed something in the dead drop, a cross through it when they left payment. Fitz had gotten twenty thousand dollars for his first cache of data. Not bad, but he always needed more. A lot more.

They'd given him a paltry two-hundred and eighty-seven thousand so far, barely enough to keep his head above water and far below what the intelligence was worth. Code for security technologies, code to new commercial software, maps of the US commercial and academic networks. They should have been able to take those and build their own technology program. Instead, they kept asking for more, and even more frustrating, for explanations about what he'd given them. What was a "bastion host," how did "parallel processing" work? He despised their stupidity. He despised that he needed them.

He thought again about the technology cache he'd come to call "the Mother Lode." A far-too-inebriated MIT colleague at a faculty party had bragged about the classified Navy project he was leading: development of an advanced acoustic analysis system designed by BBN.

Located near Fresh Pond in Cambridge, Bolt Beranek & Newman was sometimes referred to as "MIT North." They possessed the same mix of commercial, intelligence, and military research that MIT itself did, both on campus and through the Lincoln Labs out at Hanscomb Air Force Base in Lexington. Many of the projects BBN undertook came from MIT research or involved MIT researchers and faculty.

That acoustical engineering faculty member told him about the new submarine-detecting Surveillance Towed Array Sensor Systems that were replacing the old Cold War undersea SOSUS nets. BBN was well-known for its acoustics design, including the music hall at the Boston Symphony Orchestra's summer home, Tanglewood. Concert halls were great PR, but military contracts paid the bills.

When Fitz had teased the Russians that he might be able to obtain the sonar acoustic analysis design, they'd replied immediately in hurried English, less polished than in prior notes.

"For this we pay one million dollar cash. More if soon."

It was tempting. But trading military secrets was dangerous, and he'd told them so on the occasions they'd requested them in the past. He gave them commercial secrets instead. Easier to harvest, harder to detect. Plus, the government had people who watched for computer penetrations, whereas corporations had lawyers who covered them up. The government catches you spying, it can mean the death penalty. A corporation catches you? They'd as likely pay you off or offer you a job.

He'd taken the safer path. Then the well ran dry. He'd sold everything he could find on the MIT network. He didn't have access to the more interesting, classified projects MIT supported.

Fitz needed another loan and got a tip to try Banc Erin, a boutique bank on Milk Street. He was delighted with the service. In thirty minutes, he left with a check for two hundred and fifty thousand dollars in his pocket for just his signature. Then he'd missed his first interest payment. No big deal. He'd been successfully stringing Bank of Boston on for two years without a problem.

Banc Erin, however, turned out to be a different animal. Their assets didn't come from investors and depositors. They came from the Irish Mob, a fact made clear to Fitz when two beefy gentlemen met him as he walked to his car the day after that first payment was due. They made clear that he *would* make payments. That they would make sure of it.

Surprised and frightened, he'd told them his situation. That he was selling technology to fund his lifestyle, and for that he needed network access to MIT, and other places, that he didn't have. Two days later, a hard-looking man accosted him as he arrived at Building 38, introducing himself as Joey and handing him a piece of paper with a name and phone number on it.

The number was for Kenneth Frain, a former Army Signals Corps specialist and computer hacker for hire who called himself "Raven." For a fee, he got Fitz into commercial and academic networks that were gold. The Russian money started flowing in again, and he could afford to pay the Mob and pay for the Stoli. Then Frain started grumbling about more money, and before Fitz could talk him down, he was dead. Frain, as it happened, was some kind of drug dealer as well as a hacker, and got killed during a robbery gone bad.

With Frain gone, Fitz missed another payment and Joey and his goons "reminded" him he had to make payments, but then surprised him by sharing an internal FBI report on recent computer hacking incidents, with one highlighted name. A Margaret Evangeline Hayes in Maryville, MO had penetrated Northwest Missouri State's systems, though no charges had been filed.

The FBI didn't follow up.

Fitz did.

She was perfect. Young, vulnerable, trusting. And talented. Fitz had never been a programmer. That was grunt work. He was the idea guy. He got where he was by schmoozing donors, hogging budget dollars, and inflating grants. She, however, could perform the precise work Fitz needed. And did.

She'd broken into Cambridge's Thinking Machines network with ease, giving him access to specs on their Connection Machine supercomputer. That would make his Soviet friends very happy. Their next favorite thing after military intelligence was information about supercomputer design. Handy in designing hydrogen bombs, apparently.

He'd enclosed a note on the most recent diskette outlining his offering. "As you know, I have shared the best of what is available to me. You have been slow to appreciate it, and me. I am considering terminating our relationship, as you seem not to understand the value of what you have in me and in my contributions. I need a tangible expression of your faith and trust in me. As a show of my faith in our relationship, I enclose here . . ." followed by a description of the supercomputer research on the diskette. As he left, Fitz made the chalk mark on the back of the stop sign letting a driver passing by know he'd made the dead drop.

Now he was back in business, with new secrets to sell. He knew he was taking risks but felt that he had them under control. After all, the Russians wanted him to succeed, and the Irish thugs did too.

He'd get flush again. He always did.

FRIDAY, FEBRUARY 23, 1990

FINALLY, A LEAD. THINKING MACHINES CORPORATION, among the most advanced computer manufacturers in the world, had been hacked. Or at least that's how Carl explained it in the car on the way to Cambridge. In fact, he couldn't shut up about it.

"This place is legendary, building machines that are structured like the human brain. They say they are 'building a machine that will be proud of them.'"

Paul wasn't sure he wanted machines to think, much less be proud. On these matters, he trusted Carl, though, even if he didn't share his enthusiasm or understanding.

Thinking Machines was located in a former industrial building that looked onto the Charles River from First Street in East Cambridge. They were greeted and led to offices that certainly looked futuristic: bright colors, open spaces, the staff young and high-energy. On display was one of their computers—Carl called them "connection machines." Paul thought it looked like a computer should: a hulking black cube with blinking red lights. The computer, however, wasn't what they were there to see.

"Is Danny going to join us?" Carl had asked their guide as they were shown to a conference room.

"He's traveling today. Our system admin will be here in a moment."

"Danny?" Paul asked.

"Danny Hillis. The founder and designer of the Connection Machine."

"You know him? Personally?"

"Me? Heck no. It's just that everybody calls him Danny."

Like Elvis or Cher, Paul presumed.

A middle-aged fellow with a receding hairline joined them in the conference room. The system admin, presumably.

"Guy came in over the open internet and jumped past our router before he found a default admin user," the admin said in lieu of a greeting. "We wouldn't have caught him if he hadn't been hoovering a huge portion of our internet bandwidth. Users were complaining and I looked to see who was hogging our backbone connection. He'd jumped to an internal document server and was downloading designs, so I disabled him."

Paul had, much to his surprise, followed much of that explanation. Carl elicited additional information from the admin, including his name—Mike—and asked about the name "Raven" showing up anywhere. Mike said no, just the hijacking of an existing dormant user.

In the car back to the office, Carl played it out. "They got hacked, and the hacker took computer designs, which fits Raven's profile, only he didn't use the Raven handle. Maybe this was Raven, or maybe this was just run of the mill industrial espionage."

"Great, now we have more than one?"

"Trust me, we have hundreds, maybe thousands, just not all of them are part of our case."

"Did we get anything new from this at all? Anything to move us ahead?"

"Not really."

"Weaver will roast us if we come back empty handed again."

"You said you didn't get much from Jack Kane, right? We could try him again. And how about Jamie Brennan? Why can't we question her again?"

Screw it. He owed his partner an explanation. Paul recounted the conversation with Connor.

Carl shook his head and once again muttered "asshole" in reference to Connor. Paul couldn't disagree.

"And Tom Bergstrom?" Carl asked.

"He threatened to sue for harassment if we ever contacted him again. Plus, I believe him. His story is good."

"Kane, then. Let's go work him."

"He was kind of squirrelly, Carl."

"Let me try. You're not always, well, 'user friendly.'"

Paul grinned.

"Plus, these hackers love to brag," Carl said. "If we ask him for help rather than questioning him, he's bound to spill."

Assuming he's guilty.

When they knocked on Weaver's door later that afternoon, they heard "Come!" Paul inevitably found himself standing at attention, looking across Weaver's immaculate desk. A desk he'd since learned office veterans called "the killing field."

"Ostrowski, Philips, what do you have for me?"

Paul took what he hoped was a not obvious deep breath before he shared their status: the break-in at Thinking Machines, which told them nothing new, the lack of activity with the Russians, and their few open leads. Paul considered asking Weaver to overrule Connor on Jamie Brennan. He wasn't sure he had the juice for that power play, though, so he left it alone for now.

"We're going back to this Kane guy. We're going to double team him and see if we can get more information," Paul concluded.

Weaver's dismissal was curt.

FRIDAY, FEBRUARY 23, 1990

IT SEEMED IMPOSSIBLE. SURREAL. MEV HAD JUST BEEN screwing around when she'd gotten expelled from college, a joke that went too far. And she'd paid the price. But committing espionage? With the FBI already sniffing around? How long would it take for them to discover her past and link it to the present? Jamie already knew about her. Even Fitz knew about her, and he, she was coming to realize, wasn't that smart.

She'd barely left her bedroom all week, sneaking down at night to make sandwiches. Avoiding Hector's judgment, which now felt like foresight. Avoiding Jack's kindness, which felt undeserved. Avoiding Jamie, who, Mev thought, wouldn't have been stupid enough to fall for any of this.

She'd made this mess. She didn't want anyone else to get splattered with it.

If she stayed away from the lab and kept skipping classes, she'd get expelled. Again. Punishing herself didn't solve anything. But she couldn't see any way out.

When Mev stumbled into the office that Friday at 10:30, exhausted from lack of sleep, Fitz was already there. His eyebrows knit when he saw her, then he followed her into his office, closing the door behind him as she dropped her bag on the small chair at her desk.

"Banker's hours, Mev? This isn't what I expect from my best and brightest." He smiled. It didn't reach his eyes.

"I haven't been feeling well." A lame excuse, yet not entirely untrue. She did feel sick about what she'd been drawn into. She began to tear up. She was so, so tired.

The other Fitz appeared. Not the avuncular coach, not the seductive mentor. His eyes were more gray, his age more obvious. Deep furrows ran along his nose to his set jaw. This was the real Fitz, she now knew.

"I give you this all on a silver platter, and you're all boo-hoo about a few simple favors? Grow up."

He towered over her, and Mev tensed, fearing he might hit her. She was afraid of losing her position at MIT and of the police or FBI discovering what was happening. Right now, though, she was most afraid of Fitz.

But he just yanked his office door open and slammed it closed, leaving her alone, trapped.

Mev stared at her computer for the remainder of the day, walking around the lab periodically to stretch her legs. Fitz was nowhere to be seen, and she was mostly oblivious to what was going on around her as she puzzled over her options. The other students in the lab kept their distance, sensing that she was trouble, or in trouble, and wanting no part of it. She figured they'd all seen enough of the real Fitz before today.

She found it hard to touch DEMON, knowing that any work she did made it easier for Fitz to use it to commit crimes. To use *her* to commit crimes. She had the code open on her desktop all day, just doing syntax cleanup and pondering how to make it less useful for Fitz.

When she went to leave for the afternoon, Fitz was in the lab talking to Hector, who seemed pleased at the attention. With Fitz distracted, she might be able to slip out, but he noticed. He approached her and she stiffened.

"Good for you," he said, with none of the earlier dark edge. "Wrap up early today and take a break. Recharge those batteries."

Mev rushed from the lab, escaping before he changed his mind. The late afternoon had turned freakishly warm, fifty degrees, and Mev pulled off her bulky parka. Her arm sweat under the folded coat, and she was damp and demoralized by the time she reached Linnaean Street. Jack's red pickup was in the driveway. She dreaded making small talk. But she had nowhere else to go.

He was in one of the aqua leather chairs, writing longhand on a yellow legal pad, a pile of crumpled papers on the floor next to him. For once the stereo was playing music she recognized: Tom Petty, "Running Down a Dream." It ended and the announcer added "WBCN, the Rock of Boston," before the next song began.

"It's good to mix it up once in a while," Jack said, holding up his legal pad. "I'm trying to start my next chapter. I want to be on my bike, but I've got to make some kind of progress," he said in mock exasperation.

Mev tried to smile back, and knew she wasn't pulling it off. Whatever her expression signaled—exhaustion, frustration, fear—Jack noticed.

"I haven't seen you at all this week."

Mev dropped her bag and sat across from him. Some kind of progress, he'd said. That's what she needed.

"If I tell you something personal, something secret, can you keep it to yourself?" Mev said.

Jack's usual sardonic expression was gone. "Of course. You can trust me. What's going on?"

"I told you I got expelled from Northwest Missouri for hacking."

"Yeah, people are so damned sensitive," Jack joked.

"That's not the problem. The problem is that it's why Fitz recruited me." She paused.

Why was it harder to tell him this than it was to tell him about her father and her past that night at the Wursthaus? He'd been understanding. But her present was much, much worse than her past.

"I was working on a piece of software that would test vulnerabilities on a network. That could be used to fix it. Or, to break into it. Fitz brought me here to use it. To use me to hack for him. To help him steal."

"Oh, man."

"He tricked me into it."

Saying it out loud made it sound even more foolish on her part. How could she possibly have fallen for his whole act?

"It was stupid," she said. "There's more."

She was ashamed telling Jack about sleeping with Fitz. But that was hardly her biggest worry. She told him about the drinks and dinners, about her refusal to continue with him, about his deception and the Thinking Machines break in, about his threat and his promise to keep it secret as long as she continued working for him.

"If I don't keep helping him, he'll turn me in to the FBI. They'll believe him. I'll be kicked out; I'll go to prison."

"What does he do with this stuff?"

"He sells it."

"To whom?"

Mev hesitated. If she brought Jack all the way in, he was in danger too. It was probably a stupid place to draw the line. But if he knew about the espionage and did nothing, wouldn't it make him some kind of accomplice? Jamie would probably know the answer to that.

"I don't know," she said. She wished she didn't know, didn't have the words "spy" and "traitor" in her head. If she could keep Jack away of that part of the debacle, she would.

Jack sat back, fingertips steepled, silent. The silence extended for minutes as he gazed off into the distance.

"Only how do we . . ."

Hector opened the front door and conversation stopped. He looked at Jack. "Come on. I was thinking about firing up the bike, going for a quick ride before dark."

"Nah, I gotta work on my chapter."

Hector glanced at Mev, trying to discern what they'd been talking about.

"I've got work to do anyway," Mev said, taking her bag upstairs to her room, wondering if it'd been a mistake to bring Jack into this whole mess.

The knocking was polite, but insistent. Mev looked at her watch, 7:45 in the morning. She'd only fallen asleep a couple of hours earlier, after staring at her bedroom ceiling most of the night. The knocking persisted, and neither Jack nor Hector was answering the door. She put on sweats and went downstairs, aggravated that anyone would show up this early on a Saturday morning, figuring maybe it was Tom again with another crisis.

Only it was Ostrowski and a tall Black agent she'd have guessed was too young to be flashing a badge. It was one thing to relive her embarrassment and anger at how the FBI treated her and her mom, quite another to be confronted by them after learning she'd committed espionage.

"I brought Agent Philips with me to continue our discussions with Mr. Kane," Ostrowski said.

"We called several times," Agent Philips added.

And left messages. And of course, Jack didn't call them back; a fact that now angered her. She couldn't invent an excuse to turn them away, just prayed they'd keep it short.

Pointing them to chairs, she ran back upstairs, knocking insistently on Jack's bedroom door. He'd still been awake when she went to bed, reading a French literary theory book in the living room with a glass of wine in his hand.

No answer. She pounded on the door.

"Jack! The FBI is here."

She heard fumbling and he cracked the door.

"What?"

"Ostrowski is here, with another agent this time."

"What is it with these guys?"

Hector peeked out of his room.

"What's up?"

"FBI," Mev said.

"Really? Cool." Hector said, walking past them both.

Mev waited while Jack dressed, then followed him down the stairs.

"I'll make coffee," she said, shuffling into the kitchen, avoiding the agents. She turned on the kettle and grabbed the coffee. Another of Jack's food obsessions: whole Hawaiian Kona beans kept fresh in the freezer. She started the electric grinder. Usually this was what woke her in the morning, Jack persisting to get the perfect grind. For now, it made it impossible for the FBI to ask Jack a question.

Only they weren't questioning him; they were watching her, waiting for her to join them. Mev poured five coffees into mismatched cups, and put them, milk, and sugar on the coffee table in the living room. Jack put his face in the cup as he inhaled the aroma.

Agent Philips spoke first. "Thanks for letting us come by."

As if they had a choice.

The agent sipped his coffee, then stopped. "This is really good," he said in surprise.

"Of course it is," Jack snapped. Mev caught his eye, willing him to just play it cool.

"Please don't be alarmed by our presence. We're hoping you can help us."

Ostrowski was sitting on the sofa, drinking his coffee and observing. Then he pulled out a note pad. "I didn't get your name last time miss, and yours, please, as well," he said to Hector.

She hadn't told Jamie yet about everything going on with Fitz, but her words echoed in Mev's head: "They dig around enough, and they'll find or invent something on anyone." Only now it wasn't by association with a felonious parent. Now there really was something for the FBI to find.

No matter what Philips was saying, this was more than a few routine questions. She needed to get through them and get the agents out.

"Hector Cruz, sir."

"And you miss?"

No avoiding it now. "Mev Hayes."

Ostrowski looked up from his pad. "Mev?"

"Margaret Evangeline, right?" Hector said.

"And what do you each do?"

"We are in a computer research group at MIT," Hector volunteered. "I'm a PhD student, and Mev is a researcher there."

Hector needed to shut his mouth.

Ostrowski noted it, closed his pad, and nodded to Agent Philips, who continued.

"Mr. Kane, we were hoping to pick your brain, so to speak. We understand you were at the 2600 meeting with Tom Bergstrom."

"Mev too, she brought him." Hector eagerly added.

She resisted the urge to kick him. She needed the spotlight *off* her.

"I see. I had understood from Mr. Bergstrom that Mr. Kane here was a friend."

"I am. We game together sometimes."

Philips nodded, but Ostrowski spoke. "Game?"

"D&D. Dungeons & Dragons?"

Ostrowski shook his head. Philips continued.

"Why were you there Miss Hayes?"

She needed to be very careful here.

"Just curious, I guess. I'd never been to one of them before."

"I see. Do you have a special interest in hacking?"

"Like I said. Just curious."

This was going absolutely the wrong direction. Did they already suspect something? Did they *know* something? Was this a tactic to catch her off guard? She wished Jamie were here. At least she knew something about dealing with the FBI. Mev chanced a look at Jack. He was calm, even bored-looking. She tried to emulate that.

Agent Philips waited. The silence drew on.

"We're looking for connections," he said. "You see, the hacker we are tracking isn't a typical thrill seeker, grabbing a prize to show his friends: 'Oh, look, I'm elite, I hacked NASA,' or 'I can make long distance calls for free.' This is another sort of person altogether: dedicated and professional. The kind who is furthering corporate espionage. His most recent break-in was at a local supercomputer manufacturer."

Mev's heart pounded and sweat beaded at the nape of her neck. She tried to calm herself. It was hard, knowing she was being observed. The Thinking Machines hack. Did they know it was her? Or did they believe it was Jack? How was this connected to Raven? Did he even exist, or were they fishing? It didn't matter. She needed to stop this line of questioning.

In her distress, she'd missed part of what Agent Philips was saying. " . . . and that is why we need your help," he said.

"Seriously, that's why you're here?" Jack said, his indignation covering whatever fear he had to be feeling for himself and for her. "Three sleep-deprived students are better than what you have at the

FBI?" he said, sinking back into the chair, sipping his coffee, looking far more relaxed than Mev felt.

Only Raven didn't hack Thinking Machines. It gave her a touch of courage to know that despite what they might suspect, they had some of their facts wrong.

Then Hector said, "I can help." He beamed with eagerness and excitement.

Absolutely not. It was risky pushing back on the FBI, and it might well lead to greater focus on her. Nevertheless, she needed to shut this down. If they already suspected her, it wouldn't make anything worse to say nothing, whereas anything else said, any leads or evidence that she or Jack exposed would only increase her risk. And his.

"This is a bad idea all around," Mev said. "Best none of us get involved here. Tom did and look what happened to him."

Her outburst drew a sour look from Hector, who undoubtedly thought it would be cool, thought it was yet another thing she was ruining for him. Too bad.

"Yep," Jack said. "Much as I'd like to help you gents, I'm afraid my dance card is full."

Ostrowski and Philips both stood, and each put three business cards on the table. Only Hector took them.

"We appreciate your time and will reach out as we have more questions," Philips said as they left, Ostrowski giving Jack and Mev a cool look.

No question. They'd be back.

MONDAY, FEBRUARY 26, 1990

IT WAS THE THIRD JEWELRY STORE OF THE DAY. INEX-plicably, the Russians had paid him in diamonds this time. Fitz had no idea how much they were worth, and suspected his Mob loan shark would undervalue them, so he found himself going store to store in the Diamond District on Washington Street in downtown Boston trying to get the best price.

"Family heirlooms?" the older man asked, lifting a diamond from the black velvet pad with a tweezer. "They're an older cut. Edwardian, maybe. See this flat part on the tail? It's called a culet. Modern diamond cutters don't leave this artifact anymore."

Fitz could feel the flush rising up his neck. This was demeaning and potentially dangerous. He didn't want to be memorable here, didn't want to leave any kind of trail, so he just nodded.

The jeweler looked at the gem again through his loupe. "I can give you eleven thousand for them."

It was as if the jewelers had a crime syndicate of their own. It was the same price he'd gotten at two other stores. He needed more. He needed to make a dent in his loan. These damned jewelers must all talk to each other, fix prices. This had to be illegal.

"Fifteen," Fitz countered.

The jeweler pushed the velvet pad back toward Fitz. "This is not *Let's Make a Deal.* Eleven."

Who did this asshole think he was dealing with? "I need more, dammit!"

The jeweler pulled back his hands as if the diamonds were on fire. "It's time for you to go."

Fitz looked up at the camera behind the counter. Of course, now the jeweler thought they were stolen. They probably bought stolen items off people all the time, just not from Fitz.

He left that store, went back to a previous one he'd gotten the very same quote from and sold them, taking the eleven thousand and getting out. He hated taking these risks, hated that he was in this position, being sullied by spies and gangsters.

When he arrived back at MIT, he was accosted by the Mob collector, Joey, and one of the enforcers he'd seen before as he exited his car.

"We need progress, professor."

The disrespect infuriated him. What did this lowlife know about who he was, about what he'd accomplished? Fitz was known the world over for his expertise. Respected, even feared, for his dominance in the field.

He wanted to retort, to pop this punk in the mouth, only there was the beefy enforcer, clad in a Red Sox T-shirt so tight it would rip if he flexed his massive biceps. Fitz held his tongue, instead, handing him the check the jeweler had cut.

"What the fuck am I supposed to do with this? Cash only, dickhead."

Fitz had begged the jeweler for cash, only then he too had become suspicious. So, he'd taken the check.

A retort on his lips, Fitz looked at the enforcer and paused. "Give me 'til tomorrow," he said instead.

"Nah." Joey looked at his watch. "Today. 3:00. Don't be late."

Not just anybody would cash a check this large. It would have to be one of the three banks he already had a relationship with, only he had overdue loans with all of them.

At a payphone he looked through the Yellow Pages for smaller branches of Bank of Boston then drove to one in Mattapan, a neighborhood Fitz would never enter in any other conceivable circumstance. He hoped the tellers in this branch were more worried about being robbed than whether Fitz was behind in his loan payments.

Still, since it was over ten thousand, the bank would have to report it. This on top of the security cameras in the jewelry stores. This was getting too complicated, too visible.

The transaction completed, Fitz exited quickly onto Blue Hill Ave., crashing into a man on the sidewalk.

"Watch it, asshole," Fitz growled, only it was Joey, still backed by his huge friend.

"Careful there, professor," he said. "This is a dangerous neighborhood. You might get hurt."

Fitz hated that he immediately reached for the envelope in his coat pocket, hated that his hand trembled when he removed a thousand and handed Joey the remaining ten.

"Here," he said in a voice that he hoped didn't betray the feeling of exposure he felt in this neighborhood, on this street, with these two men.

Joey riffled the bills and nodded. "It's a start, but we expect weekly payments, and this doesn't catch you up." He and his companion walked away, leaving Fitz alone, shaking, and the center of attention of the entire block. A trembling white man in a cashmere topcoat walking to his luxury car. He walked faster, got in and quickly locked the doors.

He was raging. At being frightened by Joey, by having to be in this neighborhood, at the indignity of it all. He was better than this. He deserved better than this.

MONDAY, FEBRUARY 26, 1990

AFTER THE ABORTIVE INTERVIEW WITH JACK KANE AND his roommates, Paul had tried to take Sunday off. Instead, he found himself pacing in his tiny apartment, obsessing about the only thing he cared about other than the case: his daughter down in D.C. He'd placed his usual Sunday call to talk to Becky, to hear about her week. Linda wouldn't put her on the phone.

They were at an impasse. Things were tough after they had Becky. Paul worked constantly, with unpredictable hours, and Linda was overwhelmed. He didn't have a choice, had to drop everything when a case demanded it. That was the job. She said she understood when they were first together, even bragged about his job to friends. But the multiple moves for his career, starting over in a new city again and again, had worn her down. Paul's censure and indefinite posting to Boston had been the last straw.

"I've followed you to half a dozen crappy cities, and every time you get buried in work, leaving me to do the move, set up the house, and comfort Becky who's in a new school with no friends. You work nights, weekends. We never see you.

"I have a better idea this time. You go to Boston, and we'll skip the moving and uprooting Becky part. And, Paul, maybe you just stay there."

The marriage had been in trouble long before he'd punched Knightly. He'd tried hard to keep it together, to spend time with Becky whenever he could. Then he'd let his instincts get ahead of what he knew he *should* do, and punched Knightly in the face, ending his time in CID, in D.C., maybe ending his marriage, maybe his career.

And despite his efforts, he wasn't doing so well rehabilitating that career. As Paul walked into the office on Monday morning, he knew he and Carl had only speculation, and not much of that. Computer crimes and espionage had been committed, by a perpetrator known only by a hacker alias, and maybe not always using it. It had been stupid to make a big deal out of talking to Kane, since now he had nothing for Weaver, no more promising leads.

Carl was already in the office, which wasn't unusual. Paul should emulate him more—enthusiastic, engaged, on the fast track. What was unusual this morning was the shit-eating grin on Carl's face.

"You are not going to believe this," he said, waving Paul over, impatient for him to look at his screen.

Carl gave his chair to Paul, who read through what Carl showed him. "What the hell?"

What Carl had found doing background research was both unexpected and a potential breakthrough. Jack Kane and Hector Cruz were both vanilla, with a minor infraction in Kane's juvenile record that was sealed. Margaret Evangeline Hayes was a whole other story. Her father had been imprisoned during her teens for perpetrating a Ponzi scheme, a monstrous pyramid that eventually came crashing down and landed him in a federal penitentiary. And that was just the appetizer.

Last year Mev Hayes had been expelled from Northwest Missouri State University over a hacking incident. The school hadn't wanted to press charges, and no damage had been done, so the Department of Justice decided not to pursue it. Still, this woman had an FBI file. And she was a bona fide computer hacker.

"There's more," Carl said. "I widened the net, looking at other associates of Hayes. As it happens, Randall FitzRoy, her boss, is deep in debt. Several hundred thousand, with everything mortgaged to the hilt."

"He's in on it with Kane and Hayes?" Paul asked.

"Follow the money, isn't that what you say?" Carl reminded him. "I think FitzRoy is worth looking at. Kane has been outright hostile toward us, and Hayes was nervous at that last interview. Neither of them wanted us there."

Carl tapped a pen against his forehead. "I don't think we have enough to bring any of them in."

"Did we find anything more on Bergstrom's machines?"

"Clean as a whistle. As far as we can tell, his story checks. That's not to say he didn't manipulate the machines to support his story or erase evidence of Hayes' and Kane's activities."

"Then why would he report it? As I said before, my guess is he isn't involved. No reason we can't speak to Kane and Hayes again though," Paul said. "Maybe the other kid, Hector Cruz, will tell us something. He seemed to want to, so maybe he's not involved. We need to get him alone. And you're right, let's follow the money. And keep an eye on FitzRoy."

MONDAY, FEBRUARY 26, 1990

IT WAS SURREAL BEING BACK IN THE LAB AFTER EVERY-
thing that had transpired. But where else would she go? Fitz had her by
the neck. If she refused, if she didn't do what he wanted, he'd just send
her to prison and find the next patsy. Would he make her hack another
company? Or go back to Thinking Machines again and again until he got
enough money? Would he ever let her go?

Thankfully he hadn't been in yet today, and Mev tried distracting
herself by doing classwork.

She was surprised by a knock on Fitz's office door. That was nothing
compared to her surprise when she opened it to find Special Agents
Ostrowski and Philips.

"Miss Hayes, good to see you again. Your colleague told me where
I could find you," Ostrowski said, nodding back toward Hector, who was
watching this exchange carefully.

"Come in," she said, waving them in and closing the door quickly.
She sat in her desk chair, watching as Ostrowski surveyed the room, then
chose one of Fitz's side chairs and turned it to face her. In a change from
their last conversation, Philips was quiet, watching her closely.

"I have a few additional questions for you, if you don't mind,"
Ostrowski began.

Mev felt sweat beading at her hairline.

"I must say, I was intrigued by your personal history, Miss Hayes."

She swallowed.

"Despite it all, you seem to have done quite well for yourself.
Placement at MIT, a cushy research job, a nice house to share with friends,

a great future in front of you." He leaned back in his chair, pulling out his notebook, looking relaxed, in control of the situation.

Because he was.

"Seen your father lately?"

This was the reason she hadn't wanted the FBI sniffing around. Damn Hector! Once they knew her name, they'd stumble on her dad's—and her—history.

She worked to control her breathing, keeping it steady, drawing the air slowly through her nose. She would give him as little as she could.

"No."

"Don't you miss him?"

"No." She didn't, not really. She had never visited him in prison. At first her mother had forbidden her from doing so, then she hadn't wanted to. By the time she entered college, he felt almost as distant to her as a character in a novel. Part of the story of her life. Not part of her life.

Ostrowski looked down at his notes, then back up, assessing her. "Agent Philips and I have a bet. Maybe you can help us resolve it. We are working to figure out the odds of a young woman whose father is a convicted felon, who happens to enter the field of computer security, happens to be expelled from one college for hacking, happens to be invited to a much nicer college linked to hacking incidents, happens to find a room in a house owned by a man who happens to have been one of the people named on a server penetrated by known hacker Raven."

There it was. They had her.

"You see, Carl believes the odds of that being a coincidence are very low. I think the odds of it being a coincidence are, well, zero. Who do you think wins the bet?"

Actually, they didn't quite have her. Yes, she was the one who hacked Thinking Machines; no, she was not this Raven person. It opened a crack. A crack she could see a little light through.

"You don't know? I mean, come on," he leaned forward, his elbows on his knees, hands spread wide. "Isn't it too fantastic that all this comes together just like that?"

"It's a coincidence," she said. "I got a research fellowship with a professor known to find interesting candidates across the country. He saw that I'd been a winner of the Ada Promise Prize. I found an apartment I could afford by answering an advertisement from *The Boston Phoenix*. And Tom Bergstrom told you what happened on his server. Coincidence."

He flipped through his notes again. "How about friends? Surely, you've made lots of friends here."

How ironic. Her few friends at this point made her look guiltier. Jack. Jamie. Everyone else was at best indifferent, at worst hostile, like Hector. Like Fitz. "Jack, I guess."

"Not your roommate Hector?"

Mev stayed silent on that. And she definitely wasn't going to tell them about Jamie, who was already on their radar.

"No one else? None of your other colleagues?"

"It's pretty competitive."

"Oh, I bet it is. People would do anything to get a position like yours, I'm sure. How's the pay?"

"The pay?" She hadn't even gotten a full month's pay yet. And it wasn't a lot. She hadn't negotiated at all when Fitz had offered her the job. She'd been honored, as ridiculous as that sounded now.

"It's OK."

"Still, it can't be cheap living here, keeping up your little Pinto, taking friends for beers."

What was he driving at? Was this somehow about her father's fraud?

"Mev? May I call you Mev? Help me understand how those coincidences add up to anything else than you being Raven. It's just too improbable, otherwise."

Near the mark, but another miss. Or was it? Did he mean Fitz? She searched her memory for what they'd told her about Raven. Were they blaming every hack on this guy?

"Are you involved? In over your head?"

For sure. Only not how he suspected.

"I just got here. All that Raven stuff happened before, right?"

"It wasn't as if you didn't know you were going to be working at MIT. Perhaps you prepped a landing spot for yourself."

He was accusing her of being Raven. She knew she wasn't. And they couldn't connect her to it, or they'd accuse her directly. That fortified her denial.

"I had nothing to do with that," she said, this time with confidence.

"You expect me to believe this is all happenstance? That you aren't involved?"

"Are you accusing me of a crime?"

"Not at all, Miss Hayes, no. Mev. You're helping me settle a bet, remember?"

He rose, putting his notebook away. "That will do for today. I expect you'll be seeing more of us."

The door opened, and there stood Fitz, clearly startled at Ostrowski's presence.

"Special Agent Paul Ostrowski," he said, showing his credentials, a friendly warmth in his voice. The tone he'd begun with, before he'd turned up the heat.

"Dr. Randall FitzRoy III. What is this about, agents?"

Mev could see the edge of panic on Fitz's face, hoped Ostrowski and Philips didn't notice it.

"It's a pleasure to meet you," Ostrowski said. "Miss Hayes here was helping us clear up a misunderstanding. We're set for now. I'll let you all get back to work," he said with a smile as he and Philips left.

Fitz looked as if he were about to lose control, but he quietly closed the office door. His face was dark, and he stood eye to eye with her. "What the hell was that?"

"It has nothing to do with you," she said.

"The hell it doesn't. You brought FBI agents into *my* office? Are you insane? Why not advertise what we are doing in *The Boston Globe*? You have got to be the stupidest bitch on the planet."

He grabbed her wrist. "What did they want?"

"It's not related. One of my housemate's friends had his bulletin board system hacked. The FBI wants to find the guy who did it. It has nothing to do with us."

He gripped her wrist harder, pulling her closer, his arm quivering. His breath reeked of alcohol.

"You're hurting me," she said, working to keep her voice down.

He let go, angry yet still distracted. "Don't talk to them again. I'm going to get my due, and there's no way I'll let you stand in my way. Got it? You will regret doing anything to screw this up."

Mev believed him.

WEDNESDAY, FEBRUARY 28, 1990

PAUL CRESTED THE HILL ON THE GRAVEL ROAD LEADING to Randall FitzRoy's home in Carlisle, unprepared for what he saw.

"Wow," Carl whispered.

A grand white federal stood atop a rise, two large red barns cascading down the hill. The house looked over fenced meadows containing several horses, a scene from a gracious living magazine. Clearly, they should have been paying closer attention to FitzRoy's finances. Paul had no idea what a house like this cost here in Boston. Near Washington D.C. it would easily be over a million dollars.

"Professors do better than FBI agents, apparently," Carl said.

"Apparently," Paul replied, goggling at the spread.

Their unmarked Ford rolled to a gravel-crunching stop at the foot of the hill, and Paul and Carl climbed the rough granite steps toward the house. A voice hailed them from one of the barns. A woman.

She was wearing jodhpurs and tall black riding boots, a helmet in her hand. She was blonde, thin, in good shape. Although her face was youthful, her taut tanned arms told Paul she was older but "very well-kept," as Linda would have put it.

"May I help you?" she asked.

"Ma'am," he said, with a nod. He'd found the touch of southern charm he'd learned in D.C. played well pretty much everywhere.

"I'm Special Agent Paul Ostrowski, and this is Special Agent Carl Philips. Is Randolph FitzRoy here?"

She eyed them with suspicion, and Paul was half expecting a "come back with a warrant," given her squint.

"Can you tell me what this is about, agents?"

"It's a computer matter, ma'am, and we believe he can help us."

"I see," she said, turning toward the house.

The side storm door opened, framing FitzRoy, who was nudging a yapping dog back inside with his foot.

"Agent Ostrowski, what a surprise. Please come in," he said with perfect grace, holding the door open while keeping the little dog inside.

"What brings you here so early in the morning?"

They were in a tidy mudroom, with coats on pegs and boots in bins. As Mrs. FitzRoy—Donna, Paul's notes had said—struggled with her boots, Fitz led the agents into the house, calling back over his shoulder.

"Donna, would you please make the agents coffee?"

Her look back at him was hard to read exactly, a flash of anger, resentment, frustration? There was tension there. Paul recognized it. He'd experienced Linda's version of that look many times.

Fitz ignored it. "Please come in. My wife will bring us coffee. We have a few minutes before I need to get to campus. How can I help you?"

He led them into a living room—or was it a parlor?—and had them sit in two easy chairs covered in a textured fabric Paul knew was expensive. Linda had wanted their furniture upholstered like that. He'd countered that she needed to get a better job.

He'd never known when to shut up with her.

"Mr. FitzRoy," Paul began, "we have a few questions for you."

"Dr. FitzRoy," he corrected. His wife set down a silver tray with a china coffee service that looked like something out of a movie. Paul's came from a Mr. Coffee with a few years of burned coffee stains on the heating element.

Fitz poured for them, asking about cream and sugar, before pouring his own, adding two spoons of sugar, and making himself comfortable in a wingback chair. Once Mrs. FitzRoy had left the room, Paul began.

"Dr. FitzRoy . . . "

"Just 'Fitz,' is actually fine, Agent."

Paul recognized Fitz's clumsy power play here. He could make it work to his advantage. Paul spoke in conspiratorial low voice. "Fitz, we are following a lead to MIT in a computer espionage investigation."

Fitz retained his bemused smile as he sipped from the dainty china. Paul put down his own tiny cup and saucer. "Your name has come up, you see, in the investigation." He watched Fitz's expression. It barely changed. A flicker? Maybe?

Fitz put down his cup on the side table by his chair. "How, may I ask? In what context?"

"I'm not at liberty to share details with you at the moment. What I can tell you is that there's been an investigation into Boston-based computer crime that has a connection to MIT. Specifically, selling commercial secrets to hostile foreign powers."

Fitz didn't flinch and came out swinging instead. "Does this have anything to do with your conversation with Mev Hayes? What has she said to you?" he asked.

"I'm asking what *you* know, sir," Paul replied.

"Because if you'd like me to follow up with her, tell me what you are looking for and I'll be happy to see what she knows."

"No need. We're already doing that."

"I'd appreciate it if you wouldn't distract her too much. She's behind in her research work and, to be candid, she's struggling."

Paul suspected this was all a façade, but he didn't have another angle. Like with Hayes and Kane, he was looking for reactions.

"Your house is quite interesting. Is it historic?" Paul asked.

Fitz's expression changed now, evincing confusion about the direction of the conversation. Innocent non-sequitur questions often tripped up even the most prepared suspects.

"The core house itself dates from the late eighteenth century, although it was added onto during the next hundred years. The barns are from later that century, though the foundation of the upper one appears to be older. The property had been in the Bradford family for generations. Then their children sold it about fifty years ago to the Frasiers, who converted it into a horse farm. We bought it in 1981, when they had to sell."

The recession. Paul remembered it well. Linda had wanted them to move into a nicer place when houses came on the market at reduced prices, only FBI salaries lagged inflation. That only got worse when he was transferred to D.C. in '86. The sales proceeds from a big three-bedroom suburban house in Cincinnati barely covered a bungalow in Virginia.

"Really nice place, isn't it Carl?" Paul had been focused on his interaction with Fitz, and had almost forgotten about Carl, who'd been outside of his peripheral vision when he was focused on Fitz. Paul's partners always commented on his intensity, some hating it and feeling sidelined, some loving how he blasted through the bullshit with suspects, happy to stand by and catch the lies and broken alibis.

"Nicer than any place I've ever lived." Carl played the wide-eyed kid exceptionally well.

"Horses. Never got into them," Paul said. "Do your daughters ride?"

Fitz hesitated, now studying Paul. His eyes flicked to Carl then back, appearing to judge him a lesser threat.

"They do," Fitz replied. "Jessica is quite accomplished. She's won a few ribbons in dressage."

Paul needed to plant a few seeds, and then see what grew here. He wasn't going to brace Fitz in his own living room—parlor—with any success. He needed to rattle his cage, and he needed more data to do that.

Paul stood. "We appreciate your time, Dr. FitzRoy. I mean, Fitz. Please thank Mrs. FitzRoy for the coffee. We'll be on our way."

Fitz led them to the side door again, his loafer heels clicking on the shiny wooden floor. Fitz held the storm door for them.

"Gentlemen. All the best in your investigation. Do let me know if there is anything else I can assist you with."

Paul strode to the car, and Carl broke into a small jog to keep up.

"Paul, what . . ."

Paul raised his index finger and continued forward in silence to the car. Once the doors were closed, he put the Ford in gear and slowly navigated the gravel drive.

"There's something funny there. He's too slick by half," Paul said.

"And did you see that watch?"

"Fitz's?" Paul asked as he turned the car onto the narrow, paved road that ran along the property.

"Oh yeah. A Patek Phillipe. Ten grand minimum. They can run more than a hundred thousand dollars."

Paul couldn't help considering the Timex on his wrist and the Casio on Carl's. "A hundred thousand for a watch? How do you know this stuff?"

"Prior case. A computer hacker was paid with one we were pretty sure was stolen from a break-in at a German consul's house. It helped us tie all the pieces together. What next?"

"Like with your German. Follow the money."

On returning to the JFK Federal Building, they were surprised to find Hector Cruz in the lobby, nervously smoking a cigarette. He ground it out in an ashtray stand next to the reception desk and approached them.

"I want to help."

Inside the interview room, Paul gave the nod to Carl to take the lead as he had in their last visit to Linnaean Street.

"Tell us about Jack Kane," Paul said.

"Not much to tell. He's an English major. Likes music and video games. He's writing his dissertation about them. We've been housemates for a couple of years. He's a hell of a cook, thank God.

"I mean, we're friends. We hang out, ride our motorcycles together. He's really cool."

"No concerns about Jack?"

"Like what?"

"Money issues at all?"

"Jack? Oh, hell no. He owns the house we live in. And his parents are rich."

So, Kane might be just what he seemed: a nerdy English major with a bad attitude. Nothing more. Him showing up on their radar might have been a coincidence, a fortunate one that led them to Hayes and FitzRoy.

"Tell me about Dr. FitzRoy," Carl asked. "You are one of his researchers, right?"

"Yeah. He's OK. Don't get me wrong, Fitz can be a total dick sometimes, but working for him is a stepping stone to an amazing career. He's got connections everywhere."

It was those connections that intrigued Paul.

"Tell me about who he is connected with."

Hector went on for a full five minutes talking about technology companies, and names of people who Carl clearly recognized, even if Paul did not.

"How about Thinking Machines in Cambridge?" Carl asked.

Hector paused. "Not that I know of. Supercomputing is a pretty specialized hardware discipline. I don't think anyone from his lab has gone to work there, Cray Research, or any of the other supercomputer manufacturers."

Not definitive. After all, they were hacked, not schmoozed. Fitz may be just what he seemed as well: a financially over-extended, glad-handing professor.

"Tell me about your other roommate."

It was as if a dam broke. Hector's voice grew hoarse as he articulated all the ways he disliked and distrusted Mev Hayes. He was perhaps not the most objective witness. Still, they did learn two important things. First, whatever Mev was working on for FitzRoy was being done in secret. And second, the two of them appeared to be having an affair. Good additional details, but no smoking gun. He didn't have any facts directly relevant to the case.

Paul looked at his watch: 11:39 p.m. Takeout food cluttered Carl's desk, including some now-cold beef with broccoli from China Pearl that Paul knew he shouldn't have eaten. It congealed in the pit of his stomach, weighing down his brain and his gut.

"I'm going to make coffee," Paul said, needing the stretch more than the caffeine.

"Good idea," Carl said, returning to the same notes they'd been reviewing for hours.

While they'd been able to expedite the request for Fitz's financial records, they hadn't found any hard evidence. They kept trying to find another angle. This was police work, as familiar as anything Paul had done when he was CID in D.C. "To another boring day," was a common toast among the career veterans there. Excitement could make a career. It could also kill it—or the agent chasing it.

He found the coffee pot heater still on, and the typical burned crust in the bottom of the carafe from evaporated coffee. As he washed the pot, he wondered for the thousandth time why the hell they were trying this hard. He'd been one of those guys who sought excitement and look where it got him. In a new city, away from home, stuck on a nowhere case with a rookie. He filled the coffee maker with water, threw away the old grounds, refilled it, and set it to brew.

No, that wasn't fair to Carl. In many ways, he was the future of the Bureau. Tech savvy, not mired in the past. Not one of Hoover's men. It was Paul who was the zombie FBI agent, shambling around waiting to be put out of his misery.

He shook his head. This might seem like a bullshit case, but Paul was still law enforcement, still had a job to do. He couldn't let work go unfinished. Wasn't in his nature. Linda hated that aspect of his personality, urged him to let things go, to "think of your family." Not that it would have made a difference. If he thought of his family, of his daughter, he'd still be here, because he would always clock the Rick Knightlys of the world.

He brought back two black coffees, skipping the multiple creams and sugars for once. Carl was leaning back in his chair, hands behind his head, elbows winged out, staring at the ceiling, looking for all the world like a baby chick waiting for mama to drop a worm in his mouth.

"Done already?" Paul said as he handed him the coffee.

Carl sat back up straight. He still looked chipper. The joys of youth. He hoped Carl wasn't wasting his.

"No, I've been reviewing FitzRoy's financials again. He's buried in debt, and it looks like he's using personal guarantees to pay off other loans, credit card advances and bank promises piling up, paying off the minimum before the creditors come banging on the door. A house of cards, as they say."

Paul sipped the coffee. Awful. That's why he added cream and sugar.

"Once in a while, things seem to stabilize. Except for a recent transaction with some jewelry, he hasn't triggered many reporting flags."

"If you look at the history, it seems to begin in late 1987," Paul said. "I've seen this pattern before. We were chasing a multi-state drug ring, and couldn't get anything on the leader, Freddie Holmes. The guy was slick, and always had another house to escape to, another girlfriend who covered for him. The bank, though, wasn't so easily fooled. He thought he was a rock star stock trader, then after Black Monday in '87, he had to tap everything he had to cover his margins. We got him on the legitimate stuff, not his criminal activities."

"Like Capone!" Carl said.

"A lot of times, it's the boring stuff that makes cases. Freddie Holmes was over-extended, and the Colombians don't like partners who take too many risks, so he was trying to cover it all with legitimate money. I think we're seeing something like this here. Having met FitzRoy a few times, he strikes me as someone who is sure he's smarter than everyone else."

"He's in trouble, and what? He sells stuff to the Soviets? Fitz is Raven, trading computer secrets for Russian cash?"

"Sure, why not?" Paul said. "As far as I can tell, he's in huge trouble financially. And he's got to have stuff the Russians want, right? I mean, he's at MIT. He's got access to things we don't want the Russians having. Which brings us back to the Hayes girl. She's got to know something. And if they are having an affair, maybe she's involved with it."

"But like Hayes said, it started before she was at MIT. And we haven't seen Raven, or anyone using that name, since she got here. On the other hand, a known hacker comes to MIT to work with a deeply indebted professor, and they have an affair, and it's linked to a Bulletin Board System that's linked to Raven. Can't be all coincidence."

"I seem to recall that we had this conversation recently," Paul said with a smile.

"Yeah," Carl nodded. "FitzRoy is at the center of all of this. There's something there, I can feel it. And clearly Hayes is involved. But Kane might not be. He might just be a jerk."

"Harvard and MIT seems to turn them all into assholes."

Carl returned a tight smile.

"Harvard?" Paul asked.

"Class of '86."

"Sorry about that."

"No, it's OK. Lots of my classmates were assholes."

"No Ivy League insights here?"

"I was a math geek who went back to get a law degree. I didn't have time to hang with the assholes," Carl replied. "So, what next? We keep pulling at the threads?"

"Yep. We need to pay return visits to FitzRoy, Hayes, and Kane." Paul looked at his Timex. "But it's almost tomorrow. And I need sleep."

THURSDAY, MARCH 1, 1990

FITZ HAD BEEN SURPRISED, AND NOT AT ALL PLEASED, when the FBI agents had showed up at his home. Clearly what Mev had said about their visit to the lab was a lie. Of course she'd lied. When he'd grabbed her, shaking sense into her, he saw the eyes of a scared little bunny, useless against the basic facts of the world.

The strong take what they want. The intelligent find their way around any obstacle. The driven always succeed. He was all three.

Sitting in the living room of his Cambridge hideaway, Fitz was enjoying a tumbler of Balvenie by candlelight. The candles were left over from his tryst with a Physics undergraduate he'd chatted with outside Building 38. The Cyclotron particle accelerator was right across the street, and she was doing a thesis following one of the experiments running there. He'd asked her about her work, showing interest, asking probing questions. They loved it when you pretended to care.

She'd been impressed with his demeanor, his looks, and his BMW as they leaned against it and chatted. It was all too easy, really. The girls could have a frat boy they met at a kegger who felt them up, or they could spend time with an intelligent, wealthy sophisticate who would make them feel special.

Fitz was enjoying his scotch in peace, as young Chloe had to go back to her dorm to study for a Friday quiz. Just as well. It wasn't like he wanted pillow talk with the girl. Though he had appreciated how eager she was to please.

His smile widened now when he thought more about the FBI agents. Yes, he'd been concerned when they'd shown up at home; however, after talking to them he wasn't really worried. Ostrowski struck him as a man ground down by his work in law enforcement. A computer-illiterate flat foot trying to survive until his retirement. And that Black agent? He was a child, hardly older than Chloe. If that was the best the FBI had to throw at this, he didn't have much to worry about.

Plus, things just worked for Fitz. Money troubles turned to a Russian benefactor. That junkie hacker's death led to Mev Hayes. It was all about seizing the opportunities put in front of you. Wasn't that always the way? An MIT professorship turned into an award winning lab. Graduate student success ensured Fitz's name was on some of the best research coming from MIT. Recognition led to more recognition, until his actual workload was accepting grants and keeping the odd unruly grad student in line.

Sure, it was a little complicated right now, but he'd get in front of it. He always did. With Mev's program he'd get the money he needed to pay off those Mob thugs and get them out of his life. He'd find more juicy technology to share with the hapless Russians. Then he'd be back on top.

He just needed to push Mev a little harder. When he'd gone back to the Thinking Machines account to look for more goodies, it had been shut down. That was frustrating.

And Fitz didn't like being denied.

FRIDAY, MARCH 2, 1990

THE LAB WAS EMPTY AT THE END OF THE DAY WHEN FITZ came in, heading straight for his office, straight for Mev. He closed the door behind him.

"They killed the account you made me at Thinking Machines. I need you to make another one."

"No."

Mev hadn't known she was going to say that. She'd been trying not to think about what she'd do when he demanded she hack for him again. Apparently, she'd made up her mind somewhere along the way.

"What did you say?"

"No."

He grabbed her wrist and dragged her to the chair at her desk. She could feel the bones in her wrist grind against each other.

"Sit," he said.

"No."

"Sit, God dammit!"

She was afraid he'd get more violent, as he had in the car the morning he'd told her about the Russians. Instead, he hesitated, then let go of her wrist. It still ached from when he'd grabbed her before. She rubbed it, the pain hardening her resolve to give him nothing.

"Why are you making me hurt you?" he said. "If you would just do what you promised to do. To do what I hired you to do, then this would all be fine. Defying me won't do you any good. I can be good to you. I've *been* good to you. How do you not see that?"

He needed her. She sure as hell didn't need him.

And whether he sensed her determination or something else, his anger dimmed, and he left the office in a temporary reprieve.

She needed this to change. She needed to get control. Mev felt the edges of a realization. One she wanted to explore.

Fitz kept her around, kept paying her, hoping she'd still help him steal technology. Clearly that was done now. She collected the few possessions she had in Fitz's office and prepared to leave the lab for good. Mev rubbed her sore wrist. But inside she was relieved. She knew his secrets, he knew hers. He wouldn't turn her in, she wouldn't turn him in. *Mutually assured destruction.*

It was the first Friday of the month, and 2600 would be meeting. But that, like so much else, had been soured by her association with Fitz and the scrutiny of the FBI. She could never go back.

Finally home, she found the living room dark, and Hector in the kitchen eating cereal over the sink. He glanced up, then back down at his bowl.

"Hi Hector," she said, hoping to engage him. It had been an awful day, and she could use even a reluctant ally.

"Hey," he said, then resumed eating.

"How's it going?" she asked, dropping her bag on the scarred kitchen table and sitting. He looked at her. And returned to his bowl.

Silence hung in the dim house, the only sound the ticking of his spoon against the side of the bowl.

He slammed the bowl down on the counter and turned toward her. "How's it going?" he growled back at her.

She knew that look. Rage. She'd just seen it in Fitz's office.

"It's going shitty." He was seething, and Mev wasn't sure what to expect next. He turned away, dropping his bowl in the sink.

"I'm sorry, OK?" she pleaded. "I took the job. I wanted to get into MIT."

"You got it all, though, didn't you? Hey, it's your big break." He paused. "Congrats."

Mev's blush rose from her chest up her neck. She wasn't embarrassed; she was ashamed. She'd been fooled, been foolish, and now she was trapped.

He sat next to her, his anger draining away, his eyes now pleading. "I need a break. Can't you deal me in on whatever you are doing for Fitz? There's got to be enough to go around."

The irony was bitter. No doubt Fitz would happily spread the blame around.

"I don't have anything. And after today, I might be done anyway."

"You are so full of it." He stood, red-faced again, his hands clenched at his sides. "I can't fuck Fitz, so I guess I'm out of luck." He pointed a finger at her chest. "Thing is, it all comes around eventually," he said then stomped upstairs.

Trembling, she took a bottle of wine from the refrigerator and poured herself a huge glass, gulping it down. He wasn't wrong. Fitz brought her into the program. He got her into grad school. She slept with him. And then he trapped her.

Mev was sitting in the dark kitchen with a wine in her hand when Jack got home.

He sat next to her. "Looks like I'm supporting underage drinking here."

Her voice was scratchy from crying. She cleared her throat and raised her glass. "Not anymore. I turned twenty-one last week."

"No way. Seriously? Why didn't you say anything?"

"No big deal. We don't do birthdays in my house." Not after her dad went to prison.

"It *is* a big deal, and this is *my* house. And I know just the place to celebrate. Get your coat."

Jack took her glass and poured the wine down the sink.

"Stick close," Jack said as they exited the T station in Central Square. They passed Ken's Steakhouse, leaving the lights of the Square. In the dark it seemed every corner held someone who looked like a dealer, a hustler, or a mugger. Maybe all the above. Fortunately, their destination was only a few dark blocks away from the Square: a low brick building that looked like a bomb shelter with a stylized sign reading "Manray."

She was carded at the door, which gave her the first good feeling of the evening. She was, at least in this moment, not breaking the law. The club was filled with a mix of goths and punks, dressed in black, some in leather, many with piercings and tattoos. Not the crowd she'd have expected Jack to hang with, yet he was perfectly at ease.

A DJ was spinning vinyl and started mixing in a new tune.

"I love this song," Jack said, and Mev smiled again, admiring the way he embraced life, wishing she could do the same. But calamity inevitably found her.

He got them both beers and found an empty table.

"What is this?"

"Sam Adams. It's my go-to."

"No, the music."

"Fine Young Cannibals."

She'd never heard of them. Madonna and U2 were still favorites. This, though, was a different sound. And this club was a different place. The DJ put another song on, and Jack jumped up.

"Come on, let's dance."

Jack grabbed her wrist to drag her onto the floor. She yanked it back, flashing onto Fitz's earlier aggression, and Jack sensed something was wrong.

"'Love Shack' by the B-52s," he said, as if in apology. He didn't say anything else, just sat back down. Looking at her with concern, he couldn't help continuing bopping to the music. She couldn't help feeling dragged down by all the forces arrayed against her.

Jack asked if she wanted another beer and went to get them. Mev looked around the club at the people dancing with abandon, one woman her age in dark makeup, a skin-tight vinyl top, and a leather collar, bouncing to the music with friends. She reminded Mev of Jamie: self-confident, self-aware, someone who knew who they were and what they wanted. She craved that.

Jack returned with a smile and handed her the beer. She knew he was trying to be nice, trying to be supportive. He'd been sweet that night at the Wursthaus and listened with concern when she'd told him more. She sipped her beer and tried to enjoy the music. Jack didn't ask her to dance again, though he clearly wanted to, swaying to the beat.

Sensing she wasn't into it, Jack shouted over the music that maybe they could just go home. Mev nodded and they made their way back to Porter Square on the T.

Mev grabbed the bottle of wine she'd been drinking earlier but Jack gently took it from her. "Go back to wine and you will regret it in the morning. Trust me, I have experience here. If you're going to hurt, make it worth it."

He reached into an upper cabinet and removed a green glass bottle of what turned out to be scotch. Lagavulin 16 year. He poured a finger each into two squat glasses.

"This is what you toast a birthday with," he said, raising his glass.

She took hers and sniffed it, overcome with the scent of wood smoke. The taste was more of the same: sharp, then smooth and smoky-warm.

She felt her eyes water.

"Strong, I know," Jack said.

It wasn't the scotch.

It was everything else.

"What's going on here? Both you and Hector have been pretty scarce lately."

It was all her fault.

"It's bad," she whispered. She wasn't sure he'd heard.

"Tell me. We'll work on it together." Ever the optimist.

She barked an unintentional laugh.

Jack waited patiently as she thought, then poured another finger of scotch for both of them.

"Really bad," she finally said.

Fortified by the scotch—and her utter desperation—she told the rest of the story. The whole story this time. The hack of Thinking Machines. Selling secrets to the Russians. The FBI's knowledge of her past and their pursuit.

"They're coming for you, too," she said.

"I picked a perfect day to work in the library then," he said.

"I'm serious. They have this theory that it's you and me and Fitz and this guy Raven. It's wrong, yet it's too damned close to the truth."

When she was done, the full-on insanity of the situation on the table, Jack threw back his scotch and refilled their glasses again. "Right. We need to make a plan to get you out of this. You are demonstrably *not* Raven. You didn't know you were helping Fitz break into Thinking Machines. There's got to be loads of evidence implicating him. It's not like he just started committing crimes and betraying his country the day you showed up."

Another new side of Jack, one she'd have never expected: deadly serious and extremely methodical. He usually came across as scattered, a dilettante, though she was pretty sure you didn't get into MIT and Harvard without a top-notch mind.

"I don't know quite how yet," Jack said, "but we will definitely figure it out."

Mev liked the sound of that.

SATURDAY, MARCH 3, 1990

FITZ PULLED IN BEHIND THE CAR BLOCKING HIS LONG driveway, wondering if it was a lost tourist pulled off the narrow Carlisle road to check a map. Or maybe the FBI again, here to harass him. Except it wasn't the typical Ford with the generic hub caps they drove, it was a Cadillac Coupe de Ville. Not standard government issue.

He pulled into the meadow to get around the car. The passenger side power window slid down to reveal Joey and his beefy friend behind the wheel.

"Fitz, you have a lovely home. Maybe we stop by and introduce ourselves to your family since you're part of ours now."

This wasn't how this was supposed to go. Fitz had kept it all under control, had kept everyone in their place. His students, his wife, his mistresses, the banks. He had to get these assholes out of his life.

Fitz forced a smile. "Bad timing today, I'm afraid."

Joey bared his teeth when he smiled back, making him look like the predator he was. "Speaking of timing, you missed your payment yesterday."

"I just paid you."

"That was for the week before. We don't want you getting behind, now do we?"

He needed the God-damned Russians to pay. He needed Mev Hayes to do what he told her. He had "quick exit" money stashed in case he ever had to run, but he didn't want to give them that. Maybe he could give them something better.

"I appreciate that you are running a business here. My problem is the young woman you referred to me isn't doing her job. I confess, I'm having problems showing her the light. I have no doubt you two gentlemen wouldn't have that challenge."

Fitz enjoyed the image of that defiant bitch getting roughed up by these two apes.

"Help me and I'll be very appreciative."

"Pay us what you owe, and we'll think about it."

He had no choice. "Of course. Give me a moment."

Fitz ignored Donna's call to him when he got to the house. After locking his office door, he headed to his desk and removed the section of molding from the bottom. He didn't want to touch this money. It was the meager savings he'd been able to set aside in case he had to run. He pulled an envelope from the void behind the molding. Twenty-three thousand, enough for two weeks of payments. But that didn't do anything to free him from these thugs. If they could get Mev to be more agreeable, this could all be over.

He took ten thousand and got back in his car, driving down the long driveway to where Joey and his muscle waited, windows down, listening to rap music. He had fantasies of ramming their car or reaching into the window and punching Joey's smug face. Violence wasn't his style, though. He'd always relied on charm. He'd get out of this yet.

He handed the money through the window. "Here's this week's installment. Help me, and we can settle this whole thing and part ways." Hell, if Mev did what she was supposed to, he might be able to get out from under all his debt, make a new start.

"You know, all our clients say that. And yet they always come back for more." His smile faded and he gestured toward the house. "See you next Friday, professor. Don't be late, or I'll have to introduce myself to your wife and girls."

Fitz struggled to hold his temper, incensed about this scum being anywhere near his house, his life. About having to answer to these ignorant lowlifes. He needed to push Mev harder, so things could go back to normal.

He waited until they backed out onto the road before starting his car. He couldn't go back home. Not now, he was too agitated. What he needed was a distraction. He drove to the top of the hill and pulled over, dialing Lisa's dorm room from his car phone.

She was an undergraduate in the Chemical Engineering department. Brunette with a bob, smart, cute-sexy, and always in need of cash, which he was happy to provide in exchange for her attention. It was what he deserved: a nice dinner, and her complete, obedient attention at his Cambridge hideaway, his troubles forgotten.

At least for today.

MONDAY, MARCH 5, 1990

THE DAY THAT WOULD ONLY GET WORSE STARTED EARLY when the truck with the loudspeaker rolled down Linnaean Street.

"Street cleaning. No parking on the odd-numbered side of the street. You will be tagged and towed."

The first Monday of March. It had snuck up on her. Mev jumped out of bed and put on sweats, running into the cold to move her car. She should have done it the night before, but parking hardly qualified as a major concern these days.

Her Pinto's front window was completely frosted over, and the windshield wiper fluid just smeared into a blue-tinted haze, so she drove with her head out the driver's side window searching for an even-numbered side parking space.

Mev squeezed her hatchback inches behind a wood-paneled Chrysler station wagon and slightly overlapping a driveway. It might get her a ticket, a microscopic inconvenience given the rest of her problems.

One month, that was all the time required to go from a fresh, exciting start of her new life to dodging the FBI, accused of being Raven, and guilty of being a collaborator with a spy. One month for all of the bad things that had happened before she got to Cambridge to pale in comparison to the really bad things that might happen next.

She'd been avoiding Fitz: staying away from the lab, spending time in one of the many campus libraries between classes, or hanging out at Muddy Charles, MIT's on-campus bar. She knew avoiding him wasn't a real solution. Eventually, he'd find her and demand her help stealing something else. When she refused, he'd try to coerce her, threaten to hurt her, or turn her in to the FBI. Or maybe just have her expelled. Again.

After her last class of the day, Mev was too tired to find a place to study and started home instead. The T had been surprisingly empty, and she was alone on the long escalator as it rose from the deep Porter Square platform to street level. Stepping onto the sidewalk, Mev squinted at the brightness, even as she enjoyed the feel of the sun on her face.

A car pulled to the curb, matching her speed as she turned onto Linnaean Street. At first, she thought it was FBI, but the car was too fancy, almost gaudy. And the man who slid the power window down looked nothing like a Special Agent.

"Meg Hayes?"

She didn't bother to correct him on her name. "Can I help you?"

He smiled at her. It wasn't a kind expression. It was animal. Feral. "You can call me Joey. Let's stop here and talk."

His was a particularly strong Boston accent, with "here" sounding like "heah."

The car came to a stop and Mev considered what to do. No other walkers were in sight; even the car traffic was light. She turned around, intending to walk back toward Porter Square. She wasn't going to lead them home, though they clearly already knew how to find her.

"No need to be nervous, I just want a little chat." He said as he exited the car.

You-can-call-me-Joey was tall, 6'6" or more, and solid. The other guy in the car, which had turned around to slowly follow them, looked even bigger.

"What do you want?" Mev asked without looking at him. She didn't want to see that smile again.

"So, your friend. The professor. He asked me to, you know, encourage you. Helping him helps us. And you wanna help us. It's warmer in the car. Why don't we take a ride?"

She sped up her pace, wanting to be back in Porter Square in sight of other people.

"What does this have to do with me?" she asked as she power walked toward Mass Ave.

"We're from the bank. Collections. The professor has a debt. It's my job to make sure it gets paid. Don't matter who. The professor, you, whoever."

This guy was no banker. He was something else, something bad. And he knew about her, about what was going on, about how to find her. This would help explain Fitz's desperation for things to sell.

She was not that far from Porter Square where there were plenty of other people. She glanced back. The man had stopped at the corner of Linnaean and Mass Ave. "Don't let us down," he said, and walked back to the car.

Mev watched Jack coming down Linnaean in the late afternoon light, his earphones in, his Discman playing some new wave or punk album she'd never heard of, not a care in the world. How could she not envy that? She, on the other hand, was obsessively monitoring the street for the car that had found her hours earlier.

Inside, he removed his earphones. Seeing Mev, his face fell. "You look . . . "

"Freaked out?" Mev supplied.

She told him what happened. The meeting on the street. The vague yet serious threats. How she stood in the parking lot at Porter Square

Shopping Center for an hour before sprinting home while looking over her shoulder, almost running into several people.

"These were bad guys. Fitz told them who I am, where I live. Where *we* live. Fitz owes these people money and they said I was responsible for getting it."

Jack finished taking off his jacket, set his bag down, sat in the chair with the flowered bedspread cover, and closed his eyes.

"Are you even listening?"

"I'm thinking."

They sat in silence for what felt like hours, though Mev knew it was no more than ten minutes. Then Jack said exactly what she feared he might.

"I'm stumped. If you don't do it, you have these guys and the FBI on your ass."

Mev's head snapped up. "What if I do it first?"

"Do what?"

"Turn myself in to the FBI."

"That's insane. They'll throw the book at you. Hacker arrests are all over the news. It's why they're sniffing around so hard. They want another head to mount on the wall."

"People do this, right?" Mev asked. "Get immunity for evidence? Make a plea? I mean, it could work."

"Maybe. It's risky."

"Can you see another way? If I keep working for Fitz, it'll blow up eventually. He'll get destroyed by the Mob or the FBI, and he'll take me with him. Or throw me under the bus trying to save himself." Mev sighed. "Heck, I trust Ostrowski more than I trust Fitz or some Mob loan shark."

"That's not saying much, though I'm no expert," Jack said.

Right. Mev riffled through her backpack. She removed a scrap of paper, dialed a number on the kitchen phone, then put it back on its cradle. It rang in seconds.

"I need help," she said, then listened for a moment before hanging up. Turning to Jack, she said "Grab your coat."

He clearly had questions, but Mev stayed silent as they hurried to Porter Square and got on the T. At Harvard Square, she rose. "This is our stop."

The Square was hopping, the panhandlers, buskers, punks, and chess masters were all there, taking advantage of the unseasonably warm day. She and Jack listened to a banjo player for a moment while Mev looked around. She tapped his shoulder and walked toward an outdoor table at Au Bon Pain where Jamie Brennan sat.

She wore mirror aviator shades and a black vintage Red Sox silk bomber jacket. She turned to Mev, regarding her.

"You in deep shit, sister?"

Mev laughed despite her fear. "It's more than I wanted to say over the phone."

She glanced around, making sure no one was paying attention. No one was. Everyone nearby was absorbed by coffees, or books, or their own personal dramas.

"Should we go someplace more private?" Mev asked.

"No. This is perfect. Public. Anonymous. Difficult to bug. And almost impossible to grab you off the street."

"Isn't that a little paranoid?" Mev asked.

"You tell me. Do you feel safe?" Jamie replied.

"No, I'm terrified and I need help."

Mev narrated. Jamie already knew about her college screwups—but Fitz, Thinking Machines, the Russians, the FBI, the Mob—that was all new. Jamie took it all in with a series of nods.

"Deep shit, indeed," Jamie said. "The feds may not know anything about getting into computers. About getting inside your life, though, they are Goddamned experts. And if that machine is gearing up, you don't have much time. I'm on that Ostrowski guy's radar too, so I'm motivated to make sure this gets handled."

Jamie's pager buzzed. She looked at it and nodded, clipped it back to her belt. "You're not my only client," she said with a tight grin. She asked direct questions, mostly about who knew what, who was involved.

"These other guys, from today? Pretty sure that's Joey 'The Banker' Monahan. He's a debt collector for the guy my dad ultimately works for.

"Whitey Bulger," Jack said quietly.

Jamie only nodded. "And that guy, he *hates* rats."

Jack started to say something, and Jamie shook her head. "Give me a second, Kane. I'm thinking." While Mev and Jack waited, Jamie leaned back, facing the sky. What was happening behind her aviator sunglasses wasn't clear, but her body was taut. Finally, she looked back at them.

"OK, first thing we need to do is a deep dive into Fitz's life, determine exactly what he's into with the Irish and the Russians. That should tell us why the FBI is interested. And it wouldn't hurt to know what the FBI knows and who this Raven is."

"Fitz couldn't program his way out of a paper bag," Mev said. "Somebody had to have been helping him before. Maybe that was Raven?"

"Maybe." Jamie handed Mev a 3-1/2" floppy disk. "You'll need this. It's a piece of software that finds open servers on the internet and bounces your encrypted connection between them. It should make it nearly impossible to track you."

Not unlike the way DEMON worked. Great minds and all that.

They agreed to connect later in the evening, and Jamie gave Mev the IP address to a server she was sure was completely secure. "I owned it months ago," she explained.

Using the software Jamie had given her, Mev periodically checked the secure server. This communications strategy felt overly elaborate. But Mev had to admit, right now paranoia seemed prudent.

Sometime after 9:00 p.m., a file arrived. Mev downloaded it, then deleted it off the server. Jamie would know she'd received it when the file was deleted, and Mev could leave replies in the same place. Easy to use and hard to trace. Jamie called it an electronic dead drop.

It was a text file, outlining what Jamie had found so far in her research. And it was a bombshell. Mev called for Jack, and he read over her shoulder as she scrolled through the material. The research on Fitz was extensive. While Jamie said there were so many financial accounts it would take a while to go through them all, they already clearly led to one conclusion: he was in deep financial trouble. No wonder he was so desperate. No wonder he was messing with both the Russians and the Irish Mob.

In reply, Mev loaded a text file in the server dead drop: "OK, what do we do next? I'm afraid I'm running out of time."

The file was quickly deleted, and another file appeared on the server. A one-line text file: "MIT Science Library. Now."

Jack and Mev took the Red Line to the Kendall/MIT stop this time, then walked toward the river and Memorial Drive, entering the Hayden Library, one of Mev's favorite study spaces. Jamie was sitting at a table with a reference book open, still dressed in her bomber jacket, without her mirror shades.

"You got here fast," Jack said.

"I was already here, using one of the computers." She turned toward Mev. "You are in the hot seat, honey. Fitz has been dancing with two devils, that much is clear. I still can't figure out who Raven is. It's not you, and it sounds like it can't be Fitz. So, who the hell is it?"

"That's not my biggest worry right now."

"I get that. I'm just curious. Hacker's curse. You know how that is."

She did. Far too well, actually.

"You," she said to Mev, "are in a world of shit. But you," she addressed Jack. "Are you sure you want to be anywhere near this thing? This is leg-breaking, family-threatening, prison-time-with-a-side-of-shanking kind of stuff."

"I hear that," Jack said with a shrug. "Still, we have to try."

Jamie appraised him, then continued. "I'll dig into this. Don't get me wrong, I have my own motivations. Despite the parental approval, I don't want a casual visit from the FBI to turn into an actual arrest. Nor do I want the aforementioned Irish gentleman to get the slightest whiff of my involvement. In short, I was never here."

"We'll leave you out of it," Jack said.

"You're not listening, Kane. I'm not done yet," Jamie said.

"What are you thinking?" Mev asked.

"Better if you don't know. Because it's a crime to lie to the FBI, and they will take you there. Which reminds me, you need a good attorney, and I think I know the perfect fit."

It felt good to be on the offensive, with a plan. With allies she could trust.

But Ostrowski; could she trust him? It felt like the only choice. And it seemed like he followed the rules—just like a well-written program.

That she could trust.

WEDNESDAY, MARCH 7, 1990

PAUL TREKKED ACROSS THE WINTER-BEATEN GROUND
of Winthrop Square near Harvard, late for his lunch with Carl. The
location had been Carl's idea; he wanted a decent meal outside the office,
hoped it'd help them break free of their rut. They hadn't had a lead in
over a week—until today.

Paul was breathing hard when he got to Grendel's, a more upscale
place than he usually chose. Carl had insisted, said he'd treat. Paul wasn't
above letting him.

Carl pointedly looked at his watch.

"I know. Trust me, this is worth the wait," Paul said as he sat. "Just
as I was leaving, I got a call from an attorney representing Mev Hayes.
He wants to negotiate terms for a proffer."

"Wait, what? Can you back up a couple steps?" Carl said.

Paul did, explained that Hayes had hired an attorney, Francis Bishop,
and that he had contacted the AUSA, Michelle Lanza. They wanted a
proffer; Mev would tell them what she knew in exchange for a promise
of immunity.

"Will they do that?" Carl sounded skeptical.

"Maybe. They're asking for 'queen for a day.' As long as Mev tells
Lanza and the FBI everything she knows and agrees to testify against
Fitz when the time comes, they'll arrange for a plea deal with immunity."

"That could help, I suppose" Carl said, "depending on what she
gives us. Don't forget that Raven was active for months before Hayes
came to MIT."

Paul had expected more excitement. "Yeah, though you gotta ask yourself, why would she want to come in if she wasn't involved? She's gotta be guilty of something. We can decide once we see what she has to offer. Maybe it's good, maybe we can move further up the chain, wherever that leads."

Carl paused, thoughtful. "Something's changed for her."

"Yep. Hopefully in our favor."

"C'mon, let's eat while we talk. I haven't had anything today. And this place has the best all-you-can-eat salad bar in the city."

"Not usually a salad guy."

"No kidding." Carl looked at Paul's gut, which had expanded since he'd left D.C.

When they got back to the table, Carl frowned at the mountain of blue cheese dressing Paul loaded on top of his salad, but said nothing.

Paul took out his notebook, the fifth he'd started on this case, with many of the pages of the early ones filled with notes on computer arcana that he later couldn't interpret. Today the relevant notes were mostly framed as questions rather than answers: How does Fitz afford his lifestyle? Where does Kane fit? Is Hayes' background relevant? Who is Raven? Too many questions, not enough answers. And what about Jamie Brennan?

When he looked up, Carl had finished his salad, while Paul had barely touched his own.

"If you ate like this more often, you'd, you know," Carl said nodding at Paul's midsection.

"Fuck off, Philips. Help me dig into this. How do we get the most from the fact that Hayes is collaborating?"

Carl set down his knife and fork and assumed his young professor voice. That tone had annoyed Paul so much during the first computer crime lecture that he'd struggled not to tune him out. Over the last weeks, however, he'd learned to listen. This was Carl at his best. He fit right in with the eggheads at MIT.

"We know we're not going to get the whole picture. She hasn't been involved long enough, and she's not going to be motivated to give us everything. She's feeling pressure or else she wouldn't be coming to us. The problem is we don't know why. Who pushed her buttons? Which buttons did they push? What's been happening over the last few weeks that changed her mind."

"So, we don't know anything, basically." Paul said, scooping blue cheese dressing with a piece of bread. "We hear what she has to say and choose our next move."

Wing it, in other words.

Same thing they'd been doing all along.

FRIDAY, MARCH 9, 1990

JAMIE'S RECOMMENDATION FOR AN ATTORNEY HAD been inspired.

Francis Bishop was an older man, exceptionally well-dressed in a charcoal suit and highly polished shoes, with a full head of gray hair swept back with hair oil. He took up serious space in his office, substantial in both girth and presence. Jamie explained that he'd had a long and successful law career, only business had gotten softer the last few years, as his primary clients were increasingly finding themselves in prison. He'd been the attorney for the Italian Mob, who'd been gradually displaced by the Irish Mob as their capos went to prison.

Bishop hadn't mentioned any of that, of course. Jamie had given her the background, so Mev would understand why he'd fight for her.

Or, as he put it when she first visited his office and explained her situation, "sticking it to the fucking micks and godless Russkies, and running circles around the feds? That sounds like my kind of fun."

And as Jamie had also predicted, he was willing to take the case pro bono for the pleasure of doing so.

"Everything you've told me is attorney-client privileged," he'd said in that first meeting, his tone grave, "And unless I am aware of your intention to commit a crime, I cannot divulge anything you tell me. I want to make sure you are coming into this eyes wide open.

"I've sparred with the feds plenty of times. I know how they think; hell, I know what brand of boxers they're wearing. They do things a certain way. That works in our favor. And I'm not worried about the Russians. Everything I'm seeing in the news, they have their own problems at home and they're getting worse. But the Irish. These guys do not fuck around, pardon my French. Whitey Bulger ends any and every snitch he finds. And word on the street is that he's untouchable." Bishop paused for effect. It worked. "Know that you are sticking your finger in a very bad hombre's eye."

Jamie had given her much the same advice. She'd also warned Jack again to steer clear. Much as Mev appreciated his help and support, she didn't want any collateral damage. Not that he'd listen.

Bishop emphasized that negotiating with the FBI was a tricky business, and urged her to see what they had before going forward with any deal. Mev explained why she thought she had to go to them first, detailing the situation, telling him everything. Well, almost everything; she said nothing about Jamie or Jack.

She flinched inwardly when Bishop explained that if she did give a proffer for the FBI and Assistant U.S. Attorney, it would be contingent on her not lying or omitting *anything*. She would have to be very careful answering their questions.

The process, as he outlined it, would begin with him talking to the AUSA and FBI, describing a theoretical situation that paralleled hers, getting a sense of whether they'd take Fitz in exchange for immunity. They'd go back and forth, Bishop pushing, the AUSA pushing back. In the meantime, he said he was still thinking about how best to stick it to the fucking micks.

Mev waited impatiently for days while Francis Bishop sparred with the FBI and with Assistant U.S. Attorney for the district of Massachusetts, Michelle Lanza. Every time Mev called him, he said the same thing: "don't say a word until the proffer is negotiated." And he'd test her resolve, reminding her that proffers aren't iron-clad.

"The government can use your statements against you later if you're called as a witness. And if the proffer falls apart, they can use whatever you have said until that point against you. Are you sure you want me to continue?"

And each time she said yes.

In between his efforts to get a proffer agreement, they practiced her testimony in Bishop's Butler Square office.

"Weren't you just fucking Fitz to get ahead?" he asked in an obvious tone of disgust.

She sputtered in rage, cursing at him, saying Fitz had tricked her, used her. When she was done venting, he chuckled.

"Do you have that out of your system now? Better to do it here and not at the FBI, don't you think?"

And so it went, Bishop pushing her harder and harder, getting more aggressive until she knew the facts of her testimony without hesitation, until her responses were calm, cool, and automatic.

Bishop had called her the evening before to tell her he'd negotiated the proffer with AUSA Lanza: immunity based on a limited infraction by Mev. She dressed as conservatively as she could, in a new suit she'd bought for the occasion. A size 10 this time. She'd laughed when she tried it on in Filene's Basement, amazed by the effectiveness of the high anxiety diet.

Still, Mev felt her fear rise as she was escorted from the lobby of the Boston FBI headquarters in Government Square into an elevator, then into the FBI offices. Bishop strode confidently, and she tried to do the same, attempting to project a sense of calm she didn't feel. Inside the conference room was a tall, blonde woman in a gray pinstripe power suit with broad padded shoulders and 4-inch patent leather heels. She shook Bishop's hand, then looked Mev up and down, assessing her, before shaking hers.

"I'm Assistant United States Attorney Michelle Lanza, and you know Special Agents Ostrowski and Philips, I believe."

Mev didn't exactly hear an accusation in that last comment, yet there was no question Lanza had already formed an opinion.

"Let's go," Lanza said, sitting and nodding to a sound tech at the table. The conference room was arranged with microphones and a recorder, and once the tech got it going, he left.

"If we are satisfied that you are telling the truth in this session," Lanza began, "the Department of Justice will enter into a formal, written immunity agreement with you. Your attorney has provided an outline of what you are prepared to share, and if we find it consistent and compelling, we will proceed from there."

Lanza began, her questions rapid fire. When did Mev decide to come to MIT? What were the circumstances of her offer? Wasn't she suspicious about its timing? What was the first thing that felt off about the situation? Mev stumbled on a few of the first questions, nerves distracting her, then finally settled into the calm that Bishop cultivated during their hours of testimony prep.

Mev described her past, her expulsion, her arrival at MIT, her joy at the work, even though other people in the lab were jealous that she was working so closely with Fitz. About her supposed romance with him, explaining that it wasn't one, that Fitz has deceived her and pressured her into having sex with him just like he'd deceived her into hacking Thinking Machines. And she emphasized that once she'd discovered the truth, she had refused to help him anymore.

"Miss Hayes, are you expecting us to believe that you were seduced, wholly unwittingly, into using your singular expertise—breaking into computers—to spy for the Russians? All while believing this wouldn't get you into trouble? Again? Seems either monumentally stupid or depressingly naive."

"Let's be civil, Michelle," Bishop said.

"I'll handle this however I please, *Francis*. She screwed a married man and helped him betray our country."

It wasn't like what the AUSA said wasn't true.

"I was tricked," Mev said. "Maybe that does make me stupid. It's what happened. I'm here to fix it."

Unlike when Bishop had pressured her during their prep, Lanza was enjoying humiliating her, making her doubt herself.

Mev had experience identifying bullies from a distance. This one was just across the conference room table.

"And what about the Irish Mob? The bankers and their enforcers?"

She narrated that encounter. Brief as it had been, it still scared her as much as Fitz did. Lanza dug in, asking about how they operated, how Fitz had gotten involved with them. Mev didn't have answers, knew only what Fitz and Joey had told her. Lanza asked her about the Russians. Mev could say even less about them. Fitz made a big deal of the Russians to intimidate her but had never shared any details about working with them.

Lanza looked through her notes with an obvious look of disgust on her face. "Do you have anything else to add? Have you given a complete and truthful account about all criminal activities perpetrated by you or others?"

"To the best of my knowledge," Mev replied.

Lanza sat back in her chair, fingers steepled, her eyes focused out the window on the Boston skyline. Minutes passed.

"Are we good?" Bishop finally asked.

"It's thin," she said. "Most of this we already knew, though the organized crime connections are a fun bonus."

Didn't feel fun.

"I'll consider immunity," Lanza said, "I need something first."

"We're giving you a witness," Bishop said.

Lanza shrugged, the wide shoulders of her suit exaggerating the gesture. "What can I say? I want more. I need hard evidence of wrong-doing by FitzRoy, including the involvement of the Russians and Irish organized crime. Miss Hayes' testimony today is insufficient for my purposes."

Infuriated, Mev opened her mouth to speak. Bishop put his hand on her shoulder, reminding her he knew this game; she did not.

"This is bullshit, Michelle." He said. "It's not what we agreed to. And it puts my client in further danger. She has been threatened, been assaulted. That will not stop unless we stop it."

"Then I need Miss Hayes to participate in the ongoing investigation by the FBI, and only when I judge us to have sufficient evidence to proceed will I grant immunity."

Lanza rose and placed her palms on the table, towering over Mev and Bishop. "We'll give you a few moments to confer with your client."

Lanza and the agents left, and the tech returned, shutting off the recording equipment then leaving Mev alone with Bishop.

"They want me to investigate?" Mev asked. "Isn't that the FBI's job?"

"You'd think so. She seems to hate informants as much as the Mob guys do. They want you to produce evidence via a sting or by wearing a wire. Methods to be determined."

"I'll do it."

"You most certainly will not. It's extortion."

"What other choice do I have?"

"Let me talk to Lanza."

"You really think she'll change her mind? She doesn't strike me as the type to give an inch."

Bishop smiled, a tiny, tight line that barely curved at the corners. "She's not," he said.

It wasn't as if she had other options. Fitz expected her to help steal more tech and his Mob debtors wanted the same thing. She could keep refusing, but at some point, she'd get hurt. Or she could keep collaborating with Fitz, and eventually they'd get evidence to indict and convict her. It was now or never if she wanted to be in the driver's seat.

"Look, if I keep saying 'no' to Fitz, he's going to punish me. Get me kicked out of MIT, tell the cops it was all my idea. Whatever else he can think of. If I do this, at least I have some kind of chance that he's the one who pays, not me."

"It's a shit deal," he said.

"I'm in a shit situation."

Bishop stood and rapped his knuckle on the conference room window to catch Lanza's attention, waving her back in.

"My client agrees." Bishop said.

Lanza wore a triumphant smile; she knew Mev was in a jam. But Ostrowski and Philips looked uncomfortable.

"We'll draft an agreement," she said, dismissing them.

"You did exceptionally well in there given the circumstances," Bishop said once they were in the car. "I can't believe that . . ." he struggled to finish his sentence.

"Bitch?" she suggested.

"Yes. I guess I don't need to be gentle around you. You just went twelve rounds with Mike Tyson."

"Didn't he lose the title?" Jack had been obsessed with it.

Bishop laughed. "That's the spirit, my girl. Lanza's a climber. And an espionage plus organized crime case gets attention. Too bad she's willing to stand on your head in heels to make it."

"Then I better find what she wants."

"That's a tall order."

"Luckily, I'm a tall girl."

FRIDAY, MARCH 9, 1990

"YOU DON'T GET HANDED THAT EVERY DAY!" LANZA said, pumping her fist in victory as the elevator doors closed behind Hayes and Bishop. She turned to Paul and Carl, her face exultant. "You two need to work with Hayes to assemble evidence we can use. I want to nail this FitzRoy character and break up the Russian connection. And, oh yeah, take a bite out of Irish organized crime while we're at it."

Oh, is that all? Paul thought. Her reputation as a hard charger, running roughshod over anyone in her way, was well deserved.

Lanza retrieved her bag and coat, preparing to leave, then turned back to Paul. "And Ostrowski, I want a win here. Don't disappoint me."

On the way back to their desks, Carl explained that he already had an idea. "We can create fake technical and design specs that Mev can 'steal,' but of course, she'd be in on it. Now that we know Fitz is working with the Russians and the Irish Mob, we just need him to complete a transaction. She helps him get what looks like solid intelligence, he sells it to the Russians and pays down the loan with the Mob. We follow the transaction the whole way and," Carl punched his palm, "we nail 'em all."

Simple and straightforward, even if the case itself wasn't. Paul's doubts weren't put to rest by Mev's proffer; if anything, it deepened them. They still didn't know who Raven was, or what happened before Mev arrived in Boston. And Lanza's inflated immunity demands made him uncomfortable.

Mev had been tricked into committing a crime and had come to the FBI to bring the real criminals to justice. The FBI didn't indict, try, or convict people. They enforced the law and let the rest of the DOJ administer justice. But Lanza's deal didn't feel like justice.

Nailing FitzRoy, now that would be justice. FitzRoy was a predator. He'd seduced and manipulated Mev, using his position of power to coerce her. Paul couldn't help thinking of Becky. Of her as a young woman who would soon be out in the world. What if she got caught up in something? Lied to? Taken advantage of? Paul and Linda might be at odds, but woe to the poor sucker who got between them and Becky's safety. On that they agreed.

Paul knew the one sure way to feel better about this was to go after the real criminals. Lanza wanted them all. She was happy to step on Mev to get to FitzRoy, the Russians, and the Irish Mob. He'd be happy to see the actual criminals go to prison. That did not include Mev. She did the right thing; she came to the cops. And it stuck in his craw that she was being punished for it.

"Your plan is solid, Carl. I'm just not thrilled leaving Mev Hayes dangling in the breeze. If we don't get what Lanza wants, I have no doubt that she'll take convicting Mev as a consolation prize."

"I know, I feel bad about that. I can work with Mev. I can make sure we give her a ton of top cover. Plus, if the information isn't really stolen, she isn't committing any additional crimes. And if it looks like she's complying, it should keep her safe for a while."

"I'm not crazy about the 'should' and 'for a while' parts. After all, it's not just Fitz she needs to fool, it's also the Mob and the Russians."

"So, we make sure we're good at our job," Carl said.

"And we get lucky."

"That too."

"You're confident this will work?" Paul asked.

"Absolutely," Carl said. "I'll need to dig into what Mev has done with her program. I understand the principles and, working together, I'm sure we can create a solid counterfeit. After all, it's not like we haven't done this before."

"What do you mean?"

"Do you know about Farewell?"

It sounded familiar.

"It has some fun parallels to what we are doing."

Carl's idea of fun wasn't quite Paul's, but he was coming to appreciate it.

"Farewell was a Soviet defector who turned over details about the KGB's Directorate T, Line X activities to French domestic intelligence. Line X was stealing commercial secrets, like in this case. Then Farewell switched sides and gave deep intelligence to the West. Which, in turn, allowed us to institute a disinformation campaign. There was an explosion so large on the Trans-Siberian Pipeline in 1982 that it registered on seismic detectors. That was us. We funneled some flawed gas pipeline controller software to the Russians. The pressure regulators cranked the pipe up to pressures that welds and joints couldn't handle, and *Boom!*"

Carl spread his fingers in the imitation of an explosion. "The equivalent of a three-kiloton nuke. Largest explosion ever seen from space.

"We also passed them bad computer chip designs, which they gobbled like candy. And their space shuttle, the *Buran*? There's a reason it looks exactly like our space shuttle. Also, a reason it never flew."

"Farewell."

"Or what we did with it. We were successful even if Farewell, Colonel Vetrov, wasn't. He apparently stabbed a KGB agent over a woman in a public park. After that, his spying was discovered, and he was executed."

Paul didn't love the implications for Mev in Carl's story. She wasn't a spy. She was collateral damage.

"You know," Carl continued, "that may be what led us here. A revival of the Line X attempts by a suspicious KGB. We'll know more once we nail this operation down."

"We'll be passing them false info, right?"

"Yep. I'll build a server and load it with flawed computer designs. We can track them as they get copied and moved. Mev gives Fitz our version of DEMON, Fitz runs it, gets what he believes are bona fide computer specs, passes them on to his Russian friends. They'll have no reason to be suspicious since they've gotten real information so far. They do the money drop, and we grab 'em, wait for Fitz to take it and follow him to the payoff with the Mob. Roll them all up. It's perfect."

Paul didn't quite share Carl's certainty, recalling one of his instructors at Quantico who regularly quoted the Prussian General Helmuth von Moltke: "no plan survives first contact with the enemy." You could model every possible interaction, every conceivable outcome in an operation, but people were unpredictable. And unpredictable was often dangerous.

They couldn't model every possible interaction; they still had too many knowledge gaps. They had no idea who the hacker Raven was, even though he started this whole operation. Where was he now? What was his role? Despite what Paul might have insinuated to Mev when they were questioning her, he had zero suspicion that she was Raven.

"I hope you're right," Paul said.

FRIDAY, MARCH 9, 1990

ALLEN CONNOR HAD A PROBLEM, AND HER NAME WAS Margaret Evangeline Hayes. While the proffer was supposed to be confidential, the FBI gossiped like a bunch of housewives, so Connor knew the basics of Mev Hayes' proffer within hours of its completion. It created a problem for some of his friends. Which was a problem for him.

Prosecute some pansy MIT professor? Go for it. Stick it to the godless communists? Hell yes. Fuck with Irish organized crime? You'd have to be insane. There were things you *did not do* in Boston.

Connor was one of the fortunate FBI agents who hadn't been posted to multiple field offices. Born in South Boston, he'd lived there his whole life. Went to St. Monica's, hung out at Carson Beach, knew Whitey Bulger, the gangster, and his brother Billy, the President of the Massachusetts State Senate. Connor was acquainted with all the leaders in the Irish community, law-abiding and otherwise.

There was a way things were done in Boston, and an even more specific way things were done in Southie. You rooted for the Sox, the Celtics, the Bruins, the Patriots. You went to church every Sunday. You observed Lent, fed your kids fish sticks on Friday like everyone else in your neighborhood. You played along. You kept it all kosher, at least with your business partners.

And, with some minor Mob dirt from Jinx Brennan, Connor could feed into the FBI's Top Echelon Criminal Informants Program—and the FBI and the public thought they were making actual progress against the Mob.

What Connor was doing was keeping the peace, maintaining balance. That was the way. You did favors and favors were done. You kept your mouth shut. And you were taken care of.

ASAC Weaver came from somewhere down south, Texas, Connor thought. Ostrowski came from Chicago. Philips from Philly. None of them knew Boston. But AUSA Lanza had grown up here. She knew better. Or she should. An Italian girl from the North End knows you do not screw with organized crime in Boston. And if she found the proverbial horse's head in her bed, that was what she got for taking on Boston's underworld.

Connor had come to enjoy a certain standard of living the last ten years, fueled by donations from his friends in Southie. In return for a little courtesy, Connor had been treated to Red Sox box seats, jewelry for his wives and girlfriends, nice bottles of wine and good scotch.

And why not? It wasn't like anything law enforcement did would change anything. The B.P.D. or the feds would roll up one worker bee and another guy would take his place. It was a pipe dream to believe they were going to stop drugs, guns, prostitution, and loan sharking. Somebody was going to do it if the Irish weren't. Given that, there was absolutely no reason not to have a taste now and then. Better the devil he knew.

What he also knew was that you did not mess with the basic order of things. Going after Joey "The Banker" Monahan was going to upset that order big time. "When you strike at the king, don't miss," somebody famous said. And these guys were gonna miss. Ostrowski was in way over his head, Weaver too. Joey would retaliate tenfold for any threats against him. Not to mention what the rest of the Mob would do.

They just didn't understand Boston. You let stuff slide, kept the peace. People were going to do drugs, so somebody was going to sell them. Better to know who and help keep it under control. Some guy wants a hooker to get his rocks off? Keep it in the Combat Zone. You weren't going to stop any of it. At least this way, the right people made money and you avoided all-out war.

Of course, Connor had a personal stake in maintaining the existing order. If Ostrowski did get Joey to flip on the leadership of the Irish syndicate, he'd be in trouble. Part of the bargain was that Connor could not screw up. Could not let the heat come down on his friends.

The irony of the whole thing is that the Mev Hayes debacle was Joey's own damned fault. Some college professor got in deep with the Mob and was selling stolen computer technology to pay back the loan 'til he ran out of things to steal. He needed help, and Joey obliged, referred an Army vet his way, a cokehead who was a whiz with computers. Then the cokehead got greedy. And when Joey sent a guy to straighten him out, he ended up killing him instead.

So Joey comes to Connor, who's plenty happy to have The Banker owe him a favor. The FBI knew perfectly well who the most notorious hackers were. Even if Connor didn't understand exactly how all that worked, he could search for open cases. And *voilà*, an investigation in Missouri that hadn't led to an arrest. A college student, recently expelled. He passed that on to Joey so he could get paid.

Joey pitches this to FitzRoy, who eats it up. Then screws it up, sleeping with the girl and spilling his guts to intimidate her. The Russians. Seriously? His Southie friends would not be happy when they learned that's who FitzRoy was selling to. They might be criminals, but they were still proud Americans.

Now this little girl goes and drops a steaming pile of shit right in the middle of Connor's world. Coming to the FBI. To that do-gooder Ostrowski and his brainy Black sidekick. Right as a grand jury was looking at Whitey Bulger's liquor businesses. Nobody needed the extra attention right now.

Connor could easily throw a wrench into the investigation to slow things down. But if he told Joey what was going on, the Mob would definitely act, blowing this all up and potentially exposing him.

Then he had another thought. Given Lanza's reputation as a ball-buster, if a case she was chasing tanked, she'd castrate whoever was responsible. Connor smiled when he realized that it would be Ostrowski and his little buddy who'd get the hammer.

He wondered how pissed his friends would be if he didn't give them a heads up in advance. Connor couldn't know every operation underway. They couldn't blame him if he missed one.

Or could they?

MONDAY, MARCH 12, 1990

BRINKSMANSHIP. THE WORD HAD BEEN ROLLING AROUND in Mev's head. High stakes power plays with deadly consequences. The kind of game that the Soviet Union and US had been playing her whole life. The kind of game that could result in "duck and cover" when the sirens went off, pretending your school desk would save you from a nuclear blast. Maybe that game was almost done. But the game she was playing with the Justice Department, FBI, Irish Mob, Fitz, and the Russians was about to begin for real.

Having relinquished her key to the lab, she was forced to wait in the hall for Fitz. As he approached the door, she said "I'm sorry I got all turned around before. I'm working on making DEMON easier to use so you won't even need me. You can do it all yourself."

"I knew you'd come around. After all, it's the right choice. Why don't you come in and we can chat." His manner was cordial, friendly. Just two colleagues talking about work. She followed him in, keenly aware of the eyes of the other students, including Hector, watching them. Hector didn't hide his contempt; in a strange way, it helped put steel in her spine. For all of his jealousy, he had no idea what she was up against, nor what she was prepared to do to stop it.

Fitz closed the door and motioned for her to sit. She took her former desk chair and turned it toward him.

"I was worried about you," Fitz began. "You were making very bad decisions, and I feared it could end poorly. Expulsion or worse."

Worse was exactly what she was trying to avoid. Going to the FBI and the Justice Department had been a gamble, one that had become trickier when the AUSA demanded more. At least now she was making decisions, running the game.

"I needed time to get my head straight. I just hope you can forgive me." She knew she was pouring it on strong, but her new clarity told her playing to Fitz's ego was a good bet.

"Water under the bridge," he said, waving his hand. "While we had a bit of a misunderstanding, I meant what I said. I like working with you. No reason we can't enjoy ourselves."

Mev smiled, hoping it looked genuine. But she had no interest in submitting herself again to Fitz or his disgusting desires. She was here to do a job.

"Thing is, it's not safe to do the work here. Too much gossip, too many nosy neighbors," she gestured to the lab.

"I see your point. Can you keep your work confidential if you work elsewhere?"

"No problem. Besides you, no one even understands what I'm working on." A little more food for Fitz's ego.

"Don't you have roommates? I thought you lived with Hector. Won't that be a problem?"

"We barely speak."

"I'd noticed a chill between you. Lover's quarrel, perhaps?"

Fitz's expression had turned cruel. He was enjoying watching her squirm. Not unlike Lanza, she realized.

"We don't get along. And my other roommate is just an English major." An English major with one of the finest minds and caring hearts she'd ever known.

"Be careful. It's in our mutual best interest no one discover our work." He leaned back in his office chair and considered the ceiling. "If you do this for me, make DEMON user-friendly enough for me to use,

I'll call us even. You stay in school, and we go our separate ways. My grad school recommendation stands. You should get in. A fair trade."

The actual trade was hardly easier. Though, if she pulled it off, Fitz would end up behind bars.

Now *that* was fair.

Mev sat beside FBI Special Agent Carl Philips, walking him through the DEMON code on a bulky IBM PC in a conference room in the JFK Federal Building. Bishop had negotiated a temporary immunity deal that protected her during these interactions. But it still felt as if she were walking around naked.

"It's such a simple idea, yet so elegant," Carl said as she walked him through the code. "Protecting a system by breaking into it. Brilliant!"

Mev had to admit, she was warming to the agent. Young, like her. An outsider, like her. An unlikely Special Agent, she thought.

"What made you want to join the FBI?" Mev asked.

He paused, the joyful expression on his face fading. "You've seen your share of bad things. Your family situation, what's going on now. Bad shit, right?"

She nodded. This was a different side of the quiet agent.

"My family didn't, doesn't, understand my choice. I grew up in West Philadelphia, not that far from where the Philly police bombed the MOVE compound a few years ago, burning down the whole neighborhood. We're not particularly fond of law enforcement."

Mev let that sink in. If she was suspicious of law enforcement, his feelings, his family's feelings, his neighborhood's feelings, must be a whole other order of magnitude.

"Thing is," he continued, "it'll never change if someone doesn't do the work on the inside."

"I think I get that," she said, as they continued working on the code. "After Joey said he wouldn't hesitate to clean up another mess, my only choice was to come to you guys."

Carl was quiet, looking off into the distance. "Another mess?"

"Right, cleaning it up."

"No. *Another*," Carl repeated. "As if he'd done it before."

"He is a mobster, right? A bad guy."

"Still. I wonder," he said, but didn't elaborate further.

They worked in silence to create a server that DEMON would find, Carl calling it a honeypot. They filled it with the fake technical specs Carl had already prepared. Mev would give DEMON to Fitz, and Carl would monitor the server, catching Fitz in the act of "breaking into" it. Agents would follow Fitz, watching him use the dead drop, grabbing the Russian contact when they cleared the drop and left the cash. They'd watch Fitz take the money, and then snatch Joey and his muscle, along with Fitz, when he paid them off. A tidy chain of arrests.

Carl left the conference room, while Mev compiled the code. He returned with Agent Ostrowski.

"You know the plan, right?" Ostrowski asked. Both he and Carl looked at her with concern.

"I give Fitz the code and keep the heck away from him."

Carl laughed. "That's pretty much it. We'll keep an eye on him, watch the drop, the money pickup, then the payoff with Joey or one of his goons. We'll have our guys, and you'll be good. Easy peasy."

She hoped so. All she had to do was hand Fitz a floppy disk and leave.

They'd handle the rest.

And she'd be free.

TUESDAY, MARCH 13, 1990

FITZ BASKED IN THE EARLY SPRING WARMTH ON THE bustling MIT campus. This was a victory lap of a kind. There would be joy in clearing his debt with the Mob and getting them off his back. A joy in squeezing money out of the clumsy Russians. And an exquisite joy in bending a young woman to his will.

Breaking a woman's resistance, the same way Donna's horses were broken, was half the fun in fucking around. Frankly, once they were broken, he lost interest. In this moment, though, he was at the apogee of that trajectory with Mev. She was about to break, having begged to regain his favor. Now he would savor her delicious submission.

She'd wanted to meet outside of the lab in a public place, which suited him fine. It was a sign of her weakness that she couldn't face him in his domain, the very spot where she had failed. He strolled down Amherst Street, past the MIT chapel to the tennis courts, full of players taking advantage of a chance warm day. At their periphery was Mev Hayes, shifting nervously from foot to foot.

He had to give it to her, she'd shown grit in facing off with him, especially given the stakes. It was a shame that he'd had to involve Joey and his pals, though he'd have given anything to have witnessed that conversation. A conversation that led to a change of heart on her behalf. If he was honest with himself, they were intimidating guys, and he looked forward to being done with them. The Russians didn't scare him, and he was way too smart to get caught by the FBI, but the leg breakers were another thing altogether.

"Lovely day. Wonderful choice of location, Mev. Gave me a chance to enjoy the spring air."

She alternated looking at him and at the ground. In her hand she had a manila envelope.

"It's all here. A floppy disk with the code and instructions on how to load and use DEMON. I made it easy for you and gave you a first target you'll like: Cray Computer Corporation in Colorado Springs. Lots of supercomputers. I've already identified a vulnerable server for you. Follow the instructions and you'll be able to take whatever you want."

The sunlight seemed extra bright in this moment. "Whatever I want. As it should be."

"And I'm done."

Fitz tapped his lips with his index finger. "I may find use for your skills in the future."

"No, I'm done. That was the deal. You have what you need, you can do the rest."

"Whatever you say, Mev darling. I do want to make sure that our arrangement is clear, however. Breathe a word of any of this and I'll be on the phone to the authorities in a second. It is, after all, my patriotic duty to expose a filthy communist spy."

"I keep my mouth shut; you keep your mouth shut. We go our separate ways. That's the deal."

It was a shame, really, that he'd had to force the issue. Mev might have been fun to play with for a few more months. It would have been delightful to extend her humiliation a little longer. Her discomfort might have been more valuable to him even than the money he made off her assistance.

But he could always find a new plaything. One uninvolved in his business. Yes, it was time for a new girl, one blissfully unaware of anything other than her role in pleasing him. One not quite so smart or strong headed, who he could impress with his Cambridge *pied à terre*. One who enjoyed good meals, pretty gifts, and rough sex.

Or, if she didn't enjoy it, knew better than to complain.

TUESDAY, MARCH 13, 1990

WHEN MEV RETURNED HOME, JACK SAID JAMIE HAD called, looking for her. Mev called her pager and, as before, the phone rang moments later.

"I'm about to leave work. Mind if I stop by?"

Mev could hear Hector upstairs. She didn't want him overhearing whatever this was.

"Now's not a good time."

"Got it. Meet me at The Tasty in half an hour," Jamie said, and hung up.

Mev had neglected to ask what and where that was. Jack was in the kitchen pouring himself a glass of wine.

"What's The Tasty?" she asked.

"Best burgers anywhere. And it's open all night. Are you meeting Jamie there? Can I tag along?"

"I guess. Not sure what's going on. She was a little cryptic."

"Exciting," he said, exaggeratedly rubbing his palms together.

The Tasty was a microscopic burger joint in Harvard Square. Jamie had camped out at the worn Formica counter, jealously guarding an extra stool.

"Jack wanted to come," Mev said.

Giving Jack a look of mild annoyance, Jamie moved to allow all three of them to sit.

"I did some digging," Jamie said as they perused the menu above the grill behind the counter. She lowered her voice. "Raven. I know who he is. And I think I know what happened to him."

The guy behind the counter asked them what they wanted. Mev ordered a burger on Jack's absolute insistence. Jack and Jamie ordered the same, then Jamie added, "and we'll take those to go."

She said quietly, "Let's go someplace more private to chat."

They carried their paper sacks down the street to Winthrop Square, and sat on a broken piece of stonework, digging the burgers out of the bags as they talked.

"Something has been nagging at me since I first heard the name Raven," Jamie said. "I couldn't place it. I had to let it run as a background process in my brain. It hit me yesterday, but I wanted to verify it with Tomb, Tom.

"A while back, a guy came to a 2600 meeting. He was arrogant and rude, which isn't that uncommon. It's not like hackers are particularly well-socialized." Jamie allowed a slight grin.

"He used the handle Psychokiller, you know, like the Talking Heads song. He was showing off this virus he wrote, copying some stuff coming out of Bulgaria, and bragging about Patti Hoffman adding it to her virus warning list. What I didn't remember, or only dimly remembered, was that the code's embedded attribution wasn't Psychokiller. It was Raven. Somebody asked about it, and he waved it off, saying that was a handle he'd used before. I figured it was somebody else's code and he was pawning it off as his own, trying to be the big man. He never came back, and I forgot about him. Then yesterday it hit me, and Tom concurred. So, I dug."

"You found him?" Jack said, his mouth full of burger.

"I did. Tom keeps notes from the meetings, as you know, and he remembered that another member had brought him along. He made calls, and *voilà*!"

"Who is he?" Mev asked.

"*Was,* actually. Kenneth Frain. He died. December 27 of last year," Jamie continued.

"Jesus. Bastard didn't waste any time," Mev said.

"Who?" Jack asked.

"Fitz. He offered me the position days after that. I still don't know how he found me, but this makes perfect sense. How did this Raven guy die?"

"Not sure," Jamie said. "His buddy said it was something sketchy. Frain was a minor drug dealer, so it could have been related to that. I dropped by the Widener on my way here to look at their *Boston Globe* archives. The write up on his death was pretty spare. No surprise given the number of murders in Boston last year."

"And yet, somehow, the Stuart murders are the only deaths anybody seems to care about," Jack said.

Even the Missouri news had covered that story. Charles Stuart claimed he and his pregnant wife were shot by a Black man in Boston. She died, her hastily-delivered baby died, then Stuart committed suicide when the truth came out a few weeks ago that he'd committed the crime himself.

"Well, Frain's death was called 'suspicious.' And he fits the profile of someone who would hack for money. He was Raven, I feel sure of it," Jamie said.

Mev dropped her half-eaten burger back in the paper sack. What did this get them? Raven had been doing exactly what she was doing. Fitz was still a criminal, still selling secrets to the Russians, still in bed with the Irish Mob. Still, the fact that Frain—her predecessor—might have been murdered gave her pause.

"Do we tell Ostrowski about this?" Jack asked.

Would it take the pressure off her, cause Lanza to back off?

"I'm not so sure," Jamie replied. "Your AUSA sounds like a hard ass. I'm afraid it might make her rethink accepting your plea or adding extra conditions. Let them find Frain on their own. I mean, they are the FBI."

"What's a suspicious death, anyway?" Jack asked.

"Apparently it was an assault, maybe a break-in," Jamie said.

There was an aura of violence around Fitz, his uncontrolled rages, his angry assaults, Mev wondered if it had been him. Though she didn't see him killing the man supplying him bankable information. He was, frankly, far too selfish for that.

Unexpectedly, Mev thought of her father. He'd broken the law, lied, and manipulated people. Used one unsuspecting client's account balance to pay another's returns. Then another. And another. Until he was in too deep.

A feeling Mev was finally beginning to understand.

TUESDAY, MARCH 13, 1990

MORRIE WAS ONE OF THE FEW AGENTS CONNOR COULD tolerate. Plus, he was a notorious gossip, which served Connor well. Many FBI operations were confidential, eyes only. Compartmentalized. But buy Morrie a beer and a bite, and the guy wouldn't shut up. Morrie had alerted Connor to investigations he'd never have heard about otherwise, including ones outside of Morrie's counterintelligence team. He was a crappy agent, which was why he was in CI rather than one of the more important squads, but it gave him time to stick his nose in other people's business and share the wealth with Connor.

They were cramped in a booth at the Union Oyster House a few blocks from the office. Supposedly one of the oldest restaurants in the country. Connor figured people must have been a lot smaller back then. He'd have preferred to be at the big round bar with his typical lunch, a dozen oysters and a bourbon and water. But Morrie was much more forthcoming in a booth.

When Morrie's usual—clam chowder and a Sam Adams—were delivered, he began to dish. "Check this out," he said as he slurped his soup. "Ostrowski and that Philips kid? They actually found something. They got this MIT professor guy in their crosshairs and a witness who says she can implicate the Winter Hill Gang and the Russians in this sting. Big deal, right?"

Connor tried not to let the frustration show on his face. That egghead professor screwed this up, told the girl too much. He needed to act, and fast, to keep this from blowing back on his friends. Back on him.

"No kidding? I'm surprised Ostrowski and that . . ." he caught himself before he used the word that he'd normally employ. "That new computer kid made any progress. Wouldn't have thought they had it in them. What's going on with the investigation?"

"Philips and the girl made some kind of computer thing for the professor to sell the Russians so he can pay off the Mob guys. The girl's cut a deal with the AUSA for handing all three of them to her on a silver platter. Super slick!"

Connor wasn't sure how Ostrowski and Philips would approach the information the girl gave in her proffer, but this sounded like a slam dunk. Fitz was just dumb enough to fall for it. Connor didn't care if the Russians got stung, but he needed Joey to stay clean. If his friends got hurt, Connor might end up in a fifty-five gallon drum somewhere under the Big Dig.

"Sounds real slick," Connor said.

He needed to get ahead of this, thwart it in some way.

"Girl did the handoff to the professor. Ostrowski and Philips just have to follow him to his dead drop with the Russians, and then to his payoff with the Mob. Tied with a bow."

He couldn't let that happen. His Irish friends depended on him to keep them informed, safe, and out of the crosshairs of the FBI. And they wanted to get paid, so he needed to make sure the Russians and FitzRoy didn't get snagged after all. Because if the FBI came after them with no warning from Connor, they may very well come to him to cover Fitz's nut. If it happened on his watch, they'd expect him to fix it.

No, screw that. He'd handle it, make it go away quietly.

As Morrie droned on about another sting focused on counterfeit handbags, of all things, Connor thought through what to do. He could follow Ostrowski and Philips and try to intervene, only that seemed too clumsy. And he knew trying to convince them to let it go wouldn't work either. They were both Boy Scouts.

No, although Fitz was a man not to be trusted, he would have to be warned. He'd have to make sure he shook surveillance. And Connor would have to keep him from panicking or playing spy. He'd tell him as little as possible: feed Fitz an anonymous tip that he was being followed by the FBI and to be careful. Given what he knew of Fitz, the warning wouldn't scare him off from chasing a payday, but it might make him careful enough to avoid Ostrowski and Philips.

If Joey got picked up or, worse, if he flipped on his bosses, Connor would have a target on his forehead for the rest of his potentially short life.

All he had to do was keep Fitz in line. For once.

THURSDAY, MARCH 15, 1990

JOEY SLOWLY COUNTED THE BILLS IN THE FAT ENVELOPE Fitz had given him. They were sitting in Joey's Cadillac, Fitz in the back seat with Joey, one of his enforcers at the wheel.

"You're short," Joey said with the glare that was his default expression. It might have been a cultivated intimidation tactic rather than his natural demeanor. Either way, it worked. Fitz didn't like being near these guys and was anxious to get the hell out from under this debt. He knew he was short. He would take any kind of reprieve.

For whatever reason, the Cray supercomputer designs hadn't pleased his Russian handlers.

"We need more," was the only comment in spindly writing on a slip of paper in an envelope containing nine thousand dollars in mixed bills. He'd rooted around in the Cray server and found what might be relevant, but frankly he wasn't a hardware guy. Maybe he hadn't given them much of value. Still, they valued him. They wanted more. He needed to find what they were looking for.

Because he needed to wrap this up. "The FBI is watching you," the voice on his office telephone had said. His door had been closed, which was good. He was certain anyone in the office could have read his face as he took that call. Fear. Raw fear.

He'd talked himself down after the FBI had come to his office, questioning Mev. He'd never gotten a straight answer from her about that. He knew she had everything to lose, and given her background, no credibility. He wondered if the FBI had already figured that out. Maybe they were smart enough to put it together. Maybe they thought she was

Raven. The FBI had to be focused on her, not him. What could they possibly have on him?

Then that call came. Maybe they did know something. He'd been skating on thin ice, dealing with the Russians and the Mob. When it had just been throwing tidbits to the Russians for cash, it had been fun. And profitable. He'd had it completely under control. But since he took that loan from Banc Erin, he'd been slowly losing it. He'd tapped every account he had, even pillaged his emergency money, and he was still short. And now—now he was losing control, forced to deal with Joey, to try to appease him. The Mob would never let him go. They'd keep milking him. And the FBI wouldn't stop until somebody talked.

It was time to take back control. More precisely, it was time to get the hell out of dodge. Donna wouldn't miss him, though she'd sure as hell miss his money. The Mob wouldn't look too hard outside of their turf, he hoped, and the FBI wouldn't be able to locate him for future conversations. After all, he hadn't been charged with anything.

He'd had thoughts before about what he'd do if he had to flee, only they'd just been fantasies. Now, they needed to become a real plan. Until then, he just needed to keep Joey happy.

"Look, I'm good for it," Fitz said. "I just need more time. I need to get Mev Hayes to keep helping me and she's resisting."

Joey's look hardened further. "You need to learn to motivate her."

"I've tried."

"Maybe you're not using the right tools." Joey reached between his feet, retrieving an old leather Gladstone bag, removing a hammer and an icepick. "I find these to be particularly helpful in motivating people who have fallen behind on their payments. Like you, for example, professor."

He hefted the tools, testing their weight, then put them back in the bag.

"I am motivated. I just need help with her. I wouldn't have even needed her if that drug addict you guys sent me hadn't gotten himself robbed."

A grin bloomed on Joey's face, an expression far more terrifying than his stare. "I believe there's been a misunderstanding. There was no robbery. He pushed back—and paid for it. Don't do the same, professor. Now go get me my money before I decide to make you pay in another way."

As the Coupe de Ville pulled away, Fitz took off his suit coat. His sweat-drenched shirt was stuck to his back, and his collar was choking him. He loosened his tie and checked his watch. Mev would be leaving her Introduction to Algorithms class in ten minutes; he could intercept her as she left Building 38.

She would help him. He'd make sure of that. All she needed was the proper motivation.

Fitz watched Mev exit the Engineering Building, her hair shining in the spring sunlight. She did have a certain kind of innocent beauty, as long as she kept her mouth shut and did as she was told. Her smile faded when she saw Fitz.

There was risk in interacting in public, but she'd worked in his lab. Of course, he would still care about her well-being. He was just saying hello to a former research student.

"Mev, I need one last favor," he said when he reached her side. "I'm just shy of what I need to clear this loan, and then I swear, you can go do whatever you want. Keep me out of it, and I'll keep you out of it."

She walked quickly away from him. He had to hustle to catch her.

"You know you don't have a choice. The FBI is already sniffing around. They believe you are this Raven character."

She stopped and turned back toward him, almost forcing him to run into her.

"No. I'm done with all this, with you."

"Don't be such a baby. I'll keep my promise. One more little trip through Cray or Thinking Machines or some other supercomputer manufacturer and you're done."

A female student came down the sidewalk and Fitz gave her a dazzling smile, which she returned and ducked her head. Now *that* one looked like she'd be loads of fun to play with.

"Or what? You'll report me as a hacker? Tell the FBI I'm this Raven person?"

"You have no idea. I know the guy who went by that name. He's dead. Joey killed him when he wouldn't cooperate. You'll be next if you don't help me."

Now he saw fear in her eyes. It warmed him all the way down to his groin.

"I already helped you. I gave you DEMON. You don't need me."

Maybe not, but watching her cower was just so much fun.

FRIDAY, MARCH 16, 1990

JACK WAS WORKING ON HIS LAPTOP IN THE LIVING ROOM when Mev came home from class.

"Ostrowski called," he said.

"And you answered?"

"Are you on crack? This is me. He left a message and wants you to call him back. Here's the number," he said, handing her a slip of paper from his pocket. "I deleted the message. I didn't want Hector to stumble on it when he gets home."

Mev appreciated his discretion. It was getting increasingly bad with Hector. She wasn't sure how long they could keep living in the same house. But a call from Ostrowski was a good thing. It meant that he got what they needed to close her deal. That it would soon be over.

He picked up on the first ring. "Miss Hayes, I don't have good news, I'm afraid. In fact, I don't have much news at all."

"What do you mean? I just saw Fitz. He accosted me on campus, asking for more help. You got him, right? You just haven't picked him up yet."

"We haven't seen any activity from him other than his initial use of the server."

"How is that possible? He told me today he needed *more* help. That what I gave him didn't sell for enough to clear the loan. He obviously got paid and paid the Mob. You saw all that happen, right?"

Again, a moment of silence.

"We were monitoring him then lost him after he left his house. We got nothing."

"Are you kidding me? I gave you *everything* you asked for. That the AUSA asked for. This was going to set me free. You're the FBI; how did this happen?"

Jack was looking at her with concern as her voice rose.

"Surveillance is not an exact science," Ostrowski continued. "He may have known we were watching."

"Fantastic. This is why Bishop told me not to trust you guys in the first place. I gave you Fitz. And you can't even do the stuff you are supposedly experts at?"

Ostrowski again answered with silence.

"Now what?" Mev asked.

"It's good Fitz approached you for more help. We can try again. Agent Philips is ready to sit down with you and update your program to find additional bogus material. We'll catch him the second time."

She was at their mercy. "Fine. I'll be there later today."

Mev slammed the phone down, picked it up and slammed it down again. Then one more time. "Goddammit!"

"What's going on?" Jack asked.

"I have to do it again. The FBI missed Fitz. They think maybe he's on to them." She paced the room, just four steps across, and back again, whirled, did it again. When she finally stopped, she plopped onto the aqua chair.

"Fitz dodged them at the Russian dead drop, and again when he grabbed the cash, and again at the payoff. How could he have known? And all this after Fitz stalked me on campus, telling me I had to help him again. It's never going to stop."

"Fitz threatened you?" Jack asked.

"Yeah, and told me Raven was killed for not cooperating with the mob. How will I ever get out of this if the FBI keeps screwing up?"

"We'll think of something."

"I should have listened to Frank Bishop and kept my mouth shut. Only then I might already be in prison. This is impossible. I have no idea what to do next."

"Coffee? Scotch? Pasta Carbonara?"

Mev barked a laugh. "Carbonara?"

"I was thinking about what to make for dinner. And any problem is more tractable with bacon in your belly."

"You're crazy," she said, thankful for the distraction.

"I know what I like," he said, then turned serious. "Look, you're almost there. Fitz is no super spy. And Ostrowski isn't some two-bit cop."

"Clearly someone's in love."

It was his turn to laugh. "Just throwing the man respect. They may be strong-arming you, but Ostrowski and Philips seem almost OK. They're after actual bad guys. Get through this and you can go back to your life."

Whatever that might be.

"I feel like I'm completely dependent on them. I gave them everything and they still screwed it up."

Mev followed Jack into the kitchen, watched as he prepared to make dinner. Now no longer in the lab, no longer desperate to impress Fitz, she'd been home a lot. And she was enjoying having dinners with Jack, all the more now that Hector was out of the house most of the time.

She leaned against the kitchen counter as Jack started the sauce, then he poured them each a glass of wine. "*Salut*," he said, raising his glass. "Wine is even better for problem solving than bacon."

Dinner was spectacular as always, and they spent the rest of the evening watching TV, first *The Simpsons*, then *LA Law*. At some point Mev must have fallen asleep, because Jack touched her shoulder to wake her.

She'd been dreaming of being in a court room, alone at the defense table, the judge at a bench that was impossibly high, thirty or more feet above her. The prosecution was a hazy figure she couldn't quite see, and the whole thing was transpiring in silence. The judge's mouth moved, but Mev couldn't hear what he was saying.

Jack helped her up. In her bedroom, she kicked off her shoes and pulled the comforter over her, hoping to resume the dream and learn what would happen next.

She woke, still clothed, having slept more fully than she had in weeks. Downstairs, Jack was in the kitchen with Hector, who must have returned late the night before. Hector looked up from his coffee, his scowl signaling his ongoing animosity toward her. This morning it appeared particularly aggressive. She didn't get as far as the kitchen before it erupted.

"I can't believe you. I'm begging Fitz for another chance, and he lets you coast?"

The force of his anger startled her enough that it took her a moment to process what he'd said. She still didn't quite get it.

"Yesterday I'm there trying to pitch my new dissertation topic and Fitz is barely paying attention. I mean this is my God-damned life here, and he can't be troubled. I asked him outright: what's so special about you? Why should you get all the breaks? That got his attention. It's more than you just fucking him, right?"

"Hey, man. Be cool," Jack said.

"Screw you," Hector said. "You both have everything. Fitz is all worried that Mev's class load is too big, and she needs to take time off from research. I can't even get him to talk about my dissertation. Then he tells me I better work harder, or he might have to dump me from the program."

Hector's voice was loud now. "Whatever's going on, I know you are still working with him. And I'm done being shit on."

He rose suddenly, knocking back his chair, grabbing his bag and coat, and slammed the front door behind him.

"He's just . . ." Jack trailed off.

"Being a jerk," Mev said. "He thinks he's got it rough? I'm happy to trade."

She wasn't mad at Hector, not really. Fitz was, in fact, treating him like crap. He treated everyone like crap. All of this was, at the core, his fault. She didn't know how she had ever seen him as anything other than a manipulative, egotistical asshole.

Fitz was bullshitting Hector, but what he told Hector wasn't wrong. She'd been falling behind, missing classes, bombing quizzes and tests. None of it was hard; it was just impossible to concentrate. The FBI wasn't making that any easier; after class today she had to go into town for another session with Agent Philips so they could add material to the honeypot server for sting attempt number two.

If this didn't end soon, she'd fail out of MIT long before Fitz could have her expelled.

FRIDAY, MARCH 16, 1990

IMAGINING WHAT CAME NEXT FELT FREEING FOR FITZ. While he had done well in academia, won awards and accolades, the pay sucked. And this whole political correctness garbage was poisoning the campus and cramping his style. Used to be de rigueur for a distinguished faculty member to have his pick of student paramours. The girls wanted a worldly older man who would show them the ropes. But this entitled generation of students, like Mev Hayes, fought back, making it not only frustrating but dangerous.

Time to go. To leave behind the academic and suburban life—the wife, the kids, the house, the horses. Maybe go to a beach. He could ask his Russian friends about Cuba. Or maybe Indonesia. His money would go a long way there, and he could spend his days on the beach and his nights enjoying local girls who didn't speak any English and didn't talk back.

He was startled when the door to his office opened without a knock. It was that whiner Hector Cruz.

"Fitz, you need to help me."

More of that entitled crap. It really was time to leave this all behind. "I don't *need* to do anything Hector. Get out of my office," he said.

"I'm not going anywhere until you listen to me."

"You really do want me to kick your pathetic ass out of the program, don't you? So be it. We're done here."

"Oh, no, you're not in charge here."

Fitz laughed.

"I'll go to the dean," Hector said, his face reddening.

"And say what? That you can't come up with a dissertation topic to save your life. That you are a middling student and scholar? That you've been shown up by a college girl?"

Hector sputtered.

It was a pleasure toying with this punk, freely speaking his mind again. He'd leave this all behind: no more deans, whiny students, bloated bureaucracy, no bullshit.

"I know something is going on," Hector finally said.

"Oh, what is that? Excellence? Achievement? Wasn't sure you'd recognize it."

"I know all about you and Mev."

No big deal. It was hardly news that he was bedding a student.

"I talked to the FBI."

Stupid, stupid boy. Now there would have to be consequences. What was it with this generation of goody two-shoes?

"Not here." Fitz said. "We can talk, only not now. Let's wait until the lab empties. Meet me at 7:00 tonight."

He had planning to do.

At 7:00, Fitz intercepted Hector in the hallway just outside the lab. "The lab's not empty. Let's go someplace we can have privacy."

Fitz led Hector to the emergency stairwell, and they headed to the roof. On nice evenings, Fitz often enjoyed a cigar in the open air on the roof of Building 38. He had other plans tonight. The sky was dark, the moon just a tiny sliver, and Fitz felt the cold, despite his camel hair overcoat.

"OK, fine. We're alone; say your piece."

"I know you don't like me much, but you are wrong about me. I belong here. I can finish the program. And I deserve to."

"*Deserve?*" Fitz drew the word out with a sneer. "Deserve? I believe that's up to me, not you."

"I'm sure the Dean will see it my way."

"Haven't gone to him yet? Still want to grovel your way back into my good graces? You certainly aren't doing yourself any favors by sharing fairy tales with the FBI."

"I was pissed that you were blowing me off. The FBI came and talked to us at our house and wanted to know about Raven."

My God. That murdered junkie fuckup was still coming back to haunt him.

"And you know Raven?" Fitz asked.

"No. I was just at the house when they came to talk to Jack and Mev. You wouldn't give me the time of day, and I know Mev is fucking you and getting all the attention I deserve. I wanted revenge. So, I went to the FBI and told them everything."

"What's 'everything?'"

"That you and Mev were fooling around and doing something super secretive."

"Wow, that's some hard hitting evidence," Fitz said.

Nevertheless, it was inconvenient. He'd have to accelerate his timeline and go after the Mother Lode. He needed Mev's help for that, then he could escape. Only first he needed to clean things up here.

"You're right. I'm afraid I've been distracted, giving too much attention to Mev and not enough to you. First thing Monday let's sit down and review your dissertation proposal, or even brainstorm one together. How's that?"

An enormous smile lit Hector's face. His combative stance relaxed. "That's all I ever wanted."

Hector reached a hand for him to shake. Fitz went to take it, then instead brought both hands up and pushed Hector hard in the chest.

Fascinating that Hector didn't make a sound during his eight story fall to the ground.

FRIDAY, MARCH 16, 1990

AFTER CLASS, MEV SPENT THE EVENING WITH AGENT Philips, adding more fake assets to the server Fitz thought belonged to Cray Computer Corporation. He'd find the new files, drop them for the Russians, get paid, pay Joey, and hopefully this time the FBI would actually see it all happen.

The house was dark as she came down Linnaean, but Jack's truck was in the driveway. She closed the front door and turned on the living room light.

"Turn it off," Jack said from the couch, his voice slurred and rough. Was he drunk? Crying?

She snapped the light back off.

"Are you OK?"

"Not even close. Hector's dead."

"What?" Mev sat on the couch beside him. "What happened?"

"Not sure," he said between sniffs. "They said it looked like he jumped off the Engineering building."

"Jesus. When? This evening?"

"That's what the MIT Police told me. They came here after. They said it happens every year at MIT. As if that explains it somehow."

The lab, Hector's career, it meant that much?

"Did you see him today?" Jack asked, now looking at her.

"Not since that blowup this morning. I stay away from the lab now."

"Apparently, Fitz threw him out of the program. Everyone in the lab heard."

Was this her fault? "Why?"

"Fitz has been riding him for months," Jack said. "He was down on him, dismissing anything he did or said."

"Still, suicide?"

"I know. I can't go there, either. I mean, it's stupid to say he's not the type. I just don't believe he'd do it."

"Could it have been an accident? "

"Maybe. That seems even less likely. They say he fell eight stories."

"Poor Hector."

For a few minutes, they sat in the dark in silence, each lost in their own sorrow.

"Maybe it wasn't an accident," Jack said.

Mev put her hand on Jack's. "I know he was your friend. But if it happened just hours after he lost his place at MIT, then awful as it is, isn't suicide more likely?"

Jack was shaking his head slowly. "I don't know. Everything is so crazy right now."

Mev couldn't disagree. Her predicament had drawn Jack and Jamie in. She was trying hard to keep them out of trouble. Maybe her mess with Fitz had added to Hector's hopelessness, drawn him into the fray too.

Jack was quiet, yet more himself the next morning, hunched over an exceptionally large mug of coffee.

"I talked to Hector's parents late last night. They're near San Jose. They asked if I could pack his stuff and ship it to them. Once his body is released, they'll fly him home and bury him out there."

He shook his head and stared off into space. "It's all so surreal. It'll be like he was never here."

Mev left him to his thoughts, taking a black coffee into the living room. Even though Hector had been scarce lately, the house did seem extra quiet. Then it struck her: there was no music on. Jack always had some punk or alternative band's CD playing, or the television on. Not today.

Lost in her thoughts, she caught a glimpse of red. Jack was holding a bright red motorcycle helmet. And through the back door, uncovered for the first time, she saw Jack's motorcycle: a black Kawasaki 440 LTD.

"C'mon. Let's blow the cobwebs out," Jack said, handing the helmet to her. "Meet you in front. Wear your warmest jacket."

Mev met Jack in the driveway. The motorcycle rumbled low.

"Have you been on one before?" he shouted over the engine noise.

"No," Mev yelled back, putting on the helmet.

"Hold onto my sides and lean when I do."

She got on the slightly elevated seat behind Jack's, and he showed her where to put her feet, warning her about keeping them there so she wouldn't burn her ankles on the exhaust pipes. He got on, then placed her hands on his waist.

"Hold tighter," he said, then leveled the bike, kicked up the side stand, and eased them onto the street.

They started slow, and the first thing Mev noticed was how much cooler the air felt. She'd been sure the jacket Jack recommended would be too heavy, but it felt like the temperature plummeted the instant they were moving.

Jack leaned into a few easy turns as they moved west through Cambridge, down Concord Ave. to Fresh Pond. The vibration of the bike flowed through her, a subsonic drone that traveled her whole body. Her anxiety faded as Jack expertly wove through traffic, taking a chance now and then to twist the throttle, squirting them from a pack of cars into the open road ahead.

She could see everything as they accelerated out of Cambridge to Route 2. Jack leaned into the handlebars as he tweaked the throttle and the bike shot forward on the highway. There was a kind of raw power here, like a force coiled inside the machine that was gradually being let loose when Jack gave the bike gas.

They rode past Walden Pond, then cut over to the more rural Route 117, leaning into every curve. At a pullout next to a bridge spanning a salt marsh Jack slowed. With his feet now on the ground, he walked the bike over the gravel before engaging the kick stand and shutting off the engine.

Without the vibration of the bike and the rumble of the exhaust, Mev could feel her heart pounding, her fingertips buzzing.

They removed their helmets. "What do you think?"

"I love it!" she said too loudly, no longer having to shout over the engine. Then she laughed, surprised to find she was both exhilarated and calm.

"No better way to clear your head than to crank up the bike and blast out on the road."

He pulled a wool blanket from one of the bike's saddlebags, and they sat quietly looking at the still water, listening to the birds chirping about the coming spring. Mev let her mind wander, not trying to suppress thoughts about Hector, about her situation, about prison, instead letting them float by. The buzz from the ride still filled her, quelled her anxiety. She turned to look at Jack; his face was calm as he observed the birds flitting from tree to tree, the insects hovering above the still water. She was here, in this place, right now with someone who had her back. Not many people did, but she was sure Jack did. Jamie did. Even Ostrowski and Philips seemed to.

Poor Jack: it drove him crazy that he admired Ostrowski. He could barely admit having underestimated the agent. And Mev had underestimated Jack. At first, she'd thought he was just some kind of rich, flighty dilettante. But now she knew that he, like her, he was just easily bored. He just had different ways of dealing with it. He needed new music playing, new foods to taste, new trouble to get into.

Though not the sort of trouble she'd brought down on them.

After a time in silence, they rose, mounted the bike, and rode back to Cambridge.

SUNDAY, MARCH 18, 1990

PAUL WOKE TO THE RINGING OF HIS BEDSIDE PHONE. Who the hell would call him on a Sunday morning? They'd been staking out Fitz with only brief breaks since Carl had posted the new honeypot material Friday night. Fitz hadn't made a move, unless he'd slipped their surveillance again.

That would be a disaster.

He'd missed his first St. Patrick's Day in Boston. After handing the Carlisle site off to two other agents, he and Philips drove back to the city, where they saw many green-clad revelers lurching through the streets long after midnight.

"What?" Paul said into the phone, expecting Carl the eager beaver.

"Get your ass in here," Weaver barked. "It's all hands."

"What?" Paul asked again.

"Move it, Ostrowski. Call your partner and get into the office. You'll be briefed when you get here," Weaver said and hung up.

Paul looked at the clock. 7:15. He and Carl weren't supposed to relieve the other team until noon, and he could really use a few hours of sleep. What was so important on a Sunday?

Paul showered and wiped away the steam on the mirror. He wasn't surprised by the dark circles under his eyes but was by the start of a double chin. And the gray in his sideburns—when did that happen? Carl might be right. He needed to take better care of himself or he'd never make it to retirement. Though lately, he was having an increasingly hard time imagining how he'd possibly slog it out to his twenty years and a full pension.

When Paul stepped off the elevator, Carl was already there, along with what looked like every other agent in the office, including several he hadn't met yet.

"What the hell is going on?" Paul whispered to Carl.

"No idea."

They waited while Weaver talked to men in suits who radiated a look of command.

"Listen up!" Weaver bellowed, silencing the shuffling crowd of agents. Paul had been sitting on his desk but stood when everyone else did.

"This morning, sometime after 1:00 a.m., thieves entered the Isabella Stuart Gardner Museum and stole an estimated 500 million dollars' worth of paintings."

"Wow," Carl mouthed. Paul agreed. This was big.

"We'll be taking over the lead from Boston P.D. This will be an all-hands effort. If you are working cases that do not involve immediate threat to persons or property, you are to put them on hold and dedicate your resources to supporting the investigating team. See Johnson for your assignments."

Paul and Carl were attached to the site team. Gofers for whatever the agents on site needed. Paul wanted to tell Weaver they needed to be on Fitz, not standing around a museum.

Connor, who Paul had avoided since his run-in with him over Jamie Brennan, mumbled "This is bullshit. We have our panties in a bunch over some paintings?"

"It's got to be the largest art theft in Boston history," Carl said.

"Who cares?" Connor replied. "I'm working a case, and I need to get back to it, not babysit artsy eggheads worried about their fucking Picasso or whatever."

"No Picassos were stolen," Carl said, reading from the brief they'd been given. "A Vermeer, a Rembrandt . . . "

"Like I said—who gives a rat's ass? What's Mitch thinking? The Mob isn't gonna sit around and wait for me to find some drawings."

Of course, this asshole called ASAC Weaver by his first name. Still, Paul couldn't help agreeing; he and Carl were one sting away from wrapping up their case.

Carl started to correct Connor again; Paul excused himself and approached Weaver.

"What, Ostrowski? I'm busy here."

"We're in the middle of a stakeout on Longbow, and we need . . ."

Weaver's hand went up like a crossing guard stopping a truck. "Don't start. The Director himself said this is top priority and it's all hands on deck. That includes me, that includes Philips, that includes you. So, you have twice as much work? Join the club. Get it done."

"But sir . . . "

"Ostrowski. Today is not the day to piss me off. You have your assignment."

Carl was waving to him from his desk, a phone to his ear. Paul waded through the throng of agents to get to him.

"It's Mev Hayes. She says she was assaulted."

Paul took the phone from Carl. It was hard to hear in the busy office, and he caught her mid-sentence.

" . . . when we got home, and we just ran."

She sounded out of breath, and frightened. Also deeply angry, outraged at the violation.

"Miss Hayes, this is Special Agent Ostrowski."

"Agent Ostrowski, good. Fitz was here. He had a gun. He tried to grab me. I called the police, but they didn't believe me."

Fitz had slipped his surveillance. Again.

"Slow down, Miss Hayes. Where are you now?"

He couldn't help blaming AUSA Lanza for this twist in the case, Mev's safety be damned.

He signaled to Carl for something to write on. Carl handed him his notebook. "Kidnapping? Fitz. No police," he wrote and showed it to Carl.

Weaver was staring right at him. He made a sweeping gesture with his hand that Paul couldn't possibly misinterpret: hang up the damn phone and get your ass to the Gardner. When Paul didn't immediately end the call, Weaver glared.

"Miss Hayes, I'm sorry, I need to call you back in . . . " Then the line went dead.

"Dammit," Paul grunted.

"What?" Carl asked.

"Not now. In the car."

He noticed a missed call notice on his desk from "Mev Hayes." No return number, no message, just a time stamp. 2:15 a.m. She'd been on the run for hours.

He and Carl joined the queue of agents waiting for the elevators, Paul vibrating with frustration.

When they got into his Taurus, Paul slammed his fists into the steering wheel. "This is ridiculous. We're asking this woman to play cops and robbers with mobsters and spies. And now we have to go babysit art."

"You're sounding like Connor," Carl said.

"Fuck you."

"You are *definitely* sounding like Connor," Carl said with a sympathetic smile.

SUNDAY, MARCH 18, 1990

"GODDAMMIT!" MEV SCREAMED, SLAMMING THE HEAVY payphone handset onto its cradle, picking it up and slamming it down again. "When we actually need them, they don't have time for us."

Jack stood quietly watching her, and Mev slowly calmed her breathing, trying to think.

"He said he couldn't talk," Mev continued. "It's as bad as the police. What are we going to do?"

After their motorcycle ride the day before, Jack had retreated to Hector's room to pack boxes and Mev had gone to hers to work on a problem set for a class. She struggled to find a semblance of the mindfulness she'd experienced looking out over the marsh, only it wouldn't come. She decided to check on Jack.

The door to Hector's room—what had been Hector's room—was open. Jack sat on the floor among several partially filled boxes, staring off into space.

"You all right?" she asked.

It took him a moment to come back from wherever his mind had been. "I guess. How am I going to send home his motorcycle? I'm trying to remember how he got it here, and for the life of me I can't. Did he buy it here or did he have it shipped? He must have told me. I'd remember if he drove it cross country. I just can't think straight today.

"That's how we met, you know. At a motorcycle repair shop in Dorchester. He was looking for a part, and so was I. We hit it off and met for rides. Had a blast. He needed a new place to live when his roommate left school, and I told him to come here. We used to ride together all the time. I don't know what happened." Jack trailed off.

Despite the mind clearing effects of the motorcycle ride earlier that day, the facts of her life, of Jack's life, hadn't changed. Hector was still dead. And she'd heard nothing from Ostrowski. Either Fitz hadn't yet tried to sell the new tech she and Agent Philips had mocked up, or he'd dodged them again. She was still in limbo, and Jack was somewhere similar.

Jack stood, wiped his hands on his jeans. "I can't do any more of this today." He looked at his watch. "My God, it's St. Patrick's Day. I totally forgot. We need to celebrate."

"Really? Are you sure?"

"Absolutely. Let me get cleaned up."

He was doing what she was: searching for some kind of order amid absolute chaos. Maybe a little normalcy wouldn't hurt after all.

The Plough and Stars was clogged with people and cigarette smoke. Jack elbowed his way to the bar and brought back two pints of Guinness with thick layers of foam on top.

He handed her a pint, then raised his own. "To Hector. This can be his Irish wake."

Mev nodded. As fitting as anything else they could do.

"*Sláinte*," he said as they clinked their pint glasses.

"What does that mean?" She asked.

"'Health' in Irish."

She said it silently to herself.

They followed that pint with many others, listening to live Irish music and shouting to each other over the din of the crowd. They closed the place down, stumbling out into the street reeking of beer and cigarettes.

"I have good news and bad news," Jack said, his voice hoarse from the shouting and the smoke. "Bad news first. The T stopped running an hour ago. Good news, I'm drunk so I'm not feeling that cold." He had a relaxed grin that Mev was glad to see. She hadn't wanted to draw him into all of this. But he'd come willingly, for which she was deeply grateful.

She returned the smile. "We better get walking then."

Approaching Linnaean Street, she felt sleep coming on and was imagining her warm bed when a figure emerged from the dark and lunged at her, causing her to stumble backward, struggling to keep her balance.

It was Fitz in dark jeans and sweatshirt. She could smell the alcohol on his breath.

"What the hell?" she said as Jack helped steady her.

Only then did she see the revolver in Fitz's hand. Jack tugged at her coat and began to run, dragging her the first few steps, then letting go and pumping his arms to accelerate. She followed, hoping that in the dark they'd outpace Fitz. By the time they turned the corner at the end of the block, they couldn't see or hear him anymore.

It was the middle of the night, and they didn't dare go home. They stayed off Mass Ave., away from the lights, walking back toward Harvard Square. Mev stopped at a payphone and dialed 911. The male dispatcher sounded harried and annoyed, dismissing Mev's description of her attacker as "just another drunk on St. Pat's," telling her "girls shouldn't be out that late" and to "just go home."

After the dispatcher disconnected, Mev stared at the payphone receiver, incredulous. "They blew me off." She opened the phone book and flipped to the blue pages, finding the number for the FBI office in Boston. She asked to speak to Agent Ostrowski and was told they would leave a message for him. She tried to tell the FBI operator what was going on. She told Mev to call 911.

"Now what?" she said, panic rising. They needed a place to hide until she could talk to Ostrowski in the morning. Jack said he knew a place and took them to an unmarked cellar door in Central Square. He knocked and they were let into an underground after-hours club where they sipped club soda until it closed at 5 a.m. Then they walked the Cambridge Streets, killing time in Harvard Yard until it was time to call Agent Ostrowski.

Who cut her off.

Leaving them on their own.

SUNDAY, MARCH 18, 1990

THE BUS DROPPED MEV AND JACK AT THE FERRY TERMI-
nal in Rockland, Maine. The trip had taken over five hours, and they
had been silent for most of it, loath to discuss anything in the relatively
public space of the bus. Mev had been hypnotized by the hum of the
highway but grew more interested as they turned on to Route 1, passing
small towns with diners and tourist hotels touting "Vacationland."

She stood in the weak March light, gagging on the stench of rotting
fish pervading the air while Jack worked the yellow pages to find them a
taxi. They'd gotten off the bus at the wrong ferry terminal and needed
to figure out how to get fifteen miles further north.

He came back from the phone booth. "Sorry. It's been a while since
I've been here. The taxi should pick us up in a few minutes."

"Where, exactly, are we going?"

"Islesboro. It's over there." He pointed vaguely north. "We need to
get to the ferry terminal before 5:00 when the last boat leaves. We'll have
the cab run us by the Shop & Save for groceries, then we're good to go."

He had a purposeful optimism that was a welcome contrast to Mev's
own overwhelming exhaustion. She was grateful for his resourcefulness,
all his random bits of knowledge coalescing into a practical plan. He
appeared energized by having a mission. Her only mission was to stay
one step ahead of disaster.

The cab arrived, smelling of years of cigarette smoke and stale fish.

Jack chatted with the driver, a man with a leathery complexion and
slicked back gray hair. At the store, they stocked up on boxed and canned
goods, pasta, smoked fish, items that didn't require refrigeration.

"The cabin has electricity," Jack had told her, "But the refrigerator will have been off all winter, and I don't want to have to start it. Ideally, the Carters will never even know we were there."

Even though they'd traveled for only half a day, Mev felt like they were in another world. As the cab took them north, the road was lined with stretches of ragged pine and boats on jacks beside garages or in front yards, awaiting summer. After the cab dropped them at the proper ferry terminal, Mev sniffed at her jacket. She smelled like she smoked a pack a day.

They boarded a big ferry, the *Margaret Chase Smith*. Only a few other people and two cars joined them on the journey. The day was overcast, and the air grew cooler once the ferry moved away from the dock. Despite the cold, Mev stood outside on the deck watching the gulls dip and dive and the island grow larger during the twenty-minute ride.

She wondered what it would be like living on an island, and realized she was about to find out. They hadn't talked about how long they'd be here. A week, a month? Then what? They couldn't return until they figured out how to stay safe—and stay out of prison.

The sun was approaching the Lincolnville mainland horizon in the west as the ferry docked. Jack gathered his things and walked briskly down the pier, Mev working to match his pace.

"We have a ways to go, and I'd like to get there before dark," he said.

Mev was warm enough to open her jacket by the time they turned off the paved road onto a dirt one.

"Crap, I can't see anything in the trees," Jack said.

"You know where we're going, right?"

"Pretty much."

He led her back into the woods along a dirt track that gradually shrank, becoming a hint of a trail. When a house finally came into view, it was almost fully dark under the spruce canopy, and Mev could see only the outline of a one-story wooden cabin, painted white, with either green or black shutters. It was too dark to tell.

Jack strode onto the wooden porch and opened the door. He anticipated her question. "Nobody locks anything here."

Mev flopped down on a couch backed with a flannel blanket. The couch was sprung and she sank into it. A relief, nonetheless. They were away from Boston. Away from Fitz.

Safe. For now.

Jack navigated the cabin with purpose, opening and closing a fuse box, checking the rooms, and turning on the water.

"The woodstove should already be laid. Can you start it?" he said.

Mev fiddled with the small stove, trying to open the door. Jack was right. A fire was laid, with newspaper, kindling and small logs ready to go. She found a box of matches on a shelf above the stove, and she lit the paper. Smoke belched from the door.

"Chimney's cold. You want to light paper to get the air moving first. For next time," he said with a chuckle.

A small, shaded lamp on the kitchen table threw a warm light around the cabin, which was simple, but tidy. The kitchen held a small two burner stove, a porcelain sink, and three enameled metal cabinets topped by a cracked Formica counter. Living, dining, and kitchen were all one room, with doors leading back into bedrooms.

Jack opened one of the cupboards and pulled out two glasses, pouring the scotch he'd bought in the grocery store. He'd debated buying wine, despite his critical commentary on the meager selection at the Shop & Save, then decided scotch was more practical since they were "roughing it."

He handed her a Tom & Jerry juice glass. He raised his glass and they clinked. The scotch burned her mouth and throat and roiled in her stomach. They hadn't eaten all day. She was starving.

Hearing her stomach growl, he said "I'll start dinner. Sauce from a jar and boxed spaghetti. Beggars can't be choosers, eh?" he said as he banged pots and pans.

Mev sat at the table, feeling the warmth of the stove, and pouring herself another scotch as she watched Jack cook. Then she felt Jack nudging her awake. Forcing her eyes open, she struggled to raise her head from her arms crossed on the table.

"You need to eat, then sleep. Tomorrow we can plan."

She mechanically put the spaghetti into her mouth, aware, even in her sleepy state, that it paled before Jack's usual fare. He was a good cook, and a good friend. This wasn't his fight, he didn't have to do any of this, didn't have to risk prison or violence for her. Yet here he was.

Jack meticulously spun spaghetti onto his fork, cradled by a spoon, creating precise knots to neatly put in his mouth. He stopped, realizing she was watching him.

"You all right?" he asked.

"Not even close." Then the tears she'd held back all day, all the weeks prior, flowed. She didn't want to lose it in front of Jack; she didn't want to lose it at all. She was just so tired. She put her head down on her arms and wiped her face with her shirtsleeve.

Jack put his hand on her back. It felt good.

"Come on, let's get you to bed."

He lent her his shoulder, and she stumbled along to a back bedroom, dark outside the reach of the tiny kitchen lamp. Jack fumbled for a light switch and a floor lamp bloomed soft yellow light. She sat on a threadbare knotted quilt.

She was just exhausted. Just done.

Jack stood before her, silent. He too was waiting. Her thoughts were slow, tangled by the darkness in the corners and the chill of the unheated room far from the stove. He sighed and helped her pull off her shirt.

She let him, a child again, done in from too long a day, pouty, making her mother do the work of readying her for bed. He was slow, and tender, as if he feared he might break her.

They didn't speak as he folded the shirt and placed it on the child-sized dresser. He knelt and untied her sneakers, still damp with dew from the moss and grass outside. He peeled off her socks and hung them carefully on a chair back. He knelt again, unbuttoned her jeans, and worked them past her hips. Her boring underwear came down with them. He stopped, staring at the red hair between her legs.

Now Mev was fully awake, and suddenly very aroused. She grabbed his head and pulled it up toward hers, leaning over to kiss him. It was a stupid kiss, an adolescent one, missed mouths and clacking teeth. Then they found a rhythm. Even though they tasted of cheap red sauce and scotch, she was transported, excited, abandoning all the insanity of the last weeks in this one intimate moment.

She stood, pushed her jeans down the rest of the way and undid her bra, now standing naked before him. She was embarrassed by her shape, and cold, but she wanted him. Now he seemed paralyzed, uncharacteristically silent and indecisive as she undressed him.

He resisted when she pulled his wrist down to get him to join her on the bed and spoke his only words. "Birth control?"

"I'm good," Mev said. And she was. Truly.

The first time, on the top of the quilt, he was fast, and she wanted more. The second time, under the covers, he was more attentive. After, she slipped away in a dreamless, untroubled sleep.

SUNDAY, MARCH 18, 1990

PAUL PULLED OVER AND PUT ON HIS FLASHERS, JUMPING out to use a payphone. He removed his notebook and dialed a number then was quickly back in the car, driving over the Longfellow Bridge toward Cambridge.

"Where are we going?" Carl asked.

"Taking the long way to the museum."

"Weaver will . . ."

"I know. It'll be quick. She's not answering her phone."

He'd get the update from Mev and then figure out what was next. If it had weight, he'd be able to go back to Weaver and ask for more time for Longbow and protection for Mev.

Linnaean Street was quiet. Paul identified Mev Hayes' car on the street and Jack Kane's truck in the driveway. He knocked on the door and Carl offered to check around back. Paul waited, looking in the large picture window, but could see no movement, no evidence of anyone home, no evidence of violence. This case had been all about crimes with very little evidence.

Carl returned. "Nothing in the back except a couple of covered motorcycles. Everything seems fine."

Paul shook his head. Everything was definitely not fine. Mev had sounded scared. Fitz with a gun. He weighed whether they should enter the house. "Let's check around back again," he said.

The back door was in a small courtyard, not clearly visible from the neighboring residences.

"She said she was under threat," Paul said, opening the screen door and trying the back-door knob. Locked. "I think these are exigent circumstances."

Carl shook his head. "We should get a warrant. Weaver and Lanza will kill us if we taint evidence."

"You want me to call Weaver and tell him we're not at the Gardner Museum like he ordered, that instead we need a warrant to search the house for the case he told us to put on the back burner? I'd rather take my chances with a judge after the fact, thank you."

Carl nodded, and Paul put his shoulder to the door. It popped open, spilling him into the kitchen. The house was clean, tidy, quiet.

Carl searched upstairs, Paul down. Nothing out of place and the French press coffee pot was cold. Had they fled? If so, where? Was she truly threatened? He had no reason to doubt her, yet nothing appeared disturbed. On the other hand, she said she'd been threatened. Would Paul stay home if that had happened to him? Where would they go?

Carl returned downstairs.

"Anything?" Paul asked.

"The other roommate, Hector? Looks like he's packing up. Other than that, the place looks like they were just there."

Paul closed the back door as they left, making sure it was secure after his forced entry had popped the latch.

"There's nothing actionable here," Carl said. "Plus, it's not really our jurisdiction, even if she called us. Do we call Cambridge P.D.?"

"And say what? I don't *think* she was lying? We don't have any evidence. And they already blew her off once. I was stupid not to take her call."

"Weaver would've . . . "

"I know. He'd have chewed my ass. Still, I should have kept her on the phone." He got in the car. "She had something to tell us. She sounded scared. I bet she ran."

"What next?" Carl asked as they resumed their trip to the Gardner.

"We keep investigating."

"Weaver will . . . "

"I know. But we have to keep going," Paul said as he steered the Taurus across the Mass Ave. Bridge, heading back to Boston and the Gardner Museum.

At least that crime made sense.

MONDAY, MARCH 19, 1990

MEV AWOKE TO DAYLIGHT FILTERED THROUGH SPRUCE trees. She checked her watch and realized that it was all she was wearing. And that she felt lighter, less out of balance. This place might be only a way station on the journey to whatever happened next, yet here she could pause, regroup. Mev sighed, recalling the night before.

The rag rug at the side of the bed gave little insulation from the cold boards, but her shoes and socks still weren't dry, so she stayed barefoot as she got dressed. The icy wood floor burned as she walked to the kitchen and found Jack reading a tattered paperback from the cabin's bookshelves. The cover featured a woman in a ballgown, held by a man in a frock coat.

"Romance?" Mev asked.

Jack hesitated, perhaps uncertain if she meant the novel or last night.

"It's what they have. It's this or the Russians. Dostoevsky's too damned depressing in the present circumstances."

It was hard to keep it all in her head. The mob, Hector, the FBI, jail, Fitz, the gun. Now Jack and her.

"Coffee?" he asked.

"God, yes."

He poured from an old aluminum percolator pot on the stove. It was bitter and exceptionally hot. She sipped it slowly, not needing the caffeine for once, still riding the feeling of clarity she felt when she woke. She repositioned a wooden chair to face the stove so she could warm her feet.

Mev felt Jack watching her over the book he was no longer reading. Was he embarrassed? Unsure? She didn't know this Jack. Was this who Candice knew? And what about her?

"How are you doing?" he asked, tentative.

Mev laughed out loud. It was real mirth for the first time since she could remember. "Actually, I'm pretty God-damned fantastic." He regarded her with concern, and she let his attention wash over her. It could be a one-night thing or a longer thing. They'd figure it out.

She lifted the receiver from the yellow wall phone then paused before dialing the rotary dial.

Jack shrugged. "Yeah, it'll show on the Carters' phone bill. Go ahead, they're friends of my parents. I'll tell them I needed a getaway."

Mev shook her head, then dialed the number she'd memorized and hung up. She'd barely raised her coffee to her lips when the phone rang.

"Maine?" Jamie asked.

"We got in a little trouble," she said. He stood close beside her as she put the receiver between their heads so they both could hear.

Mev explained what had happened: Hector, the assault by Fitz, the police, the FBI.

"Wow, you've fallen from a world of shit into a world of really deep shit." Jamie said.

Mev laughed.

"No, I mean it. Good move going dark, though. I've been busy in the meantime, compiling a nice little dossier on Fitz. The same stuff the FBI has if they are any good. I'm pleased to share it with them in any case. Anonymously, of course.

"And you're going to have to go back to the FBI, even though they screwed up. The AUSA is going to be pissed you ran, but Ostrowski sounds like he might be a guy who will understand. And you still have something they want, so they'll work with you if you can help them land a case."

"Are we putting you in danger calling you?" Mev asked. "What if they have a trace or something."

Jamie gave a low chuckle. "Don't you worry. As far as the phone company knows, my pager belongs to a plumber in Chelsea. And they'll never know where I'm calling from."

She explained that she'd hacked dozens of corporate PBXs, internal corporate phone systems. She dialed into them, then spoofed phone numbers and locations. She gave Mev several to use when making any more calls from the cabin.

"Keep your heads down," she said before she hung up.

Jack had his hand on her shoulder. It didn't inspire the passion from the night before. She removed it gently.

"Please, Jack. Let's focus."

"Roger," he said with a two-finger salute. "And now?"

Mev was aware of the range of possible answers—what happened last night, what could happen next, the FBI, grad school, life. She picked the most pressing. They needed to let Agent Ostrowski in on what had happened yesterday.

"First, I need socks. My feet are freezing."

She found wool socks in the small dresser. She hoped the Carters wouldn't miss them. Small worries in the middle of all of this.

As she reentered the kitchen, Jack asked again, "you OK?" Solicitous and tentative.

"Just scared. We've got to get ahead of this."

She drafted what she'd say to Special Agent Ostrowski on a kitchen notepad that said "Lincolnville Motor Lodge" with a sketch of a rustic cabin. She suspected such a place was long gone.

When Mev had her thoughts clear, she opened a ratty New England Telephone book, and turned again to the blue pages. There was a toll-free number for the FBI and Mev dialed it via Jamie's PBX spoofing instructions. Should she be thinking of her as Hecate right now? Goddess of magic and the night.

She asked a general operator how to get in touch with Special Agent Paul Ostrowski in the Boston Office. She was put on hold with staticky music and asked two more times who she was and who she was trying to reach then put on hold again. She hadn't expected this would be quite so difficult.

"Your name is Hayes?"

"Yes."

"I have a directive from Agent Ostrowski to connect you with him, day or night, wherever he is. Unfortunately, I don't know where he is at this moment. We will try to find him. Can he call you back?"

"No, I need to speak with him now. Or I can call back at a specific time."

"Can you hold?"

Hold the phone, hold her breath, hold on. "Yes," Mev said. She could hold.

MONDAY, MARCH 19, 1990

PAUL WAS IMPATIENT, STUCK AS PART OF THE SITE TEAM at the Gardner Museum. He felt like a secretary, waiting for orders from his boss to type a letter or run an errand. But he knew this was how it worked. When he'd been on critical CID cases, he'd often grabbed agents to pitch in when more manpower could get the job done faster. Still, he felt frustrated by the distraction.

With Mev in the wind and AUSA Lanza setting the terms for her immunity, Paul didn't have much he *could* do. He absolutely didn't want to piss Weaver off. Didn't want to screw over Carl, who was early in his career. If computers turned out to be a big deal, then being good with them could be important in the future FBI. He didn't want a censure to rub off on Carl; the kid deserved better.

The lead agent finally gave them an assignment: sending them to talk to an art expert at Harvard who said he was too busy to come to the museum or the office. Clearly, he and Carl weren't too busy to trot over to Harvard Square.

As they were walking back to their car, the radio came alive. "Agent Ostrowski, I have a call to patch through. Operations said you wanted it if it came in. Meg Hayes."

Close enough.

"Agent Ostrowski?" It was Mev. Her voiced sounded far away and distorted through the radio patch.

"It's me. I'm here with Agent Philips. I am so sorry we couldn't talk. I was pulled into an emergency investigation here in Boston. First, are you safe?"

"We're safe."

We. She'd said in the first call "we ran." Her and Kane, he assumed.

Paul hadn't told Weaver or Lanza that she was gone yet. Lanza would blow a gasket if it looked like Mev fled. In the meantime, he hoped Operations was tracing the call. Keep her talking, give them time to track it, and he could make this good.

"I'm sorry I cut you off earlier. Can you tell me what is happening?"

"I need to know you can protect me," she said.

"I can," he said. He believed he could, but it would be complicated. "Tell me what happened."

She narrated the events of the last few days. Her interaction on campus with Fitz. The suicide of their housemate Hector Cruz. That was a surprise.

"What happened to him?"

"We're not sure. The police told us it happens all the time."

Paul looked at Carl, who shrugged. This was news to them. Was it related? He couldn't see how. He needed to understand what else had happened.

Mev continued, describing Kane's and her walk home from the bar, the encounter with an enraged and deranged Fitz waving a gun. The police assuming it was some overreacting co-ed. His own dismissal of her call.

Jesus, what a mess. And it was their fault. Technically, Lanza had put them in this position, but Paul couldn't help feeling it was his job to fix it. And it would be easier to deal with it himself than to convince the Cambridge P.D. to work it, especially since he couldn't disclose anything about the case.

"Come into the office. Let's sit down and talk about what happened and form a plan."

"No. We need to agree on the plan ahead of time, including assurances about my safety."

That was Kane's influence, undoubtedly. She was being cautious. He could hardly blame her. He wondered what, if anything, the death of Hector Cruz had to do with this. He'd figure that out later. Right now, his obligation was to her.

Carl tapped his watch and nodded. They'd had enough time for the trace. From here, he needed to have his wits about him. That was hard to do in the car on their way to another job.

"That's reasonable. I'm on the radio now. I'd like to call you back from my office and let's talk this through. Can you give me your number?"

There was silence on the other line. Talking to Kane, undoubtedly.

"I'll call you back in one hour. Be at your desk," she said, and hung up.

"She's a cool customer," Carl said.

"She's being careful."

"What are you thinking?" Carl asked.

"I have a feeling there's more going on here, and we're short of facts—as usual. Let's get back to the office."

"Weaver will have a coronary if we show up there."

"I know. Tell you what, you go see the art professor. I'll fly this one solo. I don't want you sucked down with me if I go under."

Carl shook his head. "Nope. We'll do this together. It's our case. It's our job. Let's run into the office, take the call, then go see the art professor. He's not going anywhere."

Paul nodded and started the Ford, grateful for Carl's support.

"What about Cruz's suicide?" Paul asked as he drove.

"She's right. There are a few every year at MIT. Harvard too. It's a pressure cooker and sometimes kids get overwhelmed."

"We just talked to him. He didn't seem the type."

"They never do, Paul."

"Is it related? I'm not a big believer in coincidences."

"Me either, but right now, we have other pressing issues," Carl said. "I'll look into it more when I have time."

Traffic was light in the late morning, and they soon reached the JFK Building. Weaver, thankfully, was nowhere to be seen. Paul called Operations to get the phone trace on the call with Mev.

"Cartwright Salvage," the female analyst said. "It's in South Boston, the Seaport."

No obvious connection to anything they'd found on the case, yet it was a new investigative direction. All facts accumulated to the truth over time. That worked in CID. Paul presumed it would work here. He took the address and phone number and checked his watch. Ten minutes.

"They're at an industrial site on the docks, probably squatting."

"It's kind of shady down there. Lots of abandoned warehouses, rotting docks. It's a good place to hide," Carl added.

"We take this next call, get as much additional data as we can, then go grab 'em."

The phone rang at one hour precisely. Carl was patched in from his desk.

"Agent Ostrowski?" Mev said.

"Yes, and Agent Philips is on the line with me. I'd again like to encourage you to come in."

"We aren't starting there," she said. "I need assurances you can provide protection, then we can discuss whether I come to you."

Could he provide protection? Get Cambridge P.D. to post a car? She would need to go to class, the grocery store. And how long could they keep this up? Fitz still hadn't made a move. It suddenly occurred to him that Weaver might also have pulled the agents who were watching Fitz, given the whole Gardner thing. If he didn't want Paul and Carl spending time on the case, Paul had to guess no one was. They'd miss Fitz at the dead drop and the payoff. Again. The whole case would unravel.

Without her in his sight, the only way he could provide "assurances" was to arrest Fitz. Get him to flip on his Russian handler. On the Mob. That would fulfill Mev's deal. And if he couldn't? Would Lanza honor the immunity anyway? He needed to talk to Weaver, then to Lanza, get some kind of deal put together. Even if it was with spit and scotch tape.

"I am working on protection," he said.

"That's not good enough."

If she ran, he'd have nothing. They needed her testimony to nail FitzRoy.

"Are you safe where you are?"

"Yes," she said without hesitation.

"Call me again tomorrow at 8:00 a.m. here in the office. By that point it will be safe for you to return."

"What are you going to do?"

"Figure it out. Trust me," he said.

The line was silent for several long moments.

"Is there anything else you need at this point?" he asked.

"No. Tomorrow, 8:00 a.m.," she replied and hung up.

Paul called Operations. Hopefully they were still at the docks now and hadn't only been down there to make the call to throw them off. His best bet was to grab her and bring her in, keeping his promise to keep her safe.

"Same trace?" he asked when he called back into Operations.

"Not even close."

Were they on the move?

"This one was from a trucking company in Kansas City, Kansas."

"How is that possible? You must have that wrong."

The ops analyst replied coolly, "No, agent, I do not. That's what the trace told us. Not my job to explain it. That's your department. This is mine."

Paul hung up, more stunned than stung by the analyst's rebuke.

"They're in Kansas City now."

"No, they're not," Carl said definitively. "They're probably not in Boston either and certainly not at the Seaport. They've taken over a phone system. Hackers do it all the time to get free phone calls and create huge party lines to chat with their buddies. We have no idea where they are."

"Come on, we're the FBI!"

"Yeah. They're better."

Paul clearly needed a new plan.

TUESDAY, MARCH 20, 1990

SITTING IN HIS CAR IN THE DARK, WAITING FOR THE REST of his raid team for the predawn rendezvous near Fitz's home, Paul reflected on his revised plan, rehashing the risks, second-guessing the compromises. Weaver had been surprisingly agreeable about Paul's proposal to grab FitzRoy given the evidence. He was less happy about Mev's absence but understood the logic in Paul's plan to get her back and get Fitz locked down.

AUSA Lanza was less accommodating. She had agreed to give him a few minutes before a scheduled court appearance. He hurried to flag down a cab on Cambridge Street, getting out at the John W. McCormack Post Office and Courthouse. He threw the cabbie a few bucks and hustled to the elevator, hoping to catch Lanza before his window closed.

Her office was an impressive wood-paneled acknowledgement of her station, and nicer than anything inside the FBI building. Behind her large oak desk was the requisite "I love me wall" filled with diplomas and citations, as well as a credenza featuring silver-framed photographs of her shaking hands with President Bush. With Ted Kennedy. Even with failed presidential candidate, and still Massachusetts Governor, Michael Dukakis. Paul's initial assessment of her ambition had clearly been insufficient.

He shared his proposed plan as she put on her suit coat and organized her briefcase, paying little attention to him. This would be quick but not painless.

"I understand your logic, Agent. However, let me be clear. We have a signed agreement that stipulates the terms of Miss Hayes' immunity deal. Merely delivering Randall FitzRoy does not fulfill those terms."

She paused and looked past him, considering alternatives. A wolf judging which sheep might be tastier. "But I can be reasonable."

Paul was waiting to witness that.

"Bring me FitzRoy's head on a platter and maybe we can work something out."

Maybe Fitz would confess, flip on the Mob and the Russians in return for a lighter sentence. After all, it wasn't like he was a hardened criminal. Paul couldn't imagine him withstanding a tough interrogation. A confession might be enough to back Lanza off Mev. Yet she was putting the decision, and Mev's fate, on his shoulders.

Paul hated the politics in the Bureau and had been able to steer clear of them for the most part. The DOJ felt like high school sometimes: petty squabbles, backstabbing, betrayal, anything to get ahead. No question, Lanza was playing the angles beautifully, no matter what it meant for Mev. Or for him.

Despite the uncertainty with Lanza, they were in a slightly better position than the day before. Late last night, as they were making this morning's arrest plans, Carl had received an email with previously undiscovered details on Fitz.

"Who sent this?" Paul had asked.

"Maybe Mev. Like with the calls, we'll never know. The return-path in the email header is invalid. There's no way to trace this."

Paul had no idea what Carl was talking about—nothing new there—but there were some tidbits in the email that might help throw Fitz off his game. Anything to make this all work. Understandably, Mev refused to return to Boston while an armed and angry Fitz was running around. And they'd never convict Fitz without her. Bringing him in was the only choice. Since he couldn't appeal to Lanza's nonexistent better nature, he'd have to roll the dice with Mev.

And then there was Cruz's suicide, which continued to nag at Paul. Carl had talked to both the MIT and Cambridge Police, who confirmed it. The investigation revealed a blow up with FitzRoy that same day over Cruz's place in Fitz's lab, and the medical examiner had made a determination of suicide. Of course, neither the M.E. nor the police knew about the FBI's confidential investigation, nor, given their own failure to respond to Mev's 911, about Fitz having threatened and attempted to kidnap Cruz's two house mates.

Paul had opened the conversation with the Cambridge Police Commissioner with that fact, then proceeded to upend their assumptions in the case of Cruz's death. The Commissioner was frustrated with Paul's reticence with regard to Fitz, Mev, and Jack's involvement. Nevertheless, Paul made it clear that the police had it wrong. The Commissioner, and the Chief Medical Examiner, swore they would reopen the case and investigate.

Paul had his own work to do.

Carl arrived with two other agents just before 5:30 a.m. Weaver had assigned four additional agents to the bust, two who would search the house while Paul and Carl took Fitz into custody and two who would search Fitz's office at MIT. They donned FBI raid windbreakers and drove slowly in the predawn quiet.

Paul rang the bell, then pounded on the door with his fist. Carl stood at his side, the two other agents were covering the perimeter of the house to make sure no one ran. Hard to know with Fitz. Was he crafty and dangerous, or merely greedy? Paul was wary. Still, this wasn't nearly as nerve-wracking as the domestic violence calls back when he'd been a cop in Chicago. On domestics, anything could happen.

After a few moments, the porch light snapped on, and Fitz opened the door. He had on a long silk robe and was staring at them through the glass storm door, blinking in the glare of the light.

"Agent Ostrowski?" he asked, confused.

Paul flashed his credentials. "We have a warrant to search the premises, Mr. FitzRoy, please let us in."

"I've told you before, it's Dr. FitzRoy," Fitz said as he opened the door.

Arrogant prick to the last, Paul thought, as he reached in and took Fitz's hand as if to shake it, snapped a cuff on that wrist, then turned him around and cuffed the other one. "Randall FitzRoy, I have a warrant for your arrest. In addition to the warrant to search your home, one is being executed now for your offices at MIT."

As Paul was finishing the Miranda Warning, Donna FitzRoy appeared at the foot of the hall stairs, a quilted robe wrapped tightly around her, the yapping white dog clutched to her chest. "Randy, what the hell is going on here?"

"Donna, shut up and call Greg Oster. Tell him to get his ass out of bed."

"Is he under arrest?" Donna asked Paul.

"We have a warrant for Dr. FitzRoy," Paul said, "as well as a warrant to search your home and property." He handed Fitz off to Carl and gave Donna FitzRoy the search warrant.

"Jesus, Donna, just do what I say for once. Call Greg now!"

Paul waved the other two agents in, and they moved to the back of the house, beginning their search.

Paul followed Carl up the stairs with Fitz to allow him to get dressed before they took him downtown. When they were ready to leave, and Paul had checked in with the other agents, they passed Donna FitzRoy, who was on the phone with their attorney.

"What will I tell the girls?" she asked Fitz.

"Who cares? Just get Greg down to the FBI."

Fitz was silent in the car and remained so while they processed and fingerprinted him. When they placed him in an interview room, he said he wouldn't answer any questions without his attorney. An hour passed before the lawyer, Greg Oster, showed up. He asked for a copy of the arrest warrant before conferring with Fitz.

An hour after that, the attorney waved Paul and Carl into the room. "I've spoken with my client and informed him of his rights. I've advised him not to speak with you or provide a statement. He, in turn, has told me he has nothing to hide from the FBI and will help however he can."

Oster looked exasperated, but Fitz had lost that deer in the headlights expression most arrestees demonstrated.

"Thanks Greg," Fitz said, smiling.

There it was: the fraternity boy charm that had undoubtedly kept him from being expelled when he went too far with the girls or was caught in "antics" that would have resulted in arrest and prison time for anyone else. No problem, Paul thought, as he got into interview mode. He knew how to deal with guys like Fitz.

"Our last conversation wasn't very productive Dr. FitzRoy. At that time, we asked you about an MIT connection to hacking, about possible espionage. And you denied any knowledge of it."

Paul opened his notebook. There wasn't anything he needed from it; the implication it was all written down often gave the suspect a sense the facts were incontrovertible, documented, damning.

"That wasn't quite true, was it? And, you should know, making false statements to the FBI is a crime in itself."

Paul liked to let that one sink in. Even denying your guilt to the FBI was a crime. Once that realization dawned on a suspect, that they'd multiplied their problems by acting innocent, it was easier to turn them.

"In fact, you have been using a piece of software to hack into the servers of technology companies, steal their secrets, and sell them to the Russians, isn't that right?"

"Fitz . . . " Oster started, his hand on Fitz's shoulder.

Fitz removed it calmly and didn't answer.

Fine, Ostrowski thought. Let's raise the stakes.

"Tell me. Do you know someone who goes by the name Raven?"

Fitz tilted his head like a confused Labrador. "I'm sorry agent. I have no idea who that is."

Paul watched Fitz closely. He was a damned good liar. Most psychopaths were.

"We've been led to believe you might have worked with him. Have you?"

"I don't know anything about that person or what you are talking about."

Paul pretended to consult his notebook again. "And you are sure you don't know Raven?"

"No, I've told you."

"How about Ekaterina Fedorova?" Paul asked.

Fitz visibly reacted. A link to Russian intelligence? At least a trail to follow. That was one of the pieces of information that was new to them from the email Carl had received. It suddenly dawned on Paul that Carl was the only recipient. The tech-savvy member of the team. The sender knew them. It had to be Mev. Was that information new since her proffer? He hoped so. If not, she could be in trouble.

"You might know her as Kate," Carl added. "How about her uncle?"

The email linked Fitz to Kate Fedorova. She was a student at MIT and her uncle was a Soviet Minister of Foreign Economic Relations at the Russian embassy in New York. He was undoubtedly part of the *rezidentura*, the group of spies inside the embassy, maybe even its leader, making her a "swallow," an operative who used sex to lure a man, an asset, into compromising himself and his country. And, Paul recalled, a man who seduced a woman for the same purpose was called a Raven. A coincidence, for sure, but the coincidences were starting to add up.

Fitz looked concerned. This was getting them somewhere.

"I understand you've had a few financial problems. And collections have been, let's say, aggressive."

Paul observed several emotions cross Fitz's face.

"I have it under control," he said at last.

Definitely not.

Paul again pretended to examine his notes. "Mev Hayes, your current researcher, she's involved in all of this?"

Fitz hesitated; his confidence lost for a moment like a cloud passing in front of the sun. This was a question he and Carl had debated. They didn't want to tip their hand, but Fitz would suspect her in any case.

"No. She's only a junior researcher I took in. Not very talented actually."

Excellent. Carl owed him ten bucks. Carl had been sure Fitz would throw her under the bus. Paul had bet on Fitz's ego—and won.

"You found yourself in a financial bind, so Kate Fedorova helped you, maybe made introductions to her uncle. Did you have sex with her?" The old-fashioned kind of honey trap.

"You are wasting your time," Fitz said, folding his arms across his chest. Solid defensive pose.

"We have nothing but time, Fitz."

WEDNESDAY, MARCH 21, 1990

THE BARDO. THAT'S WHAT CAME TO MIND AS SHE AND Jack walked fog-covered Islesboro the day before. Ghostly shapes formed when a breeze roiled the fog, creating a sense that there were other beings, other insubstantial presences, surrounding them inside the dense spruce woods.

At Northwest Missouri State, Mev had been required to take humanities electives, which at the time had felt like an annoying obstacle to her goal of getting a degree and getting the hell out. So, she'd picked one that sounded easy: A History of Religious Thought. Her own experience with religion had been the performative Sunday church appearances her father had required. She hoped the course wouldn't be more of that crap. She was pleasantly surprised at how interesting it actually was.

Mev was a programmer. Her discipline was grounded in logic: there were rules and if you followed them, you knew the outcome. She assumed most religions worked that way. Follow our rules and go to heaven. Don't and go to hell.

Even in computer programming there were exceptions, though: the "halting problem" for one. Alan Turing, the visionary who postulated so much of modern computing theory, demonstrated that given an arbitrary computer program and input, it was impossible to determine if the program would finish or run forever. There were certain things, it turned out, that could not be known.

What a surprise to find a similar idea in the History of Religious Thought. Sure, there were religions that forced a doctrine of faith upon their followers—believe or burn. Others, though, encouraged a more thoughtful engagement with the unknown.

Before, she'd thought she was in Limbo. That had been the wrong metaphor; she was in the Bardo. The true in-between place, between lives, between worlds, when a spirit can either progress on its karmic journey or descend into a state of lesser grace.

Mev could do nothing here except walk, breathe, eat, exist. The world before was gone, the world after was yet to come. She didn't remember all the other details about the Buddhist concept, what it included, how long it lasted. She did know she would need to face the world again soon. While it was pleasant to retreat here with Jack—to be hidden, to feel truly safe—her destiny was two hundred miles to the south.

Part of the feeling of suspension was the quiet she and Jack shared. She'd rarely known him as other than frenetic: music on, TV blaring, video games running, all overlaid with his constant commentary. It had been overwhelming at first.

She'd become accustomed to her mother's unhappy silence after her father's conviction. Mev had little idea what went on in her mother's head. She knew she struggled with resentment, despair, anger, and fear. They never spoke of any of it. Mev herself, shunned by her peers, by the community, had learned to keep her head down and mouth shut. Say nothing. Reveal nothing. But Jack was from another mold altogether.

She reflected again at how profoundly she'd underestimated him. All his odd, accumulated knowledge seemed like evidence of a lack of seriousness. But he'd known how to get them to this island safely, to make a fire, navigate in the fog and darkness. And now here she was, considering religious philosophy while fighting for her life. Maybe she'd had it backwards all along.

She'd been a happy high school girl whose only concern was making her prep school field hockey team. Then she was in the middle of a multimillion-dollar fraud investigation, broke, and mostly alone. She hadn't thought about, much less worked to understand, the consequences for her. She'd just gone into survival mode. Need money? Get the job that will give you the most hours, no matter how demeaning the work. Need to survive high school? Hide in the computer lab and blast through your coursework as fast as you can. Need to get the hell out of Missouri? Get through college and fly away. Get expelled? Take the MIT lifeline miraculously thrown to you and hold on tight. Find out all of it is a house built on sand? Reconsider your life choices.

In the fog, Jack was quiet. Waiting, as she was, uncertain what would happen to him, to her, to them. The reality of her fate wasn't going away. She would enter that next life. Still, she'd might as well get more karma before that rebirth. She took Jack's hand as they left the tree-shaded path and walked onto a small sand beach. The fog was even more dense over the water. Her future was just as opaque.

First thing this morning, she called Agent Ostrowski at 8:00.

"We have Dr. FitzRoy in custody," was his greeting.

Jack mouthed "What?"

She covered the receiver. "They arrested Fitz."

Jack pumped his fist in the air and danced around the kitchen like a goof. Mev tried not to laugh.

"That's fantastic," she said. "You caught him in the act?"

The phone was quiet, the long-distance static the only sound for a moment.

"No."

Jack stopped and again mouthed "what?" Mev shook her head.

This was bad. This meant no deal. No immunity.

"Why?"

"It was the only way I could see to make progress. There was no sign he'd sold the most recent material you and Agent Philips had assembled. You'd continue to be in danger as long as he was loose. And we need you here to testify. Otherwise, we'll never be able to bring a case against him. My boss and the Assistant U.S. Attorney agreed this was a good approach."

"And my deal?"

"I think we can still make that work."

"You *think?*"

"You've fulfilled your end of the bargain. You're not the FBI, it's not your responsibility to make the case."

Ostrowski seemed to be on her side. She wanted to believe him, but Frank Bishop had made it clear that the proffer didn't protect her from changing circumstances. She envisioned Jamie shaking her head at her naivete.

"Mev? You still there?" Ostrowski asked.

"Still here. Just thinking."

No matter how much Ostrowski might object to the AUSA's deal terms, Mev realized she was the only one who could change the outcome now. Time to exit the Bardo. Time to be reborn as the woman who would end this bullshit.

"I'll come home."

"I think that's a good call. Let's meet at our offices at 9:00 tomorrow morning and we'll discuss next steps."

She'd made her decision. She'd move forward. "OK. See you then."

After getting off the phone with Ostrowski, she filled Jack in on the details of Fitz's arrest.

"They blew up your deal without asking? What are you supposed to do next?"

"I'm done waiting for them. I'm done running."

She dialed Jamie's pager and when she called back, she held the phone receiver again so Jack could listen, too.

"I need help," Mev said.

"Our lady of perpetual disaster," Jamie replied.

Jack guffawed. Mev had to admit, it had truth to it.

"I'm trying to reform," Mev said.

"Then there's hope for you yet, babe. Tell me how I can help."

Mev filled her in on Fitz's arrest and the implications to her deal.

"Make sure Bishop is there with you. This might be a trap to get you back into custody so they can arrest you."

Bishop would be her next call.

"I guess we'll stay in a hotel until we figure this all out."

"No, the FBI can track you there, even if you pay cash. I've got a better idea," Jamie said, and gave her an address in Cambridge. And, to Mev's relief, Jamie didn't tell her she was being a fool.

Jack looked over her shoulder as she wrote down the address. "She is a resourceful one."

One last thing before they left. She used the hacked PBX to call Francis Bishop and fill him in. He wasn't exactly thrilled she'd agreed to meet with the FBI without a better guarantee but conceded that she either needed to stay on the run or come to an agreement with them. And delaying it would only serve to piss off Lanza.

"My office at 8:00 to prep, and we'll walk over together," Bishop said.

Jack closed up the house, turning off the water and electricity and putting everything back as they found it. On their way back to the Islesboro ferry terminal, Mev again considered the fog wafting through the spruce trees. It was hard to believe it had only been two days since they'd fled, and not even two months since she'd come to Cambridge. It felt like years ago, when she'd stepped into that lab and watched Fitz shame Hector. Poor Hector. Tears came into her eyes. So much loss. So much chaos.

"Hey, what is it?"

How to explain it? She shook her head. "Nothing. Everything."

Jack squeezed her hand, nodded.

The ferry was waiting at the dock to take them back to the world. As they crossed to Lincolnville, Mev had a feeling of momentum, of rolling downhill to her fate. Back to Cambridge. Back to the literal scene of the crime.

Two months from now would she be in prison? Or getting ready to graduate? And after that? The future was uncertain. She was not. She would face whatever came. Fortunately, not alone. Jamie would help. Jack would stand by her side. She squeezed his hand back.

There wasn't an official bus stop in Lincolnville at the ferry terminal; they had to flag down the bus as it came past. Mev looked around, sniffed the air, listened to the ocean. It was so quiet here, so beautiful. So distant from Cambridge and everything that had happened. Maybe after this was all over, in her unknown future, she and Jack could return, take a vacation back in the Bardo.

The bus ride to South Station in Boston felt twice as long as the ride to Maine. On the ride up her fear and fatigue had combined to make much of the trip a blur; now her decision to face her fate gave her a mental clarity that made the world outside the bus window more present.

Mev considered the small towns facing their harbors, looking toward their sailing past, yet surviving into the present. Same for her, facing what had happened, what she'd done, and figuring out how to make it work when it wasn't the future she had, or could have, imagined.

She and Jack were both stumbling with fatigue as they trudged up the Red Line T station steps at Central Square and shuffled the two blocks to the address Jamie had provided. It was on Green Street, not far from the Manray, the club Jack had taken her to for her birthday a lifetime ago.

Green Street was poorly lit, pockmarked with potholes, and lined with dilapidated buildings. Mev jumped when Jamie popped from one of the shadowy doorways. She heard Jack gasp.

"Jesus, you almost gave me a heart attack," he said to Jamie.

"That might have been fun to watch," she said, renewing their banter. "It's right here." She brandished a key and opened a padlock that secured a makeshift plywood door. They closed it behind them and waited in the pitch dark until Jamie flicked on a flashlight. She handed one to each of them, leading them up a staircase, light beams bobbing in the darkness ahead.

"No power in here, so keep the flashlights. And watch this missing step."

Mev stepped over it, Jack following suit. When they reached the third floor, their flashlight beams revealed a large open room. Dingy but swept clean, with bare wood floors and paint peeling off what had been beautiful scrollwork on the ceiling.

"What is this?" Mev asked, her voice echoing in the empty room.

"A squat," Jamie replied. "You need a place off everyone's radar. No one will look for you in this building; it's a dump. Two of the apartments downstairs have person-sized holes in the walls. The owner was behind on taxes, so the city foreclosed, and now the building just sits here and rots."

"How do you know about it?" Mev asked.

"The owner did business with my dad. Some drug thing got him five years in Walpole. I heard my dad talking about it, wishing he had the building. Wants his own little slumlord empire. I checked it out in case I ever needed a place to bolt."

Mev sighed, leaning against the wall, feeling like there were iron weights in her jacket pockets. "I'm exhausted."

"Sleep," Jamie said. "This is as safe a place as you are going to find. Central Square missed out on Cambridge's yuppification, so this is off everyone's radar. Here's the key to the padlock; lock it behind me."

WEDNESDAY, MARCH 21, 1990

ASAC WEAVER CALLED PAUL AND CARL INTO A MEETING. Usually not a good sign. AUSA Lanza was already in the room. Definitely not a good sign.

Lanza launched right in. "There has been a complaint to the DOJ Office of the Inspector General concerning your handling of the Randall FitzRoy case."

"That's ridiculous . . . " Paul started. A small calming hand gesture from Weaver silenced him.

"It's my understanding that the threat Miss Hayes claims to have received was dismissed by the Cambridge Police Department as a false report, something you failed to mention when we discussed his detainment," Lanza said. "I have concerns that we have acted precipitously in arresting Mr. FitzRoy."

Dr. FitzRoy Paul thought and hated himself for it.

Lanza had been perfectly happy for Paul to arrest him the day before.

"We had a warrant, duly signed by a judge," Paul replied.

"Nonetheless, given the complaint filed in this case and the scrutiny on it, coupled with our lack of tangible evidence and the absence of a witness against him, I don't have any other option than to release him," she said.

"We have Mev's—Miss Hayes'—testimony on record as part of her plea agreement."

"An agreement that she has not fulfilled," AUSA Lanza said. "And as you know, *Agent,* prior statements out of court are inadmissible hearsay."

Paul knew that, and also knew its exception. "We could ask for a Sirois hearing to make her statements admissible. The witness was threatened. Miss Hayes' flight was the direct result of a deadly threat by Randall FitzRoy."

"And we come full circle, Agent. No proof of any of the above. Randall FitzRoy is free to go. The only criminal we have evidence against is Miss Hayes. It's high time to consider the case against her."

Paul wanted to object, but her tone was final. This was wrong—it felt political—yet Paul couldn't quite figure all the angles. And if the obvious tension in his jaw was any indication, Carl clearly felt the same.

There was more they could get from him. He wanted to talk, and he would screw up, incriminate himself. Paul was sure of it.

"I'll ask you return to your role supporting the team at the Gardner," Weaver added.

"Sir . . ." Paul began. This time it was Lanza who cut him off.

"Don't make this worse, Agent. You let Mev Hayes slip through your fingers. She's who we need in an interrogation room. I want another crack at her. After all of this I'm not sure how complete her proffer was. We might add a few charges."

Before Paul could object again, Lanza turned and left the office. Weaver gestured to close the door.

"I'm not quite sure what's going on here myself," Weaver admitted, surprising both Paul and Carl. "This came from high in the command structure in D.C. Someone with connections made this happen, far above my level. For now, he's free. Longbow continues. In the meantime, support the team at the Gardner."

"What about Mev Hayes? She's in the wind."

"She's still coming here tomorrow morning, correct?"

"Yes, sir, I just . . ."

"We'll take it from there. Dismissed."

"Paul?" Carl asked as they walked to the elevators.

"We're done. You heard him. We let FitzRoy go and move on."

"We're quitting? Really?" Carl asked.

This was a bad move. Carl was a young agent and, so far, had been by-the-book. Paul knew well the cost of letting the job become your whole life and of striking back at the FBI hierarchy. He thought about that cost every night when he went home to his shithole apartment in Eastie and wondered how his daughter's day had been.

Carl still had a life and a career in front of him. But he made his own decisions. He might look like the computer geeks they'd been talking to. He wasn't. He was a fully qualified FBI Special Agent and deserved Paul's respect.

"I'm sure as hell not going to stop. You can. And should."

"No way, man. No way I'm stopping now."

Paul hoped that would be his answer. "Works for me, partner. Fitz is no genius. There's got to be more we can find."

"What about Mev? She's on her way back now."

Paul considered it. "She'll still be safer with us. I'm just not exactly sure how."

WEDNESDAY, MARCH 21, 1990

HOW CAN THIS BE HAPPENING TO ME? FITZ HAD REPEAT-
ed to himself as he was being delivered to the FBI holding cell the
morning before. He'd known enough to ask for his lawyer and to be
quiet in the back seat of the unmarked FBI vehicle. His panic rose even
higher as they fingerprinted him and stuck him in the interview room.

His attorney, Greg Oster, finally arrived, wild-eyed. "Fitz, what the
hell? What's going on? They told me what they're charging you with. You
didn't say anything, did you?"

Fitz felt a flash of anger, bringing him back to himself. How stupid
did Greg think he was? He wasn't some teenager pulled into the police
station with a joint in his pocket. And in that moment, he'd felt the fear
fall away. He would dodge this. Of course he would. He always came out
on top, eventually.

"I'm not an idiot, Greg. It's all bullshit."

"Fitz," Greg said, "this is the FBI, and they are telling me it's an
espionage case."

"It has nothing to do with me. I think we should cooperate with this
investigation and get it over as quickly as possible."

"That's a huge mistake. These guys are pros. Anything you say here
can be used against you in any kind of prosecution. It's better to say
nothing if you're sure they have nothing. And lying to them is a crime."

Fitz smiled. What did Greg know anyway? He was a real estate
attorney. Fitz was the expert here. Cat and mouse. He could play that
game with the best of them.

"If this is espionage, and related to my work in a way I'm unaware of, don't I have a duty to help the FBI?"

He hadn't said anything incriminating and they wouldn't find anything in their search. There wasn't any evidence at home or in his office. He wasn't sure what they had on Mev, but she'd keep her mouth shut given what he had on her. He had been surprised that Ostrowski knew about Kate, yet pleased when he went down the path of asking about Raven. Clearly, their information wasn't perfect.

And that had been borne out. They'd discovered his financial situation, so what? That wasn't a crime. All he needed to do was get free and make that final score. Then he'd be gone. He'd lull them into a sense of complacency. They'd never see it coming. Stay cool. Deny everything.

"I can't help you if you don't come clean with me," Greg pleaded.

"Don't be ridiculous. I got this." Fitz replied.

And sure enough, even after hours of questioning the day before, he'd been released this morning. His cell door had opened to reveal Greg Oster and an agent who told him he was free to go. He didn't know how or who made it happen. He figured he had a fairy godmother somewhere in the FBI, no doubt the same person who'd identified Mev Hayes for him, who had later warned him about the surveillance.

He thought back to the interview and Ostrowski fumbling around in the dark. It became more and more amusing each time he replayed it in his mind. He wished it had been Ostrowski standing beside Greg. He was a smug asshole, that one, pretending he had any right at all to accuse Fitz, that he knew anything about him.

Of course Fitz had prevailed.

He changed back into his own clothes, and he and Greg followed the agent to the elevators. When they got off in the lobby, Greg turned to him and said, "You appear to have friends in high places, Fitz. Charges dropped. You're all set.

"Oh, and that agent asked to talk to you alone. Be careful what you say," Greg said, pointing to a man smoking a cigarette in the concrete courtyard outside the JFK Building.

Fitz shook his hand, relieved. "Greg, I owe you. Lunch is on me next time."

Greg chuckled, his belly straining his suit coat buttons. "More than lunch, I think. Glad this all worked out."

Fitz walked toward the agent, a well-dressed older man with the blown capillaries of a guy who liked to drink netted across his nose and cheeks.

When he noticed Fitz, he took one last drag, flicked his cigarette butt away, and extended his hand. "Dr. FitzRoy. Let's take a stroll."

The agent walked away from the building and into the barren hardscape of City Hall Plaza before speaking again.

"I hope you appreciate what's been done for you," he said.

"Who are you in all of this?" Fitz asked.

"That's not important. What is important is that you fulfill your obligations."

Did he mean the loan? How was he connected to all of this?

"Trust me when I say that if you don't, time in a cell will feel like vacation. This is a one-time get out of jail free card."

The threat was serious. All the more reason to leave this petty bullshit behind. Flush with cash, he could enjoy his just desserts.

The agent, if he was an agent, turned to walk away, then looked back. "By the way, Mev Hayes will be in the FBI office at 9:00 a.m. tomorrow. I'm sure you can persuade her to help you."

Standing alone in the deserted plaza, Fitz mulled over a plan involving Mev, BBN, a million dollars or more, and a life of luxury in a warm, non-extradition country.

He dreamed of a Cuban beach.

THURSDAY, MARCH 22, 1990

PAUL WAITED IMPATIENTLY FOR MEV TO ARRIVE, FRUS-
trated with the cards he'd been dealt. He'd felt he had no other choice
other than to get Fitz off the street. Thought he'd had support, now
that was all screwed up. Now, Lanza was saying that even with Mev's
testimony it was unlikely they'd get a conviction. Paul disagreed, but it
wasn't his call.

They'd been ordered back onto the Gardner heist case and were
only in the office to give the bad news. Lanza had asserted that Mev's
testimony felt thin in retrospect. That was just Lanza bending in the
political wind. She didn't want to buck the higher ups in Justice, but she
wanted a win. Mev would make a perfect patsy.

Reception called to let him know Mev and Francis Bishop had
arrived, and Paul met them at the elevators. Once in the conference
room, he began. No reason to delay the inevitable.

"I'm sorry. We had no way to reach you. We didn't know where
you were."

"Reach me? Why?" Mev asked.

Bishop looked suspicious: a man steeped in punch/counterpunch.

"Randall FitzRoy. He's been released and the investigation into
him suspended."

"What?" Mev and Bishop said simultaneously.

"It's complicated," Ostrowski said. He gestured for them to sit.
"We received word from the Justice Department to back down. That
investigation is on hold."

Bishop, ever vigilant, caught Paul's careful wording. "Hang on, you said *that* investigation. Which one is still open?"

"The ongoing pursuit of the hacker Raven and any related crimes."

Not yet seated, Bishop leaned aggressively across the table. This guy must be a pit bull in the courtroom. No wonder he and Lanza tangled during Mev's proffer—two alpha predators facing off.

"This is an ambush," Bishop said. "We came here to learn about the plan to protect Mev from potential threats against her. Instead, you're telling us you've released from custody the very person you know poses an imminent danger to her, *and* that Mev's under threat of indictment—again—despite our immunity agreement? It's bad faith, Agent Ostrowski."

Bishop mopped at his forehead, then stared hard at Paul. "This is Lanza, right? You're just her messenger boy?"

Paul felt a flash of fury, the characterization cutting too close to the truth. Letting Fitz go was ridiculous. Going after Mev felt downright vindictive. Frankly, the whole thing sucked.

"Unless you're charging her with a crime, we're leaving," Bishop said. "In all my years as a defense attorney, I've never seen anything like this. And Michelle has the gall to tear up the agreement but not the balls to tell me herself. I expected better. On second thought, no, I guess I didn't. Come on, Mev, we're done here."

She stood, both hands on the conference table, staring down at Paul. "You're telling me I'm on my own? And you released Fitz despite what I told you? Despite what he did?"

"As I said, there's a Department of Justice complaint about investigative irregularities."

"You believe an anonymous asshole more than the person who handed you Fitz? More than the person he tried to grab at gunpoint?"

Paul had no good answer.

"Then we are definitely done here," Mev said, preceding Bishop out of the room.

He could hardly blame her.

Carl accompanied him to Weaver's office. "I don't see this going well," Carl said.

"Me either," Paul said as he knocked on the office door.

THURSDAY, MARCH 22, 1990

JUST AS PAUL FEARED, LANZA WAS SITTING ACROSS from Weaver.

"Agent, where are we on Longbow?" Lanza asked.

Yet again, whatever happened, it was now his fault.

"Miss Hayes and her attorney did not take the release of FitzRoy well. She is disappointed we would not protect her or honor the evidence she provided us."

Lanza was truly surprised, and looked to Weaver for support. He was his stoic self.

"Are you kidding me?" she said. "Hayes isn't some damsel in distress, Ostrowski. She is a criminal who knowingly violated the Computer Fraud and Abuse Act and aided in the commission of espionage against the United States. I want a conviction. FitzRoy is off the table for now, which is frustrating, but we can still score a win. Hold her until I get the charges finalized then we'll proceed from there."

"I released her," Paul said with no small satisfaction. "We had nothing to charge her on."

Lanza was up and out of her chair, eye to eye with him in her stilettos, her perfume not an enticement, more of a chemical attack. "What is wrong with you? You knew my intention. Longbow continues. She is our primary suspect besides FitzRoy. What did you think? That I was going to give her a tiny spank on her ass and send her on her way? She goes to prison, Goddammit."

She turned to Weaver. "Mitch, what kind of operation are you running here? Are you collecting the mental defectives from the other field offices?"

The tension in Weaver's shoulders was clear, yet he remained silent.

Lanza turned back to Paul. "You did this on purpose, didn't you? I hear you talk about this girl. You have some kind of daddy savior complex?"

Paul held his tongue. He knew she was baiting him as she would a witness in the courtroom. If her approach and her tone before made him frustrated with her, now it made him disgusted with her.

His silence, Weaver's silence, only enraged her more. "I want blood," she shouted, as she stormed from Weaver's office.

Paul was relieved she'd left. He was barely holding himself together. The strategies they'd taught in his anger management classes were wholly insufficient for this scenario. He looked at Carl, who looked stunned. This was obviously a new experience for him: front line combat in Department of Justice politics.

Weaver, however, was a veteran of those politics. He stood slowly, buttoned his suit coat. Took long, slow breaths like the ones Paul learned to use in anger management.

"That was unprofessional," Weaver said.

Understatement of the year. Paul's assessment would be far more graphic.

Then Weaver's command presence returned. "Call the Hayes girl and get her butt back in here. Let's find out what else she knows and get FitzRoy back where he belongs."

The whole floor was quiet as Paul and Carl returned to their desks. No one wanted to be near them, for fear of straying into the blast radius of Weaver and AUSA Lanza.

Paul called Mev's house in Cambridge several times, then contacted Francis Bishop, telling him that they were willing to deal—a stretch—and needed to find Mev. Bishop said they'd parted ways in the lobby of the FBI building. He had no idea where she was.

"Let's go find her," Paul said to Carl.

This wasn't about Paul's sense of burnout and betrayal anymore. He wasn't going to stand by and let a traitor, a predator, walk free and help Lanza set up a victim in his place.

When they arrived at Linnaean Street, they found the house as they had on Sunday: all the vehicles present, the house quiet and empty.

"They must be staying somewhere else," Carl said. "Makes sense, I would if I was her."

They stopped by the lab at MIT. No Mev, no Fitz. No one had seen either of them for days.

"Look, we're in Cambridge anyway, let's see if Tom Bergstrom knows something. Heck, they might even be there," Paul said, trying to convince himself.

Paul had checked his notes and found Bergstrom's work address at MIT: Building 20. Inside, they had to ask directions three times to navigate the maze of the World War II era structure, finally finding Bergstrom working in a glorified telephone closet.

"This had better be about returning my equipment," Bergstrom said.

Paul had completely forgotten about that.

"We're working on that Mr. Bergstrom. We'll have it processed and back to you soon. This is about another matter."

"Of course, there's an ulterior motive. Haven't you harassed me enough?"

"It's a simple question and doesn't affect you in any way. Do you know how to get in touch with Mev Hayes and Jack Kane?"

Bergstrom didn't hesitate. "I have no idea. They went dark a week ago. I haven't talked to either of them."

"Mr. Bergstrom, Tom, please. We need to contact Mev."

"Can't help you."

"Can't or won't?" Paul was losing his patience.

"Both."

"We're in the middle of an investigation and I need to speak with Mev. I need to know if you know how to contact her."

"Sorry," Bergstrom said, shaking his head. "I got nothing for you."

"What if I named you as a material witness and brought you in?"

Carl shifted his weight. Paul knew he was escalating and screwing this up, but needed to find her.

"Then I'd call my lawyer and we'd all sit together in silence."

He needed this to go a different way. He needed to take chances.

"She's in danger. As is Jack Kane, who is with her," he said.

Bergstrom shook his head.

"It's true," Carl added.

"How so?" Bergstrom asked.

"I can't give you details," Paul said, "but I need to find her and speak with her. Do you have any idea where she is?"

"Sorry, I honestly have no idea."

Back in their Taurus, Paul rested his forehead on the steering wheel. "Is he screwing with us?"

"I don't think so."

"FitzRoy is back out there, and he's already waved a gun at her. The officers watching his house haven't seen him since we released him. We have no idea where he is. And no idea where she is. We can't protect her if we can't find her."

Paul navigated the car through the MIT campus. "We could try Jamie Brennan."

"Connor told us to stay away from her and her family."

"We don't have anyone else connected to Mev to talk to. Cruz is dead and Kane's on the run with her. Plus, screw Connor."

Paul wound his way out of Cambridge, back over the Charles, through downtown Boston toward Southie. He didn't know if they would find Jamie at home, but he needed to put this case back on the rails. Could they reach Kane's family? He was pretty sure they lived somewhere in the area.

With no snow on the ground, they were able to find parking nearer the house in Southie this time. By the time they approached, an older man was standing behind the screen door.

"What?" the balding man said. He was wearing a ripped T-shirt Paul assumed had once been white, now a dingy gray. His hands were grimy, his fingernails blackened with grease.

Paul held up his badge. "I'm Special Agent Paul Ostrowski, and this is Special Agent Carl Philips. We are here to talk to your daughter Jamie."

"Huh," the man said, squinting at each of their badges. "She's not here."

"Where, then?" Paul asked.

The man shrugged. "Wouldn't tell you if I did know, Mr. Special Agent."

Paul didn't want to lose his shit on this guy, but he was losing patience. "What's your name?"

The man stood silent, an annoying smirk on his face.

"I'm assuming you are James Brennan, and I need to know where your daughter is. I have one simple question for her."

The man turned and walked back into the house. Paul reached for the screen doorknob and Carl stepped in front of him.

Carl spoke in an urgent whisper. "We don't have probable cause. He's done nothing. It'll be bad if we mess with him."

Paul removed his hand and the man returned to the door. He pushed an FBI business card against the screen, bowing it out, shoving the FBI seal and the name Allen Fucking Connor in Paul's face.

"Get off my porch, Mr. Special Agent," James Brennan said as he slammed the inner door.

Sliding behind the steering wheel, Paul was dreading telling Weaver they couldn't find her when she'd been in the office minutes before.

The radio chattered. "Agent Ostrowski, there's been a shooting in Cambridge. It involves your suspect, FitzRoy."

Carl grabbed the mic. "How many casualties?"

Paul accelerated and flipped on lights and siren.

"We don't have that information yet."

"Where? Where am I going?" Paul asked.

Carl repeated the question and got back a Cambridge address.

"That's Central Square," Carl said. "I know the way."

In between directions that had them zigzagging through Southie streets, Carl keyed the mic, said they were en route, and asked for more information.

"Cambridge Police are on site. We'll relay information as we have it."

THURSDAY, MARCH 22, 1990

MEV LAUGHED OUT LOUD WHEN FITZ SAID, "I HAVE a gun."

She'd left the Federal Building, relieved that she hadn't been detained. She parted ways with Bishop then joined the queue of commuter pedestrians streaming underground at the Government Center T Station, then transferred at Park Street to the Red Line on her way to Central Square. She was angry about Fitz's release and the DOJ reneging on the deal but didn't have a concrete plan of action yet. She was anxious to start brainstorming next steps with Jack and Jamie, who'd promised she'd blow off work to help them wrap things up. Not quite.

After she knocked on the Green Street plywood door, Jack peeked out next to the chain then fumbled with the makeshift lock, saying "hang on, it's stuck."

As the door opened, she heard Fitz's voice, then felt the gun barrel in her ribs and his arm wrapping around her neck. Jack, wide-eyed, off-balance, stumbled backward into the darkened hallway, and Fitz followed, closing the plywood door behind them.

When Jack recovered his balance and looked up the stairs, Fitz pointed a small revolver at him. "You first," he said.

Fitz followed up the stairs, waving the gun to urge them forward. Mev complied, careful to skip the missing step; disappointed when Fitz skipped it, too.

Jamie was at the top of the stairs. "Who the fuck are you?" she demanded, hands on hips, radiating a fearlessness Mev didn't currently share.

Maybe Jamie had seen guns before, maybe even been in a situation like this.

"Shut it, kid," Fitz snapped. He gestured with the gun. "Sit."

Mev and Jack sat together, backs to the wall. Jamie took it slow, settling away from them. She was calm and watched Fitz carefully.

"I need you one more time, like I said. Then you're done."

"I gave you DEMON. Hacking targets."

"It didn't work on what I wanted. I need your help." He gestured with the revolver.

Mev's initial fear was starting to be replaced with something else. Anger. Everyone except Jack and Jamie had failed her. Even Ostrowski, who claimed to believe her, had failed her. She was tired of it. Tired of being let down, tired of being betrayed.

Fitz was clearly desperate, and she wasn't going to antagonize him. Still, he had to know he wasn't going to get out of this a free man.

Even if she gave him real intelligence, he wasn't going to get far. Jack and Jamie would call the FBI, tell them what happened. When they realized she'd been in danger all along, they'd grab him. Hopefully quickly—before he had time to hurt her, even kill her.

"OK, OK," she said, standing.

He gestured with the gun for her to walk in front of him. As soon as he turned to follow, she heard a commotion, Jack lunging, fumbling for Fitz's gun hand, the gun going off. The sound stunned her, and it took a moment for her to realize that Jack was hit.

He was on the floor, gasping, hands wrapped around his upper thigh, blood seeping through his fingers and pooling on the dusty wooden floor.

Mev watched, unable to help, as Jamie crawled over to Jack and pulled out a bandanna which she pressed down on the wound. Fitz observed each of them in turn. Was he going to shoot them?

Jamie returned his gaze, daring him to act. Mev hadn't initially imagined Fitz would shoot. Now he was definitely going to jail, so who knew what he might do?

Fitz appeared to come to a decision. Mev tensed, waiting for the sound of the gun.

He grabbed her arm, yanked. "Let's go."

Jamie didn't move and didn't take her eyes off Fitz. Mev didn't move either, unsure what he meant. Go where?

"I'll shoot you, too," he said, pushing her ahead of him toward the stairs. If she ran, would he kill Jack and Jamie? Shoot her in the back? Screw that. She wouldn't give him the pleasure. If she went with him, she could buy time for Jamie to call an ambulance and Ostrowski.

At the outer door, Fitz put the gun in his pocket. "We're going to walk a few blocks to another house. You're going to be cool, not make a fuss, not run off, or I *will* kill you."

He kept one hand in a vice grip on her upper arm, the other in the pocket with the gun as they walked down Green Street to Western Avenue. Mev could see the Cambridge Police Headquarters just down the block as they turned toward Mass Ave. Unfortunately there wasn't a single cop in sight, and no one on the street paid them any mind, even as Fitz forced her along.

"God dammit, move!" he grunted.

Mev guessed no more than fifteen minutes had actually gone by when they approached an unremarkable multifamily house on Inman Street. Fitz pushed her up the front stairs, then fumbled in the pocket with the gun, needing to let her go and pull it out to get at his keys.

She should have run, but he had the door open and the gun back in his right hand before she could fully consider the possibility.

Or consider what would happen next.

THURSDAY, MARCH 22, 1990

PAUL DROVE AT A RECKLESS PACE, HOPING NO ONE pulled in front of him on the narrow Southie streets. He gunned it onto the Expressway and kept it at 70 mph even as he took the exit back to surface roads. The Boston drivers weren't quick enough to get out of his way, forcing him to weave between cars on Storrow Drive. The traffic on Mass Ave. was even heavier, and the Cambridge drivers refused to move over, despite lights and sirens. By the time he screeched to a halt on Green Street, he was sweating.

They'd gotten no news along the way, and he imagined a range of scenarios. Mev dead. Fitz dead. Kane dead. All bad.

Cambridge Police were all over the street, as were ambulances, but that didn't tell him anything. They'd be dispatched no matter what. Paul jumped from the car, rushing toward the dilapidated building that was the focus of activity.

"Ostrowski, FBI," he blared, badge out, as he plowed past the officer logging entry to the secured area.

Inside the building the narrow stairs were clogged with officers. Arm out like a battering ram, he mounted the stairs, shouldering officers aside, Carl following close behind. On the third floor a paramedic crew was working on a victim, blood visible beside the body. Paul muscled through the ring around the paramedics.

It was Kane, who appeared conscious. To Paul's surprise, Jamie Brennan was behind him, talking to two officers. Where was Mev? He knelt next to Kane.

"Hey, back off," the paramedic said.

"How is he?" Paul asked. It was a leg wound and they appeared to have the bleeding under control. An officer reached down and grabbed Paul's shoulder, attempting to pull him back.

"You'll lose that hand, buddy," Paul said. Carl pulled the officer aside.

"Kane. Jack. Where's Mev?"

"Don't know," he groaned. "Fitz took her."

"His gun?" Paul asked nodding toward Kane's leg.

"Yeah."

"She hurt?"

"Hope not. He took her."

"Where?"

Jack shook his head.

"242 Inman Street, Apartment B," Jamie Brennan answered.

Paul stared at her, incredulous.

She smirked. "He thinks no one knows about it."

He didn't recall that fact being in the dossier about Fitz that had been sent to Carl. The one he'd assumed came from Mev. There was so much here he didn't understand, but he needed to move. He turned to Carl for help.

"Not far. Inman Square. Maybe five minutes," Carl said before Paul could ask.

"I need officers," Paul said to the room. One of the Cambridge cops questioning Jamie was a sergeant, and he called to officers to follow.

"Go get the fucker," Kane groaned from the floor.

"You got it. Hang in there."

Paul gathered the officers on the sidewalk. "We have a hostage situation here. Randall FitzRoy, a faculty member at MIT, and currently a suspect in an FBI investigation, has shot the man inside, and taken a student known to him, Margaret "Mev" Hayes. He is armed and most likely holding her in an apartment several blocks from here at 242 Inman Street."

"I live on that block." Novak, his badge read. "The building's got three apartments. Rent controlled. Mostly working folks."

"Good. Our first responsibility is to make sure there are no more casualties, not Mev Hayes, not one of the neighbors. He believes the apartment is a secret, so we have the element of surprise."

"How well do you know the house?" Paul asked Novak.

"I walk my dog past there every day."

Tailor-made surveillance. "Here's what we're going to do. We are going to hang back, and you are going to go home and grab your dog. Keep your cruiser out of sight—we don't want to spook him. Get as much intel as you can: Is he there? Can you see Hayes? Who's at home in the other apartments? Everything you can gather. Is there anyone home at your place?"

"My wife works until eight."

"Kids?"

"No kids."

"Good." Paul's thoughts turned to Becky.

"Novak, we'll stage out of your house. Do we have good visibility to the apartment?"

"Pretty good. I'm a few houses down, on the other side of the street."

"Let's get going." He didn't call it in. Paul wasn't sure what Weaver would say and didn't want to take the chance that he would order Paul to wait for reinforcements. Better to ask for forgiveness than permission.

They entered through the back yard of Novak's house, careful not to pour into the neighborhood all at once. Nosy neighbors could ruin their chances. Novak changed into civvies, grabbed his dog. One of the officers handed Ostrowski a pair of binoculars. He opened the curtains, pulled back into the shadows, and surveilled the apartment.

"Do what you usually do. Don't rubberneck. Pay attention," Paul advised.

Novak led his shaggy golden retriever through the back door and around the house, ambling down the street, letting the dog take the lead.

He was going too damned slow. He'd be noticed.

"Anything?" Carl asked.

"We'll have to wait on Novak."

Novak had told him which door and windows belonged to Apartment B, only Paul couldn't see into the house. They needed whatever Novak could give them. Paul watched him return, walking up the near side of Inman then around to the back door.

"Jesus, I told you not to be so obvious. You were crawling down the street," Paul said to Novak as he unclipped the leash.

"Roscoe's ten years old. That's as fast as he goes. Trust me, it was a typical walk. In any case, I have good news. The Kents and Mr. Emmons don't seem to be home, so the rest of the building is empty."

"Does FitzRoy have Mev in the apartment?" Carl asked.

"I couldn't get a good view, but someone was moving around in there."

"We still have the element of surprise. We need to go now."

"Paul," Carl waved him over to the side of the living room. "Weaver won't like this."

"I know. He'll want us to wait, get a negotiator, tons of backup. Helicopters, hell, he'd want the Hostage Rescue Team. We have FitzRoy. Right there. We need to go grab him."

"Paul, I hear you," Carl said, lowering his voice. "These are city cops. They don't do hostage. That's our job."

"Couldn't agree more. Let's go do it."

Novak sketched the neighborhood for them, showing how to get behind the houses on the other side of Inman. They could stay hidden until they were just in front of the apartment. Up the stairs, in the door. Novak said it was a one bedroom, and small. They'd be able to clear the space quickly.

Paul tried not to let the recklessness of this path make him second guess himself. Carl was in, even if he harbored doubts. If it went bad, they'd both take heat.

They moved through the back yards, climbing fences and squeezing between mature bushes to stay concealed. There it was. Ten wooden steps to the door, and in. If they could navigate those stairs quietly, they could surprise Fitz, which would be critical. Paul drew his SIG Sauer and assessed the team. He and Carl in their Kevlar vests and raid jackets, Cambridge P.D. in their blues, everyone sweating from the exertion. The young sandy-haired officer in front had the ram at the ready to breach the door.

The officer with the ram climbed the stairs carefully, Paul following, his gun in a tactical grip. When they reached the top, Paul checked Carl, who gave a thumbs up. He was enjoying this.

Paul touched the young officer on the shoulder, and he swung the ram. Just not hard enough. It bounced off the door, having only cracked the frame. Paul could hear the intake of breath behind him. The officer swung again, this time with everything he was worth, and the door crashed open.

Paul rushed past it, with Carl right behind.

And Fitz waiting for them.

THURSDAY, MARCH 22, 1990

FITZ HAD PUSHED HER INTO A SMALL APARTMENT, AND dead bolted the door behind them. Gesturing with the gun to a wooden desk with a putty gray IBM PC on it, he told Mev to sit. She reached around the back to flick the big red power switch and the heard the low whir of the hard drive disks beginning to spin as the machine booted.

As she waited, Mev let herself wonder what would happen after. Would he kill her? Maybe. In any case, the FBI would catch him this time and send him to prison. And if she made it through this? The proffer deal was completely screwed up. She'd hacked Thinking Machines, and if she was about to hack again, she might very well follow Fitz to prison.

"What can't you find with DEMON that's so damn important?" she asked.

"BBN," he said.

Bolt Beranek & Newman. BBN. Thinking Machines was the third company to ever register an Internet domain name—Think.com. BBN.com had been the second. A major designer of internet protocols, and acoustic and military technologies. And undoubtedly a secure site.

Of course that wasn't why he'd needed her. The version of DEMON he had was a fake, devised by her and Carl. Even if he knew what he was doing—which he definitely didn't—he'd never get it to work. Their plan to trap him had trapped her instead.

"This is going to take time," she said.

"I'd hurry if I were you," he said, waving the gun.

"That isn't helping my concentration." She resisted adding "asshole" at the end.

He said nothing in reply.

She turned back to the computer, the green screen flickering slightly as it refreshed the DOS C:\ prompt. All she needed to do was to connect to the MIT network and she could go from there.

Nevertheless, she found herself psyched for the challenge. Hacking one of the most sophisticated sites on the internet. With a literal gun to her head. Why the hell not?

She activated the external dial-up modem, called a number at MIT she now knew by heart. The modem lights flashed, and the speaker chirped, popped, dinged, and squealed, before going silent. She was in, connected to the Unix machine on the other end.

BBN had the entire 24.0.0.0 internet IP address range assigned to them for internal use. She started there. A full IP address range contained 256 x 256 x 256 possible addresses. Even with DEMON screening them, this was going to take a while.

She remote-logged into one of the hijacked servers Jamie had shared with her and grabbed DEMON from a hidden directory where she'd stashed it. She fed the program the address range and recursion parameters and let it run against BBN's network.

She considered Fitz, gun resting on the dining table behind her, his expression lost, a million miles away.

"This has to run a while," she said.

"I need you to hurry."

"There's over sixteen million addresses on their internal network alone, so it's gonna be a minute."

MIT and BBN were on the backbone of the internet, the successor to the research ARPAnet that MIT, BBN, the Advanced Research Projects Administration, the Department of Defense, and others had created. Heck, they *were* the backbone of the internet. Even so, this could take hours.

"Look Fitz, I need more information if I'm going to make this work. You're looking for one server among millions of addresses. Knowing what I'm searching for might help speed this up."

Fitz's expression changed to one she might have called ecstasy, or maybe lunacy given the circumstance.

"There is a new technology BBN has developed for the U.S. Navy. A new kind of towed sonar array. It can detect ships and submarines from miles and miles away, making it impossible to sneak up on our fleet or our coasts. My communist friends have promised to be very, very generous in return for its plans."

Mev knew he had no morals but giving away military secrets was an all-time low, even for him. Still, Mev wasn't sure how his answer would help the search. She had no idea what file or code names Fitz was looking for, no idea whether the information was on this particular subnet. She sat in silence as the program ran, the soft grunts of the hard drive spinning and stopping the only noise in the room.

"Then what?" she asked, curious, despite recognizing the question might antagonize him. What had Jamie called it? The hacker's curse.

She tried to imagine what the hell Fitz was planning next. Would he sell this to the Russians while running from the FBI? Flee the country? He had a wife and kids. He was a famous professor. Would he disappear to Russia or Czechoslovakia or somewhere else where no one knew him? Somewhere where he wasn't the center of attention? She had a hard time imagining that.

The dreamy expression returned to Fitz's face. "I'll begin my next chapter. Somewhere new. Somewhere warm. No more snow, no more whiny students, no more academic bullshit." He sounded like a small boy who dreamt of being a pirate or an astronaut. What he was, was nuts.

His smile faded and he pointed the gun at her. "Make it go faster. I've got places to be."

"You know they'll catch you, right?" It was stupid to say it, to irritate him, but Mev really was curious. What was he thinking?

"I've always been two steps ahead. They'll never find me. You're not so lucky. You'll go to prison. Right now you're hacking a defense contractor. And you already admitted hacking Thinking Machines. Even if you blamed me."

Maybe he'd figured out what she'd done. Maybe he was delusional.

"Shooting Jack, kidnapping me, and holding me at gunpoint isn't going to help your case."

"I'll be fine." That expression of ecstasy returned. "I have a guardian angel."

DEMON continued to run.

THURSDAY, MARCH 22, 1990

HE WAS GOING TO GET AWAY WITH IT. THE IDEA FILLED
Fitz with a transcendent joy.

He had followed Mev from the FBI to the dilapidated building
on Green Street without any problem. She never turned around, never
sensed he was there until he stuck the gun in her ribs. The boy who
opened the door, the one with the priceless expression on his face, was
the same one he saw the night he first tried to grab Mev. Jack Kane, her
other housemate besides Hector.

Hector. Jesus, what a simpleton. Coming to him, threatening,
demanding. Fitz had felt out of control that night. Afraid. As afraid
as he'd been in holding at the FBI. He'd felt desperate when he'd led
Hector to the roof, overwhelmed with the sense that it was all crumbling
down around him, everything he'd worked for. Everything he deserved.
Pushing him off the roof had been a catharsis. Just like today.

Of course Mev didn't expect him to find her. Hiding in an abandoned
building wasn't a bad plan, though he liked the creature comforts of his
own Cambridge hideout more. She'd underestimated him, just like the
FBI did, just like the Russians, just like the Mob. Morons all.

He'd wave the gun about, take her back to his place, and make her
find what he needed. The desperate Russians would pay up, and he would
have a new life, giving the Irish Mob and the FBI the finger on his way
out of Boston. Sure, some of the details were still vague. That added a
certain extra thrill.

He was canny, brilliant. He'd figure it out. Plus, he had a protector in the FBI. Someone watching over him. That's how things went for Fitz; they just fell his way.

He gestured up the stairs with the gun, making it clear how this was going to go. Kane with the same stupid look of fear he'd had that night Fitz had tried to grab Mev at her house. That fear was delicious, an extra little treat.

At the top of the stairs was another girl who immediately challenged him, but he was in charge here. He told her to shut it, then had them all sit. Mev looked scared, so did Kane, but that girl glared at him like a hawk.

Maybe he could stage this like a robbery gone wrong. This was a crappy neighborhood, just like the one where Charles Stuart staged his wife's murder. Unlike him, Fitz would never, ever get caught.

When he'd made the attempt on Mev at her house, he'd planned to make her use her own computer for the theft, and would have done so today. But there were just sleeping bags and takeout containers in the dumpy squat.

No worry. A solution was nearby. He'd get what he needed and get away.

He told Mev they needed to go, but as he turned to follow her, Kane was suddenly on top of him, the idiot, trying to wrench the Detective Special from his hand. As the kid grabbed for the gun, it discharged, loud in the empty space. Then Kane was down, a bullet in his leg.

Served him right.

Fitz relished the helpless fear in Kane's eyes as he cowered, bleeding on the floor. The other girl crawled to Kane, trying to stop his bleeding. Good luck with that.

This wasn't the plan, but it would be fine. Get the tech. Get his money. Get out of town. Get on with his new life.

He had what he needed at his apartment on Inman. Plus, privacy. They walked carefully into Central Square, Fitz keeping her close. He feared she'd attempt something stupid, like Kane had, but they made it to the Inman Street apartment without incident. He was pleased with his cool-headed improvisation.

He dead-bolted the door and had her sit in front of the PC on the small wooden desk he'd taken from a dumpster. Some rich kid was throwing it away and it was still perfectly fine. It gave the place a student apartment feel, which made the girls more comfortable.

Sitting on a wooden dining chair, Fitz considered Mev Hayes. His opinion of her continued to evolve. She did, in fact, appear to be extremely intelligent. And although he'd pegged her as a naive little girl, she'd shown some steel the last few weeks.

As a rule, he didn't like strong-minded women. On the other hand, he got easily bored with his usual choices. What was the highest number of times he'd brought a conquest to this apartment before he tired of her? Five? Except for Kate Fedorova before she broke it off. Kate, the only woman besides Mev in recent memory to have thwarted his desire. Neither of them was boring, he could at least say that.

Now excitement for his next adventure was the thing driving him.

He pushed Mev to get on with it, but it was actually fine if it took some time. No one knew about this place. He'd left his car at MIT and taken the T, along with all the other proles going about their Cambridge business. Disgusting, but he needed to follow Mev. And find out where she was hiding.

Immediately after being released, Fitz made a careful trip to the dead drop, leaving not intelligence, only a note. "My next communication to you will be plans for the United States Navy's new Surveillance Towed Array Sensor Systems. Please have ready for immediate exchange $2,000,000 in U.S. currency." Sure, they'd only promised a million, but they'd said, "more if soon." After all, he deserved it.

Now it *was* soon. Soon to be paid, soon to begin a new life, free of obligations, free of all the things keeping him from what he truly deserved. Fitz closed his eyes, imagining the beach, imagining being free of all of this.

There was a sudden crash at the door; Fitz wheeled, pointing the gun head high. With a second, splintering boom, the door flew open. Ostrowski, Philips, and Cambridge Police barging in, guns pointed.

Everyone froze. Then Fitz experienced a burst of light and searing pain as something smashed into his head, toppling him over.

"Fucking bitch," he thought, just before his head smacked the table's edge with a loud crack.

THURSDAY, MARCH 22, 1990

PAUL PUSHED THROUGH THE BROKEN DOOR, STARING straight into the barrel of Fitz's handgun. Mev was standing behind him, her chair knocked back, her eyes wide, she and Fitz both fixed on his and Carl's guns, and those of the officers behind them.

As it had when he'd faced a loaded weapon as a cop in Chicago, time seemed to decelerate as Paul's perception expanded. He saw Mev make the decision. Saw the action, as if it was occurring in slow motion, watched her sweep the heavy steel-framed keyboard off the table and swing it with tremendous force against the side of Fitz's head. He had no sense of it coming, and was hurled to the side, gun hand flying up, body falling over. The crack of his head hitting the dining table edge was loud, the last sound he made before his body crumpled to the floor.

Carl moved to subdue Fitz, and Paul went to Mev, who was still holding the keyboard in her hands, panting. She inhaled, leaned forward, and furiously roared at the limp body on the floor, the blood-stained keyboard vibrating in her hands as she cried out. Mev then looked at the keyboard, seemed surprised to find it in her hands. Noticing the blood, she dropped it. She only turned away from Fitz's limp body when Paul put his hand on her shoulder.

"Are you injured?"

Her face was blotchy, pink cheeks against a sweaty, pale complexion. She was still panting, her chest heaving as if she'd sprinted the quarter mile.

"I wasn't sure anyone was coming."

"Jamie Brennan pointed us straight here." Mev was dazed. Paul righted the fallen chair, guided her into it. "Sit. I'll be with you in a sec. You're OK."

Paul knelt next to Carl. "What do we got?"

Carl had already cuffed him. "He's out cold. That table edge did a number on him. Still breathing, so I guess we'll get an ambulance."

"No particular hurry, but yeah."

One of the Cambridge P.D. handed Paul evidence bags. Paul put on gloves and picked up the revolver. He noted the position of the cylinder, then cracked it, bagging the gun, then bagging each shell separately. One empty shell spent on Kane, the rest reserved for Mev, or himself, Carl, and the Cambridge cops if things had gone differently.

"I'm cold," Mev, hunched over, said to the floor.

"Adrenaline wearing off," Paul said. "Happens to all of us. Put your head between your legs. Breathe slowly—it'll pass."

Paul would have his moment tonight, after the paperwork was done and he was back in his crappy apartment with nothing else to fill his brain. He'd feel like he'd been dropped ten feet into an icy pool.

Carl kept an eye on FitzRoy. He wasn't going anywhere. Paul told Cambridge P.D. to establish a perimeter, and he moved outside to contact Weaver. He wasn't sure how that was going to go. As he started toward the door, Mev reached out.

"Don't leave me."

"I'll stay until the paramedics get here."

In Paul's opinion, they arrived too quickly for Fitz and too slowly for Mev, yet they were brisk and thorough in examining her. Short of the shock, she appeared fine, and calmer once she was wrapped in the blanket they gave her. The pair working on FitzRoy were getting a brief from Carl, so Paul could radio Weaver and give him the update. It took him a few moments to get through the P.D. cordon, and he passed the FBI scene team as they were coming in. Weaver was already on-site.

"Sir. We're still mopping up in there."

"Give me the high points."

Paul wanted to deflect as much heat off Mev as possible. She'd been a suspect and had smacked the crap out of Fitz. It was as clear a case of self-defense as he could imagine, especially with at least five officers witnessing it first-hand.

Paul walked Weaver through their day, following leads, what they found on Green Street, and his decision to pursue FitzRoy with assistance from the Cambridge Police given exigent circumstances. He told him about the breach and the fact that Mev's quick action prevented any injuries, excluding those to FitzRoy, of course.

Weaver chewed on it for a moment. "This will get a formal review, but you made the right call going in. We had a suspected spy who'd already shot one victim and was holding a hostage at gunpoint. You had decent intel on the house and the layout. Get it all in your report and I'll be fine with it. With the espionage angle, there's going to be a lot of scrutiny, so make that report letter-perfect."

Weaver turned to confer with a higher up from Cambridge P.D. The street was filling and Paul told the scene officer to expand the perimeter. A gurney pushed through the cordon with Fitz on it, still unconscious. There was a dressing on the side of his head where Mev had clocked him and a larger one on the side where he hit the table. Paul hoped that hurt like a motherfucker when he woke. Then they'd have the pleasure of questioning him. Slowly. Loudly.

Weaver walked toward the apartment then turned back. "Ostrowski, nice work."

Mev was coming down the stairs, wrapped in a blanket and holding the railing. The paramedics were behind her with the gurney.

"Shouldn't you go to the hospital and get looked at?" Paul asked.

"I need to check on Jack. How is he, do you know?"

"The bullet grazed his thigh. Cut into the muscle. No major arteries hit. He's at Mass General. I'll have one of the officers take you there. Then he's going to take you home. They'll post a car. And please, just stay there? I need to know how to find you."

Paul waved over the young cop who had screwed the pooch on the door breach. Paul read his name tag: Simmons. "Officer Simmons, I need a favor from you. Miss Hayes' friend was shot by FitzRoy, and she needs to go check on him. After the paramedics clear her, can you do me a personal favor and take her over to Mass General then home, please?"

"Absolutely, Agent Ostrowski."

The kid stood a bit straighter now. No reason not to give him a little pride. Shit, he was part of a raiding team that busted a known spy and rescued a kidnapping victim. And Paul was dead certain that if that kid ever swung a ram against a door again, it would be like the hand of God hitting it.

FRIDAY, MARCH 23, 1990

WHEN PAUL ARRIVED AT THE FBI OFFICE EARLY THE next morning to finish paperwork, he found Carl already there, in Weaver's office. Paul had been at the scene until late, wrapping up and encouraging the Cambridge Police captain and his chief to keep details out of the news for now. Weaver waved him in.

"FitzRoy died on the table" was his greeting. He lifted a piece of paper on his desk, "cause of death was a massive brain hemorrhage due to a 'coup-contrecoup injury.' In short, the bounce off the table scrambled his brains."

Paul had been nursing fantasies of interrogating Fitz for hours and hours while his head pounded. With Fitz dead, the case was dead. "That closes Longbow, then."

"It's not the end of the case, I'm afraid."

"Jesus," Paul sighed. Lanza again? "What now? We promised her immunity for helping us nail FitzRoy." This wasn't how he should be addressing his boss, but he was done with this game. He didn't want to go after Mev. She wasn't the criminal here.

"The U.S. Attorney has a different opinion, apparently. AUSA Lanza promised Miss Hayes immunity in return for delivering FitzRoy, his Russian contact, and his Mob loan shark. Now she's saying we have nothing to show for it. FitzRoy is dead. After all the espionage screw-ups over the last few years, the Justice Department apparently wants a high-profile Counterintelligence win."

"Against a college student?" Carl asked, sharing Paul's frustration. Paul knew they were on shaky ground here but this just wasn't right.

"Based on Hayes's testimony and failure to complete her agreement, AUSA Lanza is considering charging her under the Computer Fraud and Abuse Act. With Robert Tappan Morris's indictment fresh in the public's mind, we can show we are on top of things. It's a win for the whole Justice Department.

"Lanza is also talking to the Massachusetts DA's office and checking to see if they will consider indicting on manslaughter, charging she used more force than was necessary given that the FBI and police were already confronting him."

"That's bullshit, sir, and you know it. FitzRoy's death was absolutely self-defense on her part. He kidnapped her. He had a gun on her. I was there," Paul replied.

"Ostrowski, I'm not asking your opinion."

"Well, you're getting it, sir. We promised immunity if she cooperated. You agreed, so did Lanza."

"Things change. This comes from the top. It's not up for debate, Ostrowski."

Paul was aghast. This wasn't what they'd promised. What he'd promised. It wasn't justice in any form. Why the hell was Weaver going along with this?

Weaver spread his hands. "Look, Lanza's not being unreasonable. She's willing to make a deal with Hayes, pleading to the Computer Fraud and Abuse Act violation in return for a reduced sentence and minimal prison time. She's contacting Hayes's attorney to begin negotiations. In the meantime, finish the incident reports from yesterday, organize your case notes for Lanza by end of day, then you're back on the Gardner case."

Paul stood silent, filled with rage.

"We're done here. Dismissed," Weaver said, and Paul stomped out of the office, Carl right behind him.

They returned to their desks and spent the next few hours working through their case paperwork in silence, handing over their incident report to a waiting staffer from the AUSA's office.

Carl spoke first. "I don't think . . . "

Paul held up his hand.

"I need lunch. Care to join me?" Paul asked, and Carl grabbed his coat without another word.

They passed Connor who was chatting with another agent. "Good kill yesterday, even if you had to have a girl do it for you."

Asshole.

"And I told you to stay the hell away from the Brennans. Jinx's attorney called me yesterday and told me you were hassling him about his kid again."

"His kid is involved in our case, Connor. We needed to talk to her."

"No, you didn't. Stay away from Jinx and Jamie. Stay in your lane."

Paul tamped down the anger he was carrying from the meeting with Weaver. Connor wasn't worth it. "Sure. Whatever you say."

Connor had piqued his curiosity about Jamie even more. What was her role in all of this?

"Something's weird with him," Carl said.

"I don't have time to screw with him right now."

Once they were outside, Paul realized he had no idea where to suggest for lunch. Carl took the lead, walking to a tiny café on Bowdoin at the base of Beacon Hill. It was dark and small and gave them privacy to talk, away from the office and other agents.

"This isn't right," Carl said when the waitress left.

"No, it's not. We're going back on our word."

"What can we do? Even Weaver's under orders," Carl said.

The food arrived, and Paul took a bite of a surprisingly tasty burger, though Carl's judgmental look dimmed the pleasure.

"We owe it to Mev to let her know what's coming."

"I don't want to piss Weaver off," Carl said between bites.

"I know. Maybe we can make this turn out better. Or at least less bad."

"How?"

"Not quite sure yet," Paul said.

"The AUSA is going to be furious if we interfere. And Weaver will crucify us."

And irreverent joke from Paul's altar boy days sprang to mind.

Those nails really hurt going in, but what a view from up there.

FRIDAY, MARCH 23, 1990

JACK WAS STILL IN TREATMENT WHEN MEV GOT TO MASS General Hospital, so she'd had the officer bring her home then stayed up late checking in about Jack's condition, finally being told they'd decided to keep him overnight. For a while she'd managed to ignore the other thing they'd told her. That Fitz had died on the operating table.

That she'd killed him.

She recalled being angry, with a growing disgust toward Fitz, toward his delusion and desperation. But her decision to crack him over the head with the keyboard? That came out of nowhere. One moment she was staring at Ostrowski's gun, the next, feeling the crunch of the painted steel IBM keyboard frame hitting Fitz's head and watching him bounce off the table edge before falling to the floor.

Maybe it was animal instinct when faced with a threat. Maybe that's why Jack went for the gun. Fight or flight. She hadn't meant to kill Fitz. She was sick of his bullshit, sick of his threats, sick of him. She'd swung the keyboard as hard as she could, no question. Her feelings in that moment, though, were blurry, as if an independent actor had lifted the keyboard and swung it, Mev just observing.

Still, she'd killed a man. A fact apparently not lost on Assistant United States District Attorney Michelle Lanza. Mev had received a call that morning from her attorney, Francis Bishop.

"They're coming after you," Bishop had said.

"Ostrowski told me it was self-defense. Hell, he hasn't even finished interviewing me yet. We were supposed to do that today at some point."

"I talked to him this morning. Unless he's putting on a good act, he's awfully unhappy with the AUSA's 'witch hunt,' as he called it. She's claiming you broke the terms of your immunity agreement. And for good measure they are pressuring the Middlesex County DA to pursue manslaughter charges against you."

"What's her problem with me?" Mev had asked.

"You're only a piece on the board, I'm afraid. The game makes you a headline-worthy pawn to be taken by the queen. That's what passes for justice."

Bishop went on to tell her he'd arrange the meeting with Ostrowski for later in the day and would keep working on angles to make this go away. Mev wasn't hopeful when she hung up the phone. And she worried about Jamie's supposition that they might detain her the next time she showed up at the FBI.

The phone rang again. It was Jack.

"They're discharging me early for good behavior." He sounded good.

"I doubt that," she said with a much needed smile.

He said it had been a through and through, no blood vessel or nerve damage. Just really painful.

Jack had things to celebrate. He'd come through to the other side mostly unharmed. Fitz had not.

Mev sat idling in Jack's truck in front of the lobby of MGH. She was afraid with his dressings he wouldn't have been able to fold himself into her Pinto or get back out. An orderly wheeled Jack to the truck door and Jack struggled with his crutches. He rolled his eyes at his own clumsiness. Mev jumped from the truck to help him.

"I got it," he said as he stumbled to the truck door. Hopping on one foot, he opened the door and swung in, grunting as he did so.

"Hurt?"

"Like a bear. If only a small bear. My parents wanted to bring me home, but I'm just not up for my mom babying me right now."

Mev made her way back across the Longfellow Bridge through Cambridge. "They told you about Fitz?" she asked as they approached Porter Square.

"This morning. Couldn't have happened to a nicer guy," he appeared to joke, yet his tone was somber.

She didn't disagree. Still, it had consequences for her. Serious ones.

From the driveway on Linnaean Street, she got him up the porch stairs and onto the aqua leather couch. "Home sweet home," he said, spreading his arms across the back cushions, propping his bandaged leg on the low, scratched coffee table.

There was a knock at the front door. The rest of Mev's war council. She'd talked to Jamie the night before, filling her in, then paged her again this morning before she left to get Jack at MGH.

Jamie inspected Jack's leg dressing. "Looks painful."

"It is. And I hate taking the pain meds. They make me feel stupid, like I lost twenty IQ points."

"Oh God, the temptation. Don't make it so easy for me. I don't want to take advantage of an invalid," Jamie said.

They both chuckled. Mev did not, and they noticed. Jack asked what was going on. She told them.

"Jesus," Jack replied.

"That's ridiculous," Jamie added. "I mean they honor deals with mobsters all the time."

"I'm apparently Lanza's path to promotion," she said from the kitchen, making coffee for all of them. With Jack on crutches, was she going to have to do the cooking? It wouldn't be to his exacting standards. It also might not be for long. She might be behind bars soon.

As she placed the press pot and cups on the coffee table next to Jack's bandaged leg, Mev marveled at the illusion of normality. The three of them hanging out over coffee. Like it had been at the beginning with her, Jack, and Hector. Now two people involved in all this were dead, three including Raven.

She had come to share Jack's belief that Hector's death was not a suicide, not her fault. At least not directly. Hector had been murdered. She'd seen the rage and determination in Fitz's face. If Hector had said to him anything like the last things he'd said to her and Jack, she could well imagine a confrontation that ended with Fitz shoving him off the roof.

"I need to warn you about something," Jamie said.

"Oh please, pile on," Mev replied.

"The Mob doesn't like leaving debts unpaid. If somebody welshes on debt, it passes on to their family or someone else responsible for paying it. That might be you."

"Seriously? They'd come after me for Fitz's stupid debt?" Though she remembered Joey hinting something like that when he'd accosted her on the street.

"They might go after the wife. They'll go after the person they think is the weakest, who can't fight back."

If they thought that about her, they were sorely mistaken.

Just ask Fitz.

FRIDAY, MARCH 23, 1990

LATER THAT AFTERNOON FRANK BISHOP WAS WAITING for her in the lobby of the JFK Federal Building.

"Fricking déjà vu," she said, in the way of a greeting.

"Same shit, different day," he replied, more appropriately.

An agent showed them to a conference room with blinds drawn, and Mev wondered if this was yet another ambush. She was pleased to see it was only Agents Ostrowski and Philips. No AUSA Lanza or Weaver.

Ostrowski offered her water from a carafe. Once everyone was seated, he began. "Walk me through yesterday's events as you remember them."

Yesterday? Only yesterday? Not the month it felt like since she sat in this very office and found out that they'd released Fitz while she traveled back from Maine. Not the six weeks that seemed like a year it had been since she had arrived in Cambridge, full of hope with a new start. Instead, her past infected her present, and her present infected her future. She needed to change that. Pronto.

She recounted her T ride back to the Green Street building that Jamie had found for them, a fact she'd expected Agent Ostrowski to dig into, but he merely told her to continue as he took notes.

"Fitz was suddenly behind me with a gun. He must have known I'd be here yesterday then followed me once I left."

Agents Ostrowski and Philips exchanged glances. "Go on," Ostrowski said.

"Fitz trying to grab me on St. Pat's was him needing me for one last job. A real one." Mev related the story Fitz ranted about: him trying to use the hobbled copy of DEMON to breach BBN and get the Navy's secret towed sonar plans. "He was bragging how the Russians wanted it bad. How he'd get a huge payout. And then he could run, I guess. He talked about going somewhere warm. He wasn't behaving rationally."

"Apparently not," Ostrowski said.

"So, what happens now?" Mev asked. "Fitz was breaking the law and was going to do more of that. He tricked me into doing what I thought was my job. And I think he was involved in Hector's death."

She recounted the argument she'd had with Hector hours before his death, his accusations, and the effect they'd have had on Fitz given his state of mind. Ostrowski nodded and took notes, neither confirming nor questioning her account.

"Then he threatened me with a gun, so I started searching BBN's network like he demanded. He pointed the gun at you, then I defended myself. Defended all of us. And I'm still going to be prosecuted? I'm to blame because why?"

Ostrowski didn't answer, just shifted in his chair.

If Mev had doubts the last few months about what she should do, about where she fit, they were all burned away now. She *knew* she had done the right thing.

"You didn't get Fitz, or the Russians, and the Mob never got paid. And apparently, now there's a chance the mob's going to come after me for Fitz's debt."

Bishop looked surprised. She hadn't told him what Jamie had shared. "Yeah," he said after a moment. "That's possible. It's how these guys work. The Italians do the same. There's a debt, somebody's gotta pay."

"This is Joey 'The Banker' Monahan?" Ostrowski asked.

"Yeah, and a big bruiser who drives him," Mev said. "I'm not looking forward to having them come at me on the street again."

"Personally, I'd put money on them going after the wife," Bishop said. "She's the one with the house and the horses."

Mev had never seen Fitz's home. It didn't surprise her that it was lavish, that it was a lot like where she'd grown up. Something about that kind of desperate hunt for wealth and power ended up looking the same. And ending the same.

"We can put a detail on her," Ostrowski said.

"What about me?" Mev asked. "Who's got my back?"

Again, it felt like she was an afterthought, a cog in this ridiculous machine.

"We could wire you," Philips said.

"In case Joey accosts her in the street sometime in the next month?" Ostrowski asked. "No, he's smart. He's watching and waiting, being careful."

"They won't wait long," Bishop said. "The vig on the loan is due weekly. Once they realize Fitz is dead—which is kind of hard to miss since it's above the fold in *The Boston Globe* this morning—they'll be coming for payment."

"If they go after the wife and girls, somebody's going to get hurt," Bishop said. "And you won't have anything you can use if you just scare them off. Eventually you'll move on to the next case, and they'll be sitting ducks," Bishop said.

Mev thought about that. Maybe it *should* be her in the cross hairs here. She wasn't particularly thinking of saving Fitz's wife and daughters. Still, they were innocent in all of this. Even more than she was.

"Scare them off from the family and they will definitely come after my client. She's a known quantity. Maybe not rich, but useful. Kind of their perfect mark. She'll never be able to pay it off, and will be intimidated enough to keep paying interest."

"I am not fucking intimidated," Mev said. "What I am is *done*. Done with Fitz, done with all these assholes, done with all of this."

The room fell silent, all three men considering her, making new calculations.

"Me too," Paul finally said. "We'll put an obvious patrol on the family to keep Joey and his boys away. And if you feel up for it, we can put an undercover detail on you, ready to grab him when he comes after you."

"Are you out of your mind, Ostrowski?" Bishop bellowed. "You are not going to use my client as some kind of . . ."

Mev put her hand on his shoulder, silencing him. This was her show now.

"I'll do it. Just keep them close," she said.

Bishop, his voice still strident, said, "you won't get much. He's not going to flip on his brothers for a little loan sharking and criminal intimidation."

"I have a plan for that," Paul said.

"And in the meantime?" Mev asked. "Fitz is gone. And I never had direct contact with the Russians. So, even if you get something on Joey, I'm still screwed. And now Lanza's gunning for me on Fitz's death."

Ostrowski's face darkened and his jaw tightened. He didn't appear to like AUSA Michelle Lanza any more than Mev did.

"I am—we are—working on that. To my mind you fulfilled the terms of your bargain in good faith. I have said that to Lanza and to my boss. I will not back down. If we shake Joey 'The Banker' loose, we cut a new deal, one that puts this all behind you."

He glanced at Carl again. "As I said, I have a plan."

WEDNESDAY, MAY 16, 1990

IT WAS A PERFECT SPRING DAY FOR THE PRESS CONFER-
ence, the sun shining, the sky blue, the air warm and inviting. Paul and
Carl stood off to the side behind the podium along with Assistant
Special Agent in Charge Mitchell Weaver. At the podium featuring the
Department of Justice seal stood Assistant United States Attorney
Michelle Lanza, dressed in a sharp, TV-ready double-breasted blue power
suit with a bright red scarf.

"Today, we are announcing additional racketeering charges against
former FBI Special Agent Allen Connor. As you may recall, Connor was
previously charged with alerting organized crime to FBI investigations,
falsifying FBI reports, and accepting bribes. We remain committed
to our duty to root out corruption and malfeasance anywhere in the
Department of Justice."

She turned over the microphone to Weaver.

"This would not have been possible without the efforts of the
agents standing here today. Working hand in hand with the U.S. Attorney's
office, these two Special Agents brought a known member of organized
crime and a rogue agent to justice."

Paul had won the bet. Not the one about whether Mev was a
criminal. That had been mere interrogation technique. Nor the one
about Fitz's ego. That one had been a slam dunk. No, the bet he'd won,
the one Carl handed over $100 for, was that Joey would turn over an FBI
agent, specifically Special Agent Allen Connor. Not that Paul'd had any
proof, and to be fair, maybe he only *wanted* it to be Connor. Though it
was a pleasure—and a profit—to be right.

It had played out exactly like he'd expected. And Paul got the bonus of personally nailing Joey when he went after Mev during his and Carl's surveillance shift. Sure, it was a minor set of charges against Joey, but the suggestion that he might be charged as an accessory to espionage—which could carry the death penalty—woke him right the hell up.

Bishop had also called it right: Joey refused to give any information on his brothers in crime. So, Paul offered him a different deal. Turn over his source in the FBI and they'd give him a tiny slap on the wrist. Not that Paul wanted this asshole out on the streets again, but taking down a corrupt FBI agent was too valuable. No surprise, Joey turned on Connor in seconds.

Joey spilled on Connor's advance warnings of impending investigations, and his help in finding Mev to become Fitz's new hacker after the death of the first one, Kenneth Frain, the sometimes drug dealer whose handle was Raven. The final thread, wrapping up the case. A closure, if not a perfect one.

Then filling in Weaver and Lanza. Weaver pleased, Lanza unselfconsciously greedy with her win. Then the sweetness of walking down the hall and confronting Connor, Fitz's fallen guardian angel. The look on Connor's face when Carl slapped the cuffs on him? Fucking spectacular.

And the incentive award was nice. A certificate, this public recognition, and a cash bonus. Money to move back to D.C. and put a down payment on an apartment near Linda and Becky. Linda had warmed a tiny bit when he'd told her his plan to put in his papers. He'd always imagined he'd stick it out until he got to his twenty and his pension. He saw things differently now.

Paul had believed in the FBI, in the work of the Department of Justice. Not anymore. He'd seen more of the justice system's underbelly in the last few months than in all his previous years—Lanza's duplicity,

Connor's betrayal, the bureaucracy, the prejudices and power. He'd lost his taste for it. The future of the FBI, for those who could navigate the mess, wasn't guys like him anyway. It was agents like Carl, young and computer-savvy and committed to change from within.

After they'd nailed Connor, Lanza made a big show of her magnanimity, informing Mev Hayes they were dropping the investigation and honoring her immunity agreement after all. Paul's thoughts of leaving the FBI had solidified after that, and by the time Weaver told him about the press conference and award presentation, he had his resignation letter ready to go.

As Lanza had described for the cameras the completion of a year-long investigation into espionage and computer hacking, the death of a spy and the exposure of a corrupt agent, it sounded like a clear victory of right over wrong. Paul had kept a straight face during the press conference, even smiled when Lanza shook his and Carl's hands. As the conquering hero, Lanza could let a fraction of her glory reflect onto them. Paul received it as gracefully as he could. There was a lot of back slapping and a hint of an expedited promotion for Carl.

It wasn't a totally clean resolution, though. There was speculation the Irish Mob might have pulled off the Gardner heist. That would take forever to unravel. And the Russians? They'd walked away clean. Maybe that was moot. Just as they were bringing Fitz in, Gorbachev won a democratic election. The Berlin Wall was already down, the former Soviet republics were breaking free. The world was changing.

Time for a change for Paul as well.

MONDAY, JUNE 4, 1990

COMMENCEMENT DAY AT MIT. EAGER NEW GRADUATES in their crisp gowns and mortarboards moved a tassel from one side to the other and greeted the world they would now rule.

Not Mev.

She'd graduated. That in and of itself was a miracle. She'd missed so many classes and fumbled so many exams that she'd spent all of April chasing her professors, trying to make up work, promising she was taking it seriously. It wasn't such a bad thing to be able to completely pour herself into work. After Fitz's death—and the looming indictment, arrest, trial, and prison—it had been good to have something else to focus on.

Dr. Halloway had stepped in to help, letting her gamble her entire grade in his class on her final, which she aced, and also intervening with her other instructors. He'd worked with her to finish the independent study she'd begun under Fitz, keeping his opinions about Fitz and the ethics of DEMON to himself.

He reminded her of Dave Franklin, of the people in her life who had good intentions and wanted to help, wanted her to succeed: Jack, Jamie, even Agent Ostrowski, if she was honest.

In early May the charges against her suddenly went "poof," gone as capriciously as they'd appeared. As planned, Agents Philips and Ostrowski—who now begged her to call them Carl and Paul—had maneuvered to turn Joey. The irony was that while she had been branded a traitor by AUSA Lanza, it was Agent Allen Connor, the real traitor, who had set her up. Used his FBI knowledge to steer her to Fitz in the first place. And Ostrowski had taken him down.

She was beyond grateful that her future was now her own. That the grip of the past had loosened but hadn't completely let go.

She'd killed a man. Yes, it was self-defense. Yes, Fitz had threatened her at gunpoint. Yes, she'd feared for her life. She'd also been extraordinarily angry, and that anger had undoubtedly helped accelerate that heavy keyboard.

She wasn't sorry she'd done it.

She was angry she'd been forced to.

Mev sipped at her glass of Pinot noir. Jack had told her the vineyard and the vintage, but she had just wanted something nice to bring upstairs with her for a long, hot bath. When Jack had first given her the tour of the house, she'd admired this tub. She'd never gotten around to a soak with wine and peace and quiet until today.

It had been a good day. Jack had asked her what she wanted to do when she'd told him she wasn't going to commencement. That the ceremony had nothing to do with her: with her life, with her past, with her future. She wanted to have an adventure of her own making. Make a difference. Some adventure that didn't involve Ponzi schemes, spying, Mob hits, or the FBI.

Jack said he had an idea.

The day began with Jack making breakfast for her and bringing it to her in bed. Waffles with maple syrup. She was 99% sure he wanted to put that tray to the side and join her in bed. They hadn't repeated what they'd started in Maine, though she was enjoying the emerging romance. Even if she'd almost had to knock him in the head to make it clear she was interested, just needed to take it slow.

After breakfast, in the kitchen, she poured herself another coffee, watching through the open screen door as Jack uncovered his motorcycle and began fiddling with it. While his bullet wound healed, he hadn't been able to ride. It was the first time she'd seen his black Kawasaki uncovered since Hector's death. Another end, another beginning.

"This is the next bit of celebration," Jack said.

It was a warm day, and Mev savored the way the air cooled the second they left Cambridge on Route 2 toward Carlisle, somewhere near where he'd grown up. They stopped at a diner he swore had "exquisite" patty melts and milkshakes. Stepping off the bike, her heart beating, her fingertips again buzzing from the engine's vibrations, she found herself ravenous.

Jack removed his helmet, then with a shy smile reached up to help her with hers.

They'd ridden after they'd learned of Hector's death, to find life in that speed, in the balance of loss and control. She recalled the peace she'd felt at the marsh's edge and her struggles to find it again.

She still carried guilt over Hector's death. Over the fact that his parents had no real closure, though Ostrowski said he'd spoken with them and tried to help them understand the situation. The medical examiner had re-categorized the case as a "suspicious death," Like Raven's.

Another suspicious death, another loose end.

Lunch was long and leisurely, as was the ride back, Jack flowing into the twists and curves of the roads connecting the small towns outside Boston.

Back home she found herself tired, and a little stiff. She still didn't have the knack of leaning into turns.

Jack suggested wine. She suggested a bath. And decided on both.

After, she found him downstairs in the kitchen, already starting the preparations for dinner. It was Jack, so if there was a celebration, there was food. He said he was making his special chicken pot pie recipe. Mev wondered how chicken pot pie could be special, recalling the carboardtasting frozen ones she and her mom sometimes had. But his cooking was always a pleasant surprise. Yet another recent realization: things could actually be better than she imagined.

Both of them had been intensely busy at the end of the semester, Mev working to graduate, Jack working fiendishly on his dissertation while his leg healed, surprising Mev as well as his dissertation director. It had been fun to talk over wine at the end of each day about what he'd been working on; to explore his theories around computer entertainment and how that would change everyone's lives.

Tonight, as she now often did, Jamie would be joining them. They had lots to talk about. Somehow the events of the past few months had motivated Jamie to go back and work to finish the degree she'd abandoned out of boredom a few years earlier. She'd been admitted to MIT long after the application deadline. Mev hadn't asked—and Jamie hadn't volunteered—how that particular computer record got updated.

Mev wouldn't be there with her. While she waited to be cleared by the Justice Department, and Dr. Halloway worked his magic with her grades, the higher-ups at MIT had decided the crimes, deaths, and FBI investigations linked to the Advanced Concepts Lab weren't the best PR. They were closing the lab. They didn't want any lingering evidence of Fitz or their complicity in his crimes. And while they'd let her graduate, they'd quietly rescinded her acceptance to graduate school.

That future, the one Fitz had sold as a way to control her, was gone. Mev was fine with that. Even so, Jamie said if Mev wanted her MIT email address back, she could definitely make that happen, no problem.

As for Jack, he was scheduled to defend his dissertation and graduate in the fall. He'd look for an academic appointment somewhere, teaching and doing research, a direction Mev had decided was not for her. And for the two of them? All in good time. On her schedule.

And Jamie was going to move in with them later in the summer, before school started. She'd offered to talk to the folks at the Harvard–Smithsonian Center for Astrophysics about Mev taking her old job there. It might be a good fit.

In the meantime, Mev was keeping her hands clean, leaving the computer hacking alone. Frank Bishop had explained that the DOJ had five years, until the statute of limitations ran out, to come after her for lying to the FBI, so she would keep a low profile. But she'd seen the press conference. The FBI and the Justice Department called the whole thing a win and seemed to be moving on.

So was Mev.

ACKNOWLEDGEMENTS

I am indebted to so many generous friends and colleagues whose suggestions and encouragement made this book possible. First to my stellar editors at High Frequency Press, Scott Wolven and Shanna McNair, who saw a partial draft of the book at their conference—The Writer's Hotel—then asked me to join them as one of the inaugural authors at their new press. Thank you both for your friendship and the care you put into getting my work out into the world.

A deep thank you to all my fellow writers: my Master Class teachers, friends and colleagues at Maine Crime Wave, New England Crime Bake, ThrillerFest, the many fine members of the Maine Writers and Publishers Alliance, as well as my colleagues at Maine Crime Writers. These wonderful, warm writing communities made it possible to believe that this book would someday see the light of day.

My profound gratitude to my early beta readers—Brenda Buchanan, Matt Cordes, John Hirsch, George Smith, and Mitch Thomashow. Your generosity made a huge impact on this project.

A shout out to Jessica Vest, Archivist at the B.D. Owens Library at Northwest Missouri State University, who helped me get my facts right on that university's 1980's electronic campus.

And finally to Margot Anne Kelley, my fellow writer, my first reader, my greatest champion, my dearest love.

Robert T. Kelley spent 30 years in the technology industry, building multiple companies before turning to writing and working with startups. Formerly the publisher of the quarterly literary journal, *The Maine Review*, Rob now regularly blogs for Maine Crime Writers. He received his undergraduate degree in Mechanical Engineering from the University of Missouri-Rolla and his PhD in English from Indiana University.

Rob lives in Midcoast Maine with his wife, writer Margot Anne Kelley, and an indeterminate number of cats. *Raven* is his debut novel.

Find out more at roberttkelley.com.